Bookweird

Bookweird

Paul Glennon

Doubleday Canada

Library and Archives Canada Cataloguing in Publication

Glennon, Paul, 1968–
Bookweird / Paul Glennon.

ISBN 978-0-385-66547-6

I. Title.
PS8563.L46B66 2008 jC813'.6 C2008-901083-3

Cover image: Gillian Newland
Cover design: Jennifer Lum
Printed and bound in Canada

Published in Canada by
Doubleday Canada, a division of
Random House of Canada Limited

Visit Random House of Canada Limited's website: www.randomhouse.ca

TRANS 10 9 8 7 6 5 4 3 2 1

To Nicholas

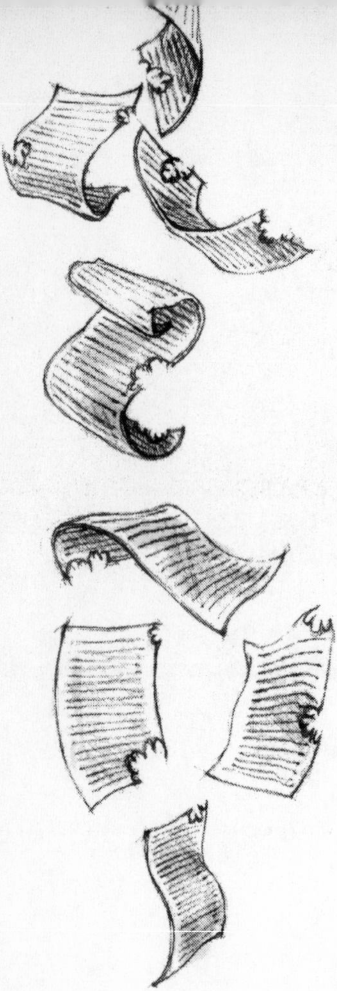

Contents

Bookweird

Things Begin to Fall Apart

1

The weekend *started* out well for Norman Jespers-Vilnius. Saturday morning and the first one out of bed—Mom, Dad and Dora were still sleeping when he climbed the stairs back up to his bedroom with a stack of peanut butter and toast. The toast lasted maybe half an hour and three hand-to-hand battles through the third level of Castle Keep. He played with one hand on the controller, the other shuttling toast to his mouth from the plate on his lap. When last of the ice moths of level 3 had been dispatched, Norman paused the computer, freezing his character in mid victory celebration, fist and battle axe raised, eyes blazing with orange pixels behind the hoisted visor of his helm. This called for more toast, which Norman supplemented this time with a large glass of milk and a bowl of pretzels. A hero's work is hungry work.

Norman spent the next few hours like this, seated sideways in his desk chair, skinny legs dangling off the side, a plate of peanut butter toast balanced in his lap, milk and pretzels within reach of his left hand and his right hand gripping the controller. The food required no attention at all—it would be eaten whether he was conscious of it or not. His eyes never strayed from the computer screen before him.

Level 4 of Castle Keep had some surprises in store. The broadsword that had dealt destruction to the beasts and enemies of the first three levels was useless to him here. The phantasmagorical warriors of level 4 were immune to sharpened steel, and Norman's character had precious little magic to keep them at bay. Only his shield, bathed in the magical waters of Avalon on level 2, was of any use to him against the Spirit Knights.

It took some getting used to. Norman lost track of the number of times he was killed, overwhelmed by the massed phantasmagoricals and enveloped in a mist that sent him back to the start of the level, but he was getting the hang of it. The trick was speed. You couldn't stand and fight against these things; you just rushed through the castle labyrinth as fast as you could, ducking swiftly behind the shield when necessary.

He was vaguely aware of the rest of the house waking around him, but the world outside his bedroom door was so much less real than the world within the computer screen. He didn't count how many times he told his sister Dora bluntly to go away. It was his instinctive reaction every time the door squeaked, and it usually worked. Some whiny retort always came back, but he ignored it. Dora might have said "I'm going to tell Mom." Or "Mom and Dad are mad at you." Usually it was something like that. It was only a background annoyance, but he was at a particularly tricky part when the door squeaked again.

"I *said,* go away," Norman snarled through his teeth. If she made him lose here, he thought, he'd kill her.

"Pardon?" It was his mother's voice. Norman glanced up, surprised to see her standing in the doorway. Her arms were crossed and an eyebrow was raised. It could have been worse.

"Sorry, I thought you were Dora." He just about kept it together, eyes back to the screen now as his hero leapt across a chasm to a ledge.

"And that makes it right?" Meg Jespers-Vilnius asked. Norman could tell that she wasn't really mad. He focused on climbing the wall toward a small niche carved into the dark stone near the ceiling.

A golden chalice flickered in that small high alcove—a magical one, Norman hoped. His magic stores needed replenishing, and if he was lucky it was also a save point.

"She was driving me crazy."

"The only person who can drive you crazy is you." It was the sort of thing his mother said. It might make sense, but it was best not to think about it. "Anyway, it's time to wrap it up." She casually messed his already ragged head of hair. "We're leaving in ten minutes."

Norman heard what his mother said. He even understood it, but he didn't have time to think about that now. He just stored the information away until he could process it properly. First things first: he had to get that chalice or he was a dead questor.

He still hadn't found a way to the chalice niche when his mother appeared at his door again.

"We're all ready to go. Hurry up and get dressed and get down to the car."

"I just have to get to a save point," Norman whispered. He ducked around his mother's arm, trying to keep his eye on the screen while his mother reached across to pick up his empty plate and glass.

"Make it quick. We'll be in the car in two minutes, and your dad isn't happy that you drank the last of the milk."

Norman twisted as the plate came back across his line of sight. His knight was mid-leap. This was something that required a precise touch.

He didn't hear his father shouting from the bottom of the stairs, didn't hear the thump of shoes that should have warned him. He was almost there, his questor's fingers stretching for the chalice, when the door burst open.

"You're still not dressed?" His father was incredulous.

Norman took his eyes off the screen and his knight slipped a few feet down the wall. He only just managed to catch a handhold.

"Just a few seconds, I have to—"

The screen flickered, its light closed to a point and it blinked out.

Norman turned to see his father holding the plug.

"Put these on and get to the car." Norman's father threw clothes at him. Hearing the growl of real anger in his father's voice, Norman struggled into them hastily. How could this have happened? He had been nearly there. He was still stunned as his father frogmarched him down the stairs and to the car.

Norman slumped into the back seat.

"Where are we going, anyway?" he asked, unable to disguise the resentment in his voice.

"For coffee, then shopping," his mother replied from the front seat.

"Why do I have to come? I can look after myself."

"Because," Dora explained in her know-it-all voice, waggling her ponytailed head for emphasis, "you drank the last of the milk so Dad couldn't have his cappuccino at home."

"I didn't ask you," Norman muttered. In his heart he blamed Dora for all this mess. If she hadn't kept bothering him all morning, he would have reached the chalice a long time ago.

His dad cut the argument short. "Come on, guys. We're not even out of the driveway yet. Just sit quietly and read your books."

Dora flashed Norman a taunting grin and picked up her stupid pony book.

"I don't have a book," Norman said.

Edward Vilnius put the car back in park. "Where is it?" His eyes met Norman's in the rear-view mirror. He was doing that professor thing where he looked over the glasses that had slipped down his nose. His normally kind grey eyes were now cold and hard.

Norman opened the door and unbuckled his seatbelt. "It's in my room. I'll get it."

"Stay where you are," his father sighed. "I'll get it." There was no arguing with him in this mood. Norman watched sulkily as his father returned to the house.

"I was ready ten minutes ago," Dora announced for no other reason than to annoy him.

Norman wanted to punch her, but he wouldn't. He could feel the anger building up in him, but he wouldn't do it. He had made up his mind to take her book and lose her page for her. His mother put an arm over the car seat and looked back.

"Now, Norman, I did warn you that we were leaving, right?"

Norman shrugged and allowed a single grudging nod.

"You haven't forgotten your father's curse?" his mother asked.

Norman folded his arms and rolled his eyes. He wasn't in the mood to be cajoled.

"He really *is* cursed," Dora affirmed gleefully.

"It's true," his mother continued. "When he was born, some evil nurse at the hospital put an irascibility curse on him, the foulest of moods possible. There is only one cure."

"Coffee," said Dora melodramatically. "Three times a day."

"Preferably in its most potent espresso or cappuccino form," his mom added, finishing the oft-told family joke. "It is our duty as his family to ensure that he never goes without coffee—for the sake of humanity."

Norman thought the old joke was lame, but he couldn't help smirking. As Edward Vilnius strode out of the house, tall but hunched over at the shoulders, he really did look as if an evil curse lurked over him. He heaved the car door open, fell into the front seat heavily and drew his arms back as if to toss Norman's book back at him, but he caught Norman's eye and passed the book to him gently. His father would never damage a book.

"Okay," he said, putting the car in gear. "Can we all keep ourselves out of trouble now?"

That should have been the end of it. On another day Norman might have put his head down and read quietly. He might have stayed out of trouble. But today he couldn't help himself. His ejection from Castle Keep still rankled. If they had only waited a few more minutes, he could have reached the chalice and saved the game. He glanced over at Dora. She was only eight and skinny, but she still managed to find a way to take up more than her half of the seat, slouching against the door, curling her feet under her, piling stuff beside her. She was doing it on purpose. Norman wasn't fooled by her silent squinting into her book. It was better when they were both in trouble. It was better to spread it around. He'd find a way.

It wasn't that Norman minded reading. He was looking forward to this book, anyway. *The Brothers of Lochwarren* was the latest in the Chronicles of Undergrowth series. He'd been 137th on the library's waiting list. Thankfully, the paperback had just come out. Norman's dad had brought it home the night before and already Norman was seventy pages into it. He didn't get much farther that day in the car, though. He was restless and bitter. In the coffee shop, his father finally got his cappuccino and biscotti and temporarily lifted the curse. Norman knew better, but he asked for a slice of cheesecake. He was politely refused. The refusals became less polite as the day continued, as in each store he asked for something he knew he couldn't have.

He couldn't see why he had to be here anyway. His father could buy coffee by himself. His mother could shop without him. At eleven, he was old enough to stay at home and look after himself. He couldn't stop reminding his parents of this as they dragged him from the coffee shop to the building supply store, to the grocery store and to a hundred clothes stores. He spent the morning trailing around after them sulkily, subtly insulting his sister at every chance until she was as miserable as he.

"Sometimes it's just nice to do things together as a family," his mother said when he complained for the umpteenth time.

"Nice for who?" Norman muttered bitterly. He knew even at the time that it was a step too far. Nothing made his father angrier than him mouthing off at his mother.

"Norman," he said, "you've been miserable all day. Your mother and I have had some errands to do. We thought we'd do them as a family. You had most of the morning to do what you like, and once we got home you would have been free to do as you please."

Norman noticed the "would have been," but he still couldn't stop himself.

"So I'm just supposed to pretend I'm happy to be here?"

His father grimaced and took a deep breath. He was clearly thinking about what punishment was appropriate.

In the pause, his mother repeated one of her little sayings: "You determine your attitude. Everyone does. Don't be at the mercy of events." Norman's mother had written a self-help book called *Unthink and Undo* and now made a living as a motivational speaker saying things just like this. Norman usually tried to ignore them.

At this point her comments weren't ignorable.

His father had decided on his punishment. "You can spend the rest of the weekend without your computer. Maybe this will remind you how lucky you are."

It will remind me how all of you messed up my game, Norman thought to himself, but his father wasn't done. This was to be one of his compound punishments.

"And when we get back home, you can rake all the leaves in the back yard. Hopefully this will teach you not to be so selfish."

It taught him nothing of the sort. It was nearly dark when Norman had finished with the leaves. The rake was ancient, and the grey wood of its handle had split and cracked. Norman felt a bitter sort of justice when the blisters started to erupt. There, that would be proof that he'd suffered, if that's what they wanted. Before the afternoon was done, he had removed two splinters from his hands. The second one went deep and caused a bubble of red blood to form in his palm. He squeezed it, almost enjoying the sting. Inside the house he could see his father working at his computer in the den. He typed with one hand and sipped espresso from a tiny cup with the other.

Norman didn't want to hear a thank you from his dad when he came in. He wanted to be angry. He rubbed his hands, hoping someone would comment on his blisters. No one did. He ate supper silently and went to bed without being told. If he was going to be punished, he wanted to look the part.

A Passage to Lochwarren

In bed that night, Norman finally buried enough of his resentment to manage to read. He really had just got to the best part. The Undergrowth books started slowly. They always began by describing the lands of Undergrowth in great detail, from the Western Sea and the Fisher Kingdoms of the coast to the Obsidian Desert in the east, from the Fastness of the south to the Forbidden Highlands of the north and everything in between. What was important in this bit was always the last part, which described the setting of this particular book in more detail. A few of the countries and cities, like Caernavon and Brunswick, turned up in multiple volumes, but more often than not each book explored a region barely mentioned in previous books. Norman skipped over the general geography. He knew it by heart and had a wall poster of the map of Undergrowth. The description of Lochwarren itself he read in more detail.

Lochwarren was, for centuries, part of the Kingdom of Stoats, one of the lines descended from the ancient Mustelid dynasties. The stoat kings had their summer palace at Lochwarren. Covered in snow much of the year, Lochwarren was nevertheless glorious in summer, a high cold lake surrounded by tall pines and forbidding mountains. Isolated in the highlands of the northeast, the Kingdom of Stoats was one of the last countries to preserve the Mustelid traditions. Decades of war with first fox then wolf invaders had reduced the Mustelid Kingdoms to one. With the death of the stoat king, Malcolm Sharp Sword, at the battle of Tista Kirk, the last remaining Mustelid kingdom fell and the dynasty crumbled.

The flower of stoat knighthood marched with Malcolm, and every stoat yeoman who could hold a longbow or short sword too. This was the stoats' last stand. They would fight until the army was shattered, but if they lost, their kingdom would be overrun. The princes, Duncan and Cuilean, were eager to go to war with their father, but he would not be moved. Before King Malcolm had marched out from Lochwarren to meet the wolves at Tista Kirk, he had given his instructions to his sons. If the battle was lost, the king would die on the field of battle. The princes must live so that the Kingdom could rise again. If the news from Tista Kirk was bad, they must flee, taking the singular gifts he had left them. Each prince had been assigned a bodyguard, in stoat language a "swordfriend," who would protect them in their flight from the highlands. In ten years they must return for the unveiling of the gifts, the crowning of the new king and the reconquest of the highlands.

The news from Tista Kirk was not good. The trumpets told the story. The stoats had fought bravely. Urged on by their indomitable king, they withstood wave upon wave of wolf attacks, their sharp swords flashing out, dealing death to the fanged invaders, but in the end it was too much. The wolves were too big and too many. Outnumbered and out-toothed, the stoats slowly succumbed. Finally, inevitably, the stoat lines broke and the wolves rushed in. King Malcolm saw his standard-bearer fall, one of the long barbed lances of the wolf cavalry piercing his light mail vest. The red and gold pennant of his kingdom fell into the grim mud of Tista Kirk field. No king of Malcolm's blood would stand to see his banner laid low. Shrugging off his own attacker, the King grasped the standard with his shield hand and raised it high.

"To me, my brave stoats, to the glory of our forefathers and the great maker, rally to me!"

He gazed across the field at the horde of wolves that still surged toward them. He could not win this battle. As the last of his warriors rallied to their king and their flag, the King whispered to his trumpeter, and the great, sad anthem of the Mustelid dynasties rang out. In the hills above Tista Kirk a messenger heard the signal. His name was James, sword-friend to Prince Cuilean. He paused only momentarily in silent salute to his king before departing in a flash, with his solemn message, for Lochwarren. As he dashed through the forest, he heard stoat trumpets above the howl of blood-mad wolves behind him on the battlefield. When the last note blew, James knew the King had fallen and the day was done for the stoat army. Then there was only the massed howl of the victors and, later, as night fell, the fearsome sound of their pursuit.

James reached Lochwarren only minutes before the wolf hunting parties, but when the wolf scouts arrived, the castle was empty. The stoats had scattered. The princes parted ways by the shore of the loch. Cuilean and Duncan had never been close friends. They had squabbled their way through childhood, but beneath their rivalry was the close bond that ties all brothers, and twins more especially. They embraced quickly and nodded their goodbyes before leaping to the boats. James, the messenger, sword-friend to Cuilean, guided the small skiff carrying his lord to the west stream pouring out of the loch toward the fertile lands and the League of Five Cities.

Duncan and his fighting companion took the east stream, toward the swamps and tangled waterways of Rivernest. The prince's sword-friend, Falk, piloted the boat while Duncan kept watch. It was just sinking in now that his father was dead, and half of him hoped that they would come across a wolf sortie party, so that he could make good use of the broad cutlass at his side to exact some revenge.

On the west stream, Cuilean kept a light rapier strapped to his belt, a quiver of arrows and a longbow over one shoulder. Between his feet at the bottom of the boat lay the small chest that contained his father's gift. Sadness consumed him as he peered at it and remembered his father. He had no idea what the chest contained. Duncan had an identical one. The keys lay beneath a concealing stone in the King's Chapel near Lochwarren castle. In ten years they would know, no sooner. In ten years they would return to Lochwarren for the unveiling of the gifts and the crowning of the new King.

Norman had read this far the night before. It had been a good place to stop. The next chapter picked up again ten years later, when Duncan and Cuilean began their journeys of return to their kingdom. Cuilean had spent ten years in the Five Cities. He had finished school in Oviedo and taken a degree at the university at Santander. For the last four years he had worked as a clerk for the Duke of Logorno. City life suited the exiled prince—he appreciated the great architecture, the libraries and the civilized conversation. But he never forgot where he was from. The people of the great cities were mostly hares and moles. The stoat prince never felt completely at home among them. Sometimes, during the festivals and the great celebrations, he would think of his homeland and his own people. Such thoughts put him in no mood to celebrate, and he retreated to his lodgings to practise fencing with James. Nor did he neglect the bow. Every year since he'd taken employment with the Duke of Logorno, Cuilean had competed for the Archers' Palio, an archery tournament held yearly in the city. He had won it three out of four times, competing under the colours of the Duke of Logorno, three silver towers on a cornflower blue field.

It was under the same colours that Cuilean left Logorno, taking the road toward the mountains, but after the last toll gate of the city's demesne, he rolled up the fine blue cloak of his hosts and drew out the cloak of his own house. James patted the young prince on the shoulders solemnly as he donned it. James too kept in his luggage a cloak that he had waited ten years to wear again. Those ten years had made their mark on the man who had heard the last trumpets of Tista Kirk. He did not move with the same spring in his step, and his fur had grown grey around his eyes and beneath his whiskers. Still, his confident smile was all Cuilean wanted to see before they returned to the road, and he strode onward with the gold-trimmed red mantle of the stoat kings upon his shoulders.

The other Prince of Stoats did not spend his ten years of exile in the cities learning law and competing in tournaments. Duncan had taken the advice of his companion, Falk, and had joined Falk's cousins in the crew of Rufus Singewhiskers, the weasel captain of the river raiders. For ten years Duncan learned the ways of the river pirates, harassing the treasure convoys that brought gold and diamonds from the edge of the Obsidian Desert to the merchant camps of the delta. Duncan had studied his craft well, and for three years had commanded his own ship and crew.

The *Hastewind* had been more than a ship to Duncan these past years. It had been his home and his academy. It was where he had become a man and learned that he could shape his destiny. At the helm of the *Hastewind,* Duncan had become as respected and feared as Rufus Singewhiskers himself. It was a sad day when he and Falk walked ashore and took leave of the river raiders. Rufus Singewhiskers bid his trusty lieutenant adieu: "Goodbye, my friend, and may the Maker protect you in your travels. Remember, you always have a friend in Rufus Singewhiskers."

Like the rest of the river raiders, Duncan did not consider himself an outlaw. The riverboats were crewed with stoats, weasels, ermines and other exiles from the ancient Mustelid lands. When they boarded a merchant ship, they announced themselves as representatives of the Mustelid Empire and demanded their taxes. They attacked only when forced to, if the merchant crew resisted or came looking for a fight, but that did not mean that the river raiders shirked battle.

The merchant ships carried treasure from the mines of the Obsidian Desert. Those were Canidae mines now. Prairie wolves and coyotes were rulers there and reaped the profits, but the mines were worked by slaves—weasels and stoats brought down from the mountains, grasshopper mice and kangaroo rats enslaved in their own ancestral lands. More than a few of the crewmen among the river raiders were escapees from the mines, and none of them missed a chance to exact their revenge.

When Duncan left the *Hastewind* behind, a dozen stoat comrades accompanied him. Like Duncan, they had in mind a greater revenge than harassing a few boats and thieving some wolf profit. In Duncan they saw the chance of their kingdom's rebirth. Unlike Cuilean, Duncan did not march in the red cloak of the Stoat Kingdom. He travelled with a larger party and knew that this alone called attention to them. He did not want to announce to the wolves that the Prince of Stoats was returning—not yet, at least.

As Norman read on, he was drawn further and further into this new instalment of the Undergrowth saga. It was familiar territory, but strange and new enough for him to want to know more. He huddled under the covers and brought the book as close to his face as he could. If he were there with the heroes themselves, he couldn't have felt more involved. The excitement rumbled in his stomach and he picked nervously at a page farther into the book, ripping tiny triangles of paper from it as he read and putting them in his mouth. Without knowing it, he was actually devouring the book.

Norman was prone to little quirks like this. At school, kids told him that he made noises while he was reading or studying, mumbling barely intelligible words or making little squawks. Norman didn't believe them, or mostly didn't believe them. They exaggerated, but maybe he did spaz out a little bit when he was nervous or absorbed. His mom often reprimanded him for sucking on the collars of his shirts while he read or played on the computer, and the damp patch of T-shirt was pretty conclusive proof. He wasn't gnawing on his collar this night. He was eating a page from his book, methodically ripping it apart bit by bit and chewing the tiny balls of paper between his slightly crooked teeth while he read. When Norman put the book down that night, he had no idea what he'd done.

The Voyage of the Brothers

Norman didn't even bother getting out of bed the next morning. The rest of the family was sleeping in as usual. Maybe if he stayed in bed long enough, someone would make pancakes. Rubbing the sleep out of his eyes, he sat up in bed and found his place in *The Brothers of Lochwarren*. Norman already had a favourite brother. Pirating didn't seem like the best training to be a king. It might have made Duncan a good fighter, but he seemed rough and uneducated. Norman hoped that old King Malcolm had chosen Cuilean to succeed him. Duncan would make a good general, perhaps, but Cuilean was smart and educated. He had worked with the Duke of Logorno—he knew what it meant to govern. Surely he would make the better king. Norman was no novice reader, though. He was well aware that authors liked to set you up and turn things around against your expectations. He'd read enough Undergrowth books to know that things were not always as they appeared. Who, for example, would expect ferrets, stoats and rats to be heroes while voles and shrews were villains?

The gifts were a crucial clue. There was a reason that the author hadn't described them yet. It built suspense. One gift was a gift fit for a king. Whatever it was, it would make it clear to both brothers which one had been chosen. Norman wondered what

Duncan would do when he opened his chest and found the consolation prize. The pirate-prince seemed so sure that he was destined to be King. He had been planning his return and the battle to take the highlands for years. From what Norman had read so far, he didn't think that the river warrior would take disappointment too well. Duncan had a short temper and a quick sword. As for Cuilean, for all his practice with the rapier, he had never fought a real battle. Norman doubted he could best his brother if it came to that. But perhaps it never would. The brothers had other things to think about.

The journey back to Lochwarren was no easy one. The terrain on either side was treacherous, the lands unruly and bandit-ridden. The wolves too had heard rumours of a stoat revolt. Old King Malcolm's sons had not been among the corpses at Tista Kirk ten years before. In the decade since, their reappearance and return had become the stuff of stoat legend and fervent hopes. Lately, whispers of the Princes' return had become all too common among the stoat rabble. Spies were sent out by the wolves, and all the roads were watched. Stoats were still numerous in the highlands, but without a leader they could do nothing against their wolf overlords. The wolves aimed to make sure that the Princes never returned to challenge them.

The Princes were no fools. They had no intention of taking the old King's Road to the highlands. They travelled on long-forgotten paths and secret byways, keeping out of sight and under cover of night. Duncan's road was the most difficult. His plan was a bold one: he aimed to strike the wolves in their old territory. They would never expect this. The new rulers of the highlands believed that any revolt would start at Lochwarren, that the stoats would regroup at their ancestral home and march out to meet them as they had ten years earlier, but Duncan had learned a few things among the river raiders. His plan was to strike the mine at Scalded Rock. In the foothills at the edge of the Obsidian Desert, Scalded Rock was the richest mine in the Wolflands. Hundreds of stoats laboured there in slavery. Duncan planned to take the mine by surprise, seizing the diamonds and releasing the labourers. The diamonds would finance his war and the labourers were all loyal stoat men who would bolster his fighting numbers, but it was the victory that counted. Stoats would hear of it and take heart. When he arrived in Lochwarren, the people would be ready to follow him.

The surprise attack on Scalded Rock required Duncan to lead his party over the Glace Mountains. The paths over the peaks were treacherous and steep. Many had not been travelled for decades, and no one knew if the narrow passes at the summits remained clear. At the foot of one of these high passes, Duncan's party pulled up before a pile of rock and debris, an avalanche. Duncan stood staring at it for minutes, his hands upon his hips and his eye-whiskers knitted in fury, as if he meant to frighten the rocks into moving. Behind him some of his men were beginning to mutter about turning back when Duncan shouted, "Bring me ropes."

Silenced by their captain's command, his crew scrambled to do his bidding. Duncan had spent the last years climbing slippery masts. No mere wall of rocks would deter him. While his men fetched ropes, Duncan reappraised the cliff. His sharp eyes darted over the cliff, tracing imaginary paths for many silent minutes, but when he had found his course, he did not hesitate.

With a rope clamped firmly between his teeth, the muscular stoat began his ascent in a confident leap to a handhold above his head. From there he moved assuredly up the rock wall along a path no other stoat could see. He seemed to float along the rock face as he scampered up the near-vertical cliff. It looked effortless, but every man below felt a knot in his stomach at the thought of having to follow him.

Duncan, however, had no intention of forcing his men to scale the cliff as he did. He had brought the rope for this purpose. He would haul the first man up himself. It would only get easier after that. This was the strength and bravery that Duncan was renowned for. This was why men followed him. This was why he would be a great king.

Half the men were up the cliff when they started hauling the baggage, the armour and the bundles of swords that they had left at the foot of the cliff to make the climb easier. They hauled Duncan's battered chest up first, the one he had kept close to him for ten years, the one that held his father's gift. He could have prised it open long ago, and many times he had been tempted to, but he had kept the promise to his father. While he watched the chest being heaved up the cliff face, Duncan imagined, for the thousandth time, that day at Lochwarren when the gift would be revealed. What legendary sword, what storied weapon of his ancestors would declare his right to lead?

Suddenly there was a jerk in the rope as the chest caught on something. The men below shouted up in alarm as they saw what was happening. The knot was slipping. What ship rat has not learned his knots? thought Duncan angrily for a moment. Before he could hurl any insult or instruction, the knot gave way completely and the chest broke free. He watched it plummet unhindered to the jagged rocks below. He was already on his way down again when he heard the crash. He knew the chest had burst. He must get to it quickly. He must know if the gift was damaged.

Norman turned the page quickly. His stomach was rumbling and he could hear the rattle of cups and the slamming of cupboard doors downstairs, but he could not stop here. The chest had burst open. Duncan's gift was revealed. This was much sooner than he expected. The whole story would change here.

He hunkered down lower in the bed, turned the page and brought the book to his face again. But something was wrong. Something was missing—a whole page, in fact. The book was defective. The previous page had ended mid-sentence, but the next page began a new chapter. The action had moved to Cuilean and James.

Had he not looked a little closer at the spot where the missing page should be, Norman would have called out to his father right away to share his outrage and order an emergency trip to the bookstore. But there had been a page there once. A jagged edge remained, close to the binding. It looked as if the page had been ripped or bitten. Maybe the bookstore had mice. Maybe there was a vandal. Norman peered at the torn page and wondered—was he dumb enough to have done this himself? He put the thought out of his mind. Perhaps he could just keep reading. He'd know soon enough what had happened on the missing page, wouldn't he?

Norman began the new chapter, following Cuilean half-heartedly down the merchant road out of the realm of the Five Cities, but his head wasn't in it. He couldn't help thinking that he had lost the story. He wasn't reading the book the author had intended. There was something he was supposed know that he didn't. Without this clue, what else would he miss? Norman managed to stick with Cuilean for a few more pages, to the edge of the stoat lands, but his heart wasn't in it either now. He couldn't go on without knowing. He laid the book face down on the floor beside his bed and slouched down to breakfast.

The Replacement Librarian

"Morning, Spiny," Edward Vilnius said cheerfully as Norman sat down heavily at the table. Obviously his father had had a coffee already and the curse had been lifted for the morning. Perhaps it had been transferred to Norman himself. Usually he just ignored it when his dad called him Spiny. He didn't really know why his father did it, but he could say that about a lot of things. This morning being called Spiny seemed like a deliberate provocation. Norman put both elbows on the table and stared down at the flat surface.

"Is everything all right, Norman?" his mother asked. Meg Jespers-Vilnius didn't call him Spiny, but somehow her being nice to him was just as annoying.

"He's mad because he can't use his computer," Dora announced with her usual tone of self-satisfaction.

"I am not," Norman barked, but it reminded him that he had other reasons to feel that disgruntled.

"I thought you were reading your new book." Norman's father slid a few pancakes in front of him. A grunt was as close as Norman was going to get to a thank-you this morning.

"What's it called? *Grokloman*? *Rabbitrover*? *Flatweasel*?" In a better mood, Norman might have seen that his father was trying to humour him, but this morning it just sounded like teasing. Norman cut his pancake savagely, scraping his knife along the plate.

Dora held her ears theatrically and squealed, "Mom, he's doing that on purpose!"

Norman's father put his hand gently on his shoulder and whispered, "You don't have to slaughter the pancakes. I dispatched them already. They can't have survived the heat of the griddle."

Norman shrugged his father's hand away but knew better than to screech his knife against the plate again.

"Is there something wrong, Norman?" his mother asked again. She was dressed in her running gear and was stretching against the kitchen counter. At least she'd be gone for an hour—one less person to pester him.

"I'm just having a bad weekend is all," Norman said, enunciating each word, just like his dad did when he was trying to make a point.

Norman's mom just raised an eyebrow and answered cheerfully, "And who can change that?" She was out the door before Norman could think of a surly retort. What she meant, of course, was that only he could change that. Who could believe that his mother got paid to say things like that? It was a joke. Norman would gladly pay her *not* to tell him these things, at least this morning. He wolfed down the rest of his pancakes and chugged some milk to try to dislodge the knot of food his hasty eating had left at the bottom of his throat.

"I'm going to the library," he shouted as he headed for the door.

He ignored his sister's "Can I come?" but it slowed him down enough that he was able to hear his father say, "Maybe you should change out of your pyjamas first." Norman looked down. His father was right. He was still wearing his pyjamas. It didn't make him any happier to have to be reminded.

Only twenty minutes later, Norman was locking his bike to the rack outside the library. He headed right for the computer terminal. Norman knew the system by heart. He was here at least once a week. At the search screen, he pecked out "Lochwarren" in the title field and brought up the result page, showing that his local library had one copy. He fully expected it to be signed out. He almost didn't stop to look at the details, almost didn't believe the status was "Returned." Blinking just once to make sure, Norman didn't stop to write down the shelf location. He knew where the Undergrowth series was shelved better than most librarians did. Only years of coming to the library and his father's solemn training on proper library behaviour stopped him from shouting for joy and running to the fiction shelves.

There were nearly twenty books now in the Undergrowth series. The library had multiple copies of some, so that they filled nearly a whole shelf, just above Norman's eye height. He checked them alphabetically at first, then, when *The Brothers of Lochwarren* was not in its place, went through them methodically from left to right, his finger sliding along their spines. *The Brothers of Lochwarren* was not there. He returned to the computer terminal and confirmed the status. It still read "Returned." This had happened before to Norman, and he knew exactly what to do. *The Brothers of Lochwarren* just hadn't been reshelved yet. This was excellent luck. If it had been reshelved, it would have been snapped up by now. It must be in the reshelving stack behind the desk. All he had to do was ask.

Norman was somewhat taken aback when he arrived at the desk. His usual librarian, Mrs. Balani, the kind but taciturn Indian lady who always recommended excellent books that Norman had never heard of, was not there. Maybe she was on vacation. Maybe she had been promoted. Behind the desk in Mrs. Balani's place was a tall teenager dressed completely in black. When he turned around, Norman could not help staring at his lip piercing and the circular earrings that made a huge hole in his earlobes.

"I can stick a pencil through them," the librarian said nonchalantly.

"Pardon?" Norman managed. When he was intimidated he tended to be very polite.

"See," the teenager said, threading a pencil through the hole in one ear. "Fits right through."

Why anyone would want to do this, Norman could not guess. Maybe puberty did make you crazy, like his friend Jean said.

"I'm looking for *The Brothers of Lochwarren,* the new book in the Undergrowth series."

"It's out," the teenager replied without glancing at his computer. He flipped a long bang of dyed black hair out of his face and continued to stare at Norman.

"The, um, computer says it's returned," Norman stuttered.

The librarian in black curled his pierced lip and turned to his terminal. His typing was so quick that Norman almost believed that he was just pretending.

"It's reserved. The person's already been called," he replied after only a few seconds. "That's a good book. It's almost as good as *The Wastrel* and *Thorsten's Brood*. You should read it."

"I *am* reading it," Norman replied, a little annoyed.

"Then why do you want to sign it out?" the young librarian asked suspiciously.

"I don't want to sign it out. I just want to see it," Norman insisted.

"To see it?" The librarian made a face as if Norman was the crazy one.

"I just want to read one page."

"One page?" the new librarian asked. "Is that a special reading program you're on for school?"

Norman bit his lip in frustration. Did the whole world want to wreck his weekend? "It's just that my sister scribbled on a page in my copy," he lied. "I just wanted to read that one page here."

"You want to check something? Why don't you ask me? I read it last week."

"I'd rather read it myself."

The strange librarian typed again on the keyboard. It sounded like he was just hitting keys blindly, the way Dora did when she was pretending to be writing on the computer.

"It's damaged," the librarian said. "It's out for repairs."

"You just said it was reserved and that you'd called the person who reserved it."

"Unlucky for him, I guess."

Norman stared at the black-clad librarian in disbelief. He probably thought this was funny.

"You sure you don't want me to tell you what happened?" the librarian asked, faking sympathy.

Norman shook his head, unwilling yet to walk away.

The pierced librarian changed his tone and ran a pencil through his ear hole again. "What if," he asked, as if offering a special bargain, "I could arrange for your copy to be fixed."

Norman knew he was joking now. "Sure, go right ahead."

"All right, but you know you have to give something up, right? I'll replace the page you lost, but you have to give me another page."

"Sure," said Norman sarcastically. "I'll bring it right over." Norman turned his back now and walked away, before he did something that would get his borrowing rights revoked.

"No need for that," the librarian called after him. "I'll look after it."

It was only when he had cycled halfway home that Norman wondered how the librarian in black knew the page was missing. He was sure he'd told him Dora had scribbled on it. Not that it mattered. Librarians shouldn't make fun of the clients. Norman told himself that he'd report the new guy to Mrs. Balani. He'd never find the courage to do so, but for the duration of the ride home it made him feel better to imagine that he might.

Between the Pages

A chill rippled up Norman's arms and legs. Without opening his eyes, he reached for the covers but found them out of reach—kicked off the bed again, probably. His mom could never believe how he twisted sheets. "Who were you wrestling with?" she always asked.

It was the whispers that finally made him decide to get up.

"By the Maker, what creature's that?" one nervous, hoarse voice asked.

"Must be a bear, by the size of it," another replied unconvincingly.

"That's never a bear. Just look at it. It 'as hardly a hair on it. What manner of bear looks like that?"

"A sickly one, per'aps?"

"Aye, mebbe a sickly bear, mebbe."

At this point Norman opened his eyes.

"You've done it now, Makkie. I told you to keep quiet. You've gone and wakened it."

There was a rustling in the bushes in the direction of the voices, but Norman could see no one. Norman's bedroom did not normally contain bushes, nor was he used to sleeping on damp moss, but it was the sort of things a few blinks usually sorted out.

He rubbed his eyes and looked out again wearily. Blinking was apparently losing its magic. Norman climbed to his feet from his unfamiliar moss bed. His pyjamas were damp and grimy, but they were still his pyjamas. Nothing else was familiar, though. Pale sunlight streamed through a forest of pine trees. Somewhere behind him was the sound of a swiftly churning stream, but that was it—no other forest sounds, no insects or birds, certainly no people. If there had been people in the clearing when Norman woke, they had run away now.

Norman took a few tentative steps in the direction from which he had heard the voices. Gingerly, he poked a bush with a stick. No one emerged from it. He had imagined the voices, like he had imagined all of this. And imagined things, he knew, disappeared as easily as they appeared. He wouldn't worry about the voices, he decided. He'd worry about the forest. There was really only one question: was this the sort of imaginary forest you were supposed to try to find your way out of, or was it smarter just to stay here in this little clearing? It seemed safe enough. Nothing had tried to eat him yet.

He patrolled the clearing for a while, examining the tops of the trees and straining his ears until he thought he could hear his own blood rushing through his veins. Occasionally he stepped on a twig, making himself jump into a stance that he imagined a ninja or a black belt would take when faced with peril. When no danger presented itself, he stood up straight again and pretended to himself that nothing had frightened him. What he was feeling was not yet fear, but there was something growing in the pit of his stomach, something maybe worse than fear. Fear was for things you knew and understood.

Waiting finally became too much.

"I can't stand around in my pyjamas all day," Norman told himself. Talking to himself out loud might have been meant to calm his nerves, but the sound of his reedy, trembling voice was hardly reassuring.

The clearing had no obvious entrance. If the bushes seemed less thick in any spot, it was in the direction from which he'd first heard voices, but he could not force himself to go that way.

He retreated the other way, away from the imaginary voices and into the imaginary forest. Very quickly he found his route covered with thick, thorny brambles. And only just quickly enough did he discover it also concealed a deep ravine that almost guaranteed a twisted ankle. For a moment he considered climbing a tree to see if he could get a better view, but the saplings around him weren't quite tall or strong enough for climbing, so, slowly and carefully, he pushed into the bush where it appeared most sparse.

This was only slightly better than the opposite direction, but at least the ground seemed level. The thick brush forced Norman to shuffle forward with his arms in front of his face, to avoid poking his eyes out on a branch. He tried to bend the pine boughs out of the way and edge through the gap he made, but the trees got their share of swipes in. The beating he took at least kept his mind off the weirdness. He couldn't think about getting out of the dream of the forest at the same time as he thought about getting out of the forest itself. After a few minutes his pyjamas were ripped in two places and he had a nice scratch on his forehead from a branch he'd failed to duck.

It was slow going and tiring work. Maybe if he hadn't been concentrating on keeping his eyesight, he might have seen what was coming next, but it's unlikely. What was coming next did not want to be seen yet and was very good at keeping itself concealed when it wanted to. A gap of sunlight finally opened up in the brush, just a small one. Above and around it the bushes seemed thicker than ever. Norman got down on his hands and knees to get through, keeping his head down and his eyes half shut as the brambles and bushes grazed his head. He kept going, steadily, his teeth gritted and his eyes squinting toward the growing gap of sunlight, until an authoritative voice commanded him to stop.

"Heel, beast," it ordered. "Advance no farther."

Norman blinked and looked up. He half recognized the shape that stood before him. This half recognition only made him blink again. Once he started this blink, he found it hard to open his eyes again. He kept his eyes shut tight and prayed to wake up from this dream.

"Is this the beast you spied?" the commanding voice asked.

"Aye, that's the foul thing," a somewhat squeakier one answered. "'Tis a hideous creature, to be certain, and ungodly huge."

Norman opened his eyes fully and gaped at the figure that stood before him. He knew what it was, but he refused to believe it.

The impossible figure continued to speculate about Norman. "But hardly fearsome. If it is a bear, it is a sick one or a cub. 'T'has only a patch of fur. I wonder if its eyes have only just opened."

"If it is a cub, then likely its sow might be looking for it," a quavering voice added. Norman recognized it from when he'd first woken in the clearing.

"I'm . . . I'm not a bear," Norman said. He didn't want these strangers to be any more nervous than they already looked, but his squeaky, stuttered words had the opposite effect. The welcoming party took a collective step backward, leaving its leader alone at the forefront. Only he remained still, his legs steady on the boulder, his cape swept back over his shoulder and a steady sword arm holding a blade at the level of Norman's eyes. His eyes narrowed with curiosity, or perhaps suspicion.

"'Tis no baby, then. 'T'has the power of speech. Yet 'tis a mighty weird creature still."

Norman made a move to rise to his feet and wave his hand in friendly greeting, but the swordsman warned him with a waggle of his sabre.

"We'll have none of that. Stay where you are." He stood about two foot tall on his hind legs. His sharp little eyes squinted slightly as he appraised his captive, and his jaw was set at an angle that exposed a sharp canine tooth on one side. His whiskers rippled just slightly as he sniffed Norman from a safe distance. On his head he wore a black Cavalier hat with a broad brim and a long white feather. The rest of the animals kept their heads bare. It was the hat that gave him away.

Norman wondered if there was anything he could do or say to let them know that he was no danger to them.

"I know you," he said in a voice that surprised him with its wavering. "You're Duncan."

A dozen more blades were instantly drawn from their sheaths.

"My name's Norman," he continued uncertainly. "I don't come from here, but I'm a friend."

Duncan's whiskers bristled as he crouched even more threateningly. "Many's the varmint that claims to be a friend when faced with the blade of River Raider," he growled.

"Really, I am," Norman insisted rather lamely. "I'm a friend to the stoats. I'm on your and your brother's side."

Duncan thrust the tip of his sword toward Norman, stopping just short of his throat. "What do you know of me and my brother?" he muttered.

Norman gulped, feeling the air around his throat disturbed by the sword blade. "I know you are going back to Lochwarren, to reclaim your kingdom."

"And *how* do you know this, beast?" There was a sharp note of threat in the buccaneer's voice.

Norman could see how this was suspicious. His mind raced. He couldn't really say that he'd read about them in a book. No one would believe this.

"I'm a seer," he said quickly, hardly knowing where the inspiration came from. He had read enough Undergrowth books to know it might work, though. "I'm an apprentice seer. I saw your journey in a vision. I saw you and your company leaving from Rivernest, and Cuilean and James leaving from—"

"Enough of that, beast. Keep your tongue," Duncan commanded. And then, in a low voice, to himself he murmured, "And so Cuilean lives too." His face became thoughtful. "Stand up, beast. Let's see the height of you." Duncan made an upward motion with his sword.

Norman staggered slowly to his feet. The stoats took yet another step backward and sucked in a deep collective breath.

Duncan shook his head in disgust or wonderment.

"By the Maker, you have some altitude, don't you? What manner of beast are ye?"

Norman decided to tell the truth. "I'm a human."

Duncan nodded his head. "Aye, I've heard of such things—read of them in books when I was a bairn. Never thought to lay my eyes upon one. Are all your kind of such mass?"

"I'm average height for my age. My father is six feet tall."

"Merciful Maker," Duncan muttered. "Six of *your* feet, perhaps. You look to be fifty paws yourself. I hope I never meet your father."

Norman assured him that it wasn't likely.

They led him back to their encampment. They didn't tie him up, but they made him sit alone on the edge of the camp with two armed guards for company. Duncan's war party seemed to be readying itself for travel. There may have been twenty or thirty stoats in all. Some packed weapons and cooking utensils into bags, while others carefully erased all trace of their fire. When they were ready to depart, Duncan brought two of the larger packs over to Norman. Norman didn't mind carrying them. They were light, and he welcomed a chance to show that he could be useful.

"Keep your seeings to yourself for the time being, apprentice seer," Duncan growled as they set off.

Norman nodded obediently. "My name's Norman," he reminded him.

The stoats made Norman walk at the head of the column, where they could see him. They were leaving the forest behind now and heading into the more barren region of the Glace mountain peaks. The rocks and low scrub afforded little cover, and the stoats could not count on their stealth to conceal them. Norman served as their lookout, keeping an eye on the path ahead, as they kept an eye on him. He walked slowly and absorbed the situation while the stoats bustled behind him. He had daydreamed like this before, when a book got really good. You wanted to help the heroes. You thought you could give them advice, tell them about action going on in other parts of the book that they didn't know about. But this was more than a daydream. He couldn't tell what it was yet, but it was no ordinary dream either. It was strange how easy it was to accept it, to just go along as if it was normal and push away that awful anxiety that had started to fidget in his belly. It was better to give in to the story than to his fear.

Norman found himself wondering about the contents of the chest. What had fallen out of the shattered box at the bottom of the cliff? Duncan's mood was no real indication. Secretly Norman hoped that Duncan already knew that Cuilean was destined to be King. The pirate-prince's dour mood tempted him to think so, but Norman had read enough to know that Duncan was always this cantankerous.

As the day dragged on, Norman was lulled with the dullness of it all. His legs ached and his bare feet stung. He wished he'd entered the book with Cuilean and James. No one had offered him breakfast, and the anxiety in his belly now fought with the grumblings of hunger. He didn't dare ask for anything to eat. He knew what stoats normally ate.

Cuilean, he was sure, would have offered him a sandwich. Cuilean would have talked to him properly and invited him into his confidences. After a morning's march, Norman was more sure than ever of who was the rightful king of the highlands. And in his wistful sulk, he wasn't overly focused on the path. Perhaps if he had been paying more attention he would have recognized the danger on the road ahead. When a bird settled at the crest of the hill before them, Norman saw only a bird. It wasn't until it spoke that Norman remembered where he was, and what a large black bird like this must be.

"Alarm, alarm!" the black bird cried in its raspy voice. It fixed an inscrutable black eye on Norman, and paused a moment before taking to the air.

"Raven!" Norman cried, turning back toward the stoats, but his warning was late. Duncan and his men had already drawn their weapons.

The Battle of the Ravens

The stoat archers took position by the side of the path, sheltering behind whatever boulder or overhang they could find. Like them, Norman moved to the side, but he was too big for the soccer ball–sized rocks to offer him any protection. He had read about raven warcraft in *The Helm of Bildung,* book IV of the Undergrowth saga, and he had no desire to be part of it. Duncan and the swordsmen formed up in a circle in the centre of the road, their backs against each other and their blades bristling. All eyes were on the sky. For a moment it seemed that nothing might happen. No bird called out. The only sound was of the wind howling through the pass. Norman relaxed his shoulders and prepared to step forward, until he noticed that the stoats remained still and vigilant.

Duncan's warning cry came first. "Wits about you, lads. Here they come."

Then came the sound of a great bustling of wings, like water rushing through rapids.

Norman crouched down as a black form wheeled into view around the curve of the mountain. The raven flock moved like a single entity, coming in high and circling the assembled stoats below.

"Fire, fire! What are you waiting for?" Norman muttered, but the archers were experienced warriors. They waited patiently, arrows nocked.

Norman squinted into the brisk alpine sky trying to tell how the ravens were armed. In *The Helm of Bildung,* the fox engineer Daedalus had built crossbow harnesses for his raven warriors. The weapons had been devastating. The ravens had been able to attack from a distance and height beyond the reach of ground archers. Only the owls and the hawks had been able to defeat the crossbow ravens. That was the only time that the micelings of Undergrowth ever allied themselves with their archenemies in the air. But this had been a long time ago in Undergrowth history, and Norman knew there was no chance of hawks or owls coming to their rescue today.

"Draw," the steady voice of Duncan finally commanded. The archers drew back their strings and planted their back paws.

"Take aim."

A dozen arrows slowly tracked the sweep of the ravens, as the attackers made their approach.

"Loose!" the Prince cried, and those dozen arrows took flight. They were too fast for Norman to track them—he only heard their whoosh through the air. The enraged cries of the ravens were the first sign that some arrows had found their target. Norman watched as a few black shapes tumbled from the sky. Surely if the ravens had crossbows the bolts would have been unleashed by now. The thought gave Norman some hope, but he had little time to savour it. The remaining ravens continued undeterred on their attack run, swooping overhead, unleashing a hail of rocks as they closed in.

The missiles flew in along low trajectories, whistling through the air toward the ambushed party of stoats. The sound of them ricocheting off shields was shockingly loud. The swordsmen had anticipated the attack and defended themselves. The archers were not so lucky. They had admired the flight of their arrows too long and had ducked behind their boulders too late. Norman heard high yelps as three or four of them were struck and fell to the ground. In front of him a stoat archer lay motionless and unprotected in the middle of the path.

Shock and pity made Norman act without thinking. He dashed out into the open to the stricken archer, who was not heavy. He's about the weight and size of our old housecat Moggy, Norman thought incongruously as he lifted the furry little body. The thought made it worse. They had taken Moggy to the vet for the last time three months earlier. It still brought a lump to the top of his throat, but as he shuffled backward to the side of the cliff, his pity was shaken from his head—by a sharp blow and a stinging explosion in his temple. It made him stop for a moment to look up. A crow wheeled away from him now, shrieking victoriously.

A curious thing happened then. The throbbing in his forehead made Norman realize that he was in real danger, but instead of frightening him, it only made him angry. Carefully he placed the unconscious stoat in a sheltered spot and turned to avenge himself.

The ravens had circled again and were coming in for a second run. They had not had time to reload with rocks. This would be hand to hand.

"Fire on your own marks, archers," Duncan called out.

Arrows were unleashed singly now as each archer tracked a diving bird. There were more ragged cries and more falling ravens before the squadron struck again, but still they struck, racking the little formation of swordsmen with steel-tipped talons that glinted in the high mountain sun. The swordsmen slashed at the sky, but the birds moved too fast.

The force of the ravens' attack was enough to knock a few of the stoats to the ground. They were still being helped to their feet when a second wave of rock launchers hurtled in. There was no sound of rocks bouncing off shields this time. Norman looked in dismay as more stoats fell. A trick, he thought—they'd held some back from the first attack. It was a clever ploy. The stoats were in disarray. The formation looked ragged, and at least half the archers were disabled. Another attack like this might break them.

The ravens seized this chance to bring the fighting in close. They came in at all angles, each bird lining up a stoat. Bows and arrows were useless in such close quarters, and even the archers drew their swords now. Formations and battle plans were forgotten. The melee had degenerated into single combat, stoat against raven, sword against armoured claw.

Through it all, Duncan called out encouragement to his fighters: "Have heart, men—remember what blood runs through those veins!" He swatted his own assailant away with a mighty swing of his sword, slicing across the angry bird's face. The battling prince did not wait to see his attacker stumble and cover his blood red beak with a bent wing. Duncan knew what his blow had done and was now leaping to the aid of the man who fought beside him. Seeing it with his own eyes, Norman could not help but be reminded of Duncan's father, Malcolm, battling on bravely at Tista Kirk, back in chapter one.

Norman's head still smarted. He longed to do something to avenge himself and the little archer slumped beside him, but he hadn't a clue how to make himself useful. He watched helplessly as the battle raged around him. The ravens tried to pull their prey away from the main body of the fighters, where they could set upon them in murderous groups of three and four. The stoats tried to hold together, forming up around their leader and beating the ravens back, but the ravens' cowardly strategy began to work. They singled out one wounded warrior, a tactic they must have learned from their wolf allies. Norman's rage bubbled as he watched three ravens drag the poor stoat away from the main battle. His companions rushed forward to reclaim him, but more ravens intervened, slashing at the rescuers' eyes with their claws. Norman was close enough to see the terror flash momentarily in the captured stoat's eyes before the defenceless creature raised his arm to shield them. His attackers tugged his arms with their beaks. They meant to blind the poor thing.

This was too much for Norman.

"Get off him, you scum!" he screamed.

His voice boomed through the canyon. Startled, the ravens stopped and looked. They regarded him disdainfully for just a moment, then set about their victim once more. What had the pink giant done in this fight yet? they must have thought.

Their contempt only made Norman angrier. Without a thought of what he might actually do, he ran at the three ravens at full speed. Some instinct took over as he hurled himself at them, as if he was charging down a loose ball on the soccer field. He followed through with a swift kick, connecting firmly with one raven's flank and sending it hurtling into the cliff wall. The black bird struck the rock hard, then tumbled to the ground, shook itself from the blow and staggered back as if confused, one wing hanging at a sharp angle. The two other birds hopped back in surprise.

Somewhere a stoat voice cried out in alarm, "'Tis young Malcolm!"

Norman stepped over the prone stoat protectively. The ravens eyed him viciously and hopped tentatively where they stood, but neither advanced nor retreated. Their victim was still alive, but covered in too much blood for Norman to know where the wounds might be. Norman crouched down and stroked its ears instinctively as he would any pet. It was only now that he noticed how small the stoat was, not even fully grown. Once again, the unfamiliar battle rage surged in his belly.

"Bullies!" he cried, facing the ravens again. His hand found a handy rock, and he stepped forward to hurl it side-arm at the defiant birds. If he tried a hundred times he would never again be able to throw another rock with that velocity and accuracy, with such deadly effect. The stone struck one raven full force on the head. It let out half a cry before falling still to the ground. Norman kept going, rushing toward the remaining raven, screaming once again, "Filthy vermin!" It was Undergrowth's worst insult, and he meant it. What sort of creature picked on a poor kid like that?

Norman's charge turned the battle. The ravens had never seen anything like him—nothing so tall and so loud that wasn't a bear. They would never dare face a bear, and Norman at this moment seemed as fierce and as deadly. They stumbled back toward the crest of the pass. Stoats harried them all the way. The blur of battle was slowly lifting for Norman. He sank to a knee beside the bloody stoat. The young creature was stirring, rising with the aid of two companions who had rushed to his side.

Norman tore his gaze from the recovering stoat, his eye drawn reluctantly to the bird he had felled. Its repulsive glossy eye was motionless and unblinking. A sick churning tumbled through Norman's stomach. He had killed that bird. It was just sinking in, as the cries of the ravens became distant and the pursuing stoats returned. Norman had never killed anything before. He knew kids who threw stones or fired BB guns at birds, and he hated them. Was he one of them now? For a long time Norman just stood there, looking but not really seeing anything.

A deep growl of a voice disturbed his reverie. "You do more than see, then."

"Huh?"

"You are a fighter as well as a seer." It was Duncan who spoke.

"Not usually," Norman said slowly. "But I had to. They would have poked out—"

"I know what they would have done, and I thank you for it. You fought bravely and well. You have saved my boy's life. I will honour you for this." Duncan crouched to feel the young stoat's wounds. The youngster smiled woozily as Duncan introduced him.

"My boy, Malcolm. He will remember his first battle, and I your part in it."

"Malcolm, named after your father," Norman said softly.

"Indeed, seer." Duncan nodded as he spoke. "Indeed he is. And what are you called by your people?"

"My name's Norman." He had told him twice already, but he didn't mind repeating it.

"Welcome, Norman Strong Arm, and thank you. Let's be moving now. Those blackwings will be warning their masters."

Norman Strong Arm

By some miracle all of Duncan's stoats had survived the battle at the pass, although several had to be shaken back to consciousness. They rubbed their heads and grumbled, but they found their feet soon enough. Those that had taken cuts from the ravens' steel-tipped talons and beaks were patched up and bandaged. They too would be able to hobble their way down the path. Only Duncan's son, Malcolm, needed help to continue. Duncan ordered his men to make a stretcher for him. A piece of canvas sail was found, and a single pike for one handle, but they needed a second. All the other pikes had been broken during the confusion of the battle.

"Well, find some other stick then!" Duncan was beginning to anger. "We've to be moving from this place."

Norman stood over the stricken stoat. He could not shake the uncanny memory of his lost pet cat. "I'll carry him," he said quietly.

The animals looked up at him, still surprised every time he spoke.

"Make a sling, like a hammock, that I can put around my neck," he said more loudly. Norman had seen human mothers carry their babies in such contraptions. He didn't see why it wouldn't work for the wounded stoat.

Duncan too saw immediately that it would work. "Aye, do as he says. Let Norman Strong Arm bear the bairn. We'll travel faster for it."

And so the canvas sail was fastened into a sling and the half-conscious creature was slung around Norman's neck. The weight was no burden at all. If anything, it was comforting to have the thing breathing slowly against his chest.

Duncan regarded Norman curiously while he adjusted the sling. He held Norman's eye for a moment then turned away. "Right, then, let's be off," he ordered gruffly, obviously eager to be away from this place. If they were lucky, the ravens would want to deal with the stoats' incursion themselves. Scouting parties would be sent out, and a larger force mobilized against them. If they were unlucky, the ravens would pass the intelligence on to their wolf allies, and Duncan's surprise attack on Scalded Rock would be no surprise at all.

The barren mountaintops offered no protection. They needed to crest the mountains and descend to the tree line on the other side before sunrise. The party marched as quickly as it could, eating and drinking on the move. Bread was found for Norman, and a sort of salad was made from the weeds at the side of the road. It was enough to stop his stomach grumbling. The stoats were reluctant, though, to share the water from their skins with their giant companion. Norman could tell that they feared he would drain it all. When Duncan noticed this, he dropped back, handing his own water skin over to Norman before returning to the head of the column. The other stoats looked away, embarrassed.

The animals still could not fathom what sort of beast Norman was, but at least they had a name they could call him now. Norman Strong Arm was the hero of the battle with the ravens. He had saved two stoats, one of them Duncan's own son, and his throwing arm had driven off the birds when the battle seemed lost. Norman tried not to think about that moment. The ugly, plaintive squawks of the dying raven reverberated in his head and filled him with remorse. Death was strange and frightening to him. His sister Dora's three goldfish had died, one after the other. He had had nothing to do with it, but he had still felt guilty when his mother had flushed them down the toilet. And there had been Moggy. The cat had been older than Norman himself. She had always been part of his family. Norman had not been able to understand why the vet could do nothing for her at the end. Dora had cried for a day and began asking for a new kitten the next morning, but Norman wanted no replacement. He had always felt that they should have done more. He didn't know what, but something.

Carrying the injured stoat made Norman feel like he was helping somehow. The animal's body heat against his chest felt familiar and comfortable. Its body rocked with the rhythm of its breathing, and with each deep breath it let out a high-pitched little wheeze. It sounded like Norman's father's quieter snores.

The party continued quickly along the path, the stoats dropping to all fours to pick up the pace. They dashed ahead in quick spurts, stopping at each corner or outcropping to quickly spy or sniff out danger. They looked more like animals this way, less like people, and it reminded Norman just how strange this whole situation was.

I am in the book, he thought to himself. *I really am in it*. It might have been just his hunger, but the thought of having fallen into the book made him feel oddly dizzy. He found himself looking up at the sky now, not for signs of the raven pursuit, but half expecting to see the eyes of the readers looking down on him.

I wasn't always in the book, he mused—*not in the original version. The book has changed because I'm in it*. He wondered if the actual physical book had changed due to his presence, whether the other kids higher on the library waiting list were wondering what a human boy was doing in the world of *Undergrowth*.

Norman had not read this far. Would Duncan's party have crossed the Glace Mountains without him? Maybe finding Norman had delayed Duncan's party. Perhaps they would never have stumbled across the ravens if they hadn't spent the morning dealing with him. But what if they had met the ravens in the book? Would they have fared as well? And what about young Malcolm? Was the young prince meant to die in the book?

The human boy patted the sleeping body of the stoat he carried. "I don't care whether it was meant to happen," he said quietly. "I'm glad I saved you." He scratched the little stoat's ear gently, as you would a cat, and like a cat the animal let out a low purr. "Don't worry, Malcolm. I'll look after you," he promised, reassuring himself as much as the stricken animal he carried.

It wasn't hard keeping up with the stoats. They were capable of intense bursts of speed, but they were sprinters, not cross-country runners, and their cautious instincts didn't favour careening on heedlessly at full tilt. After every burst of speed there was a pause and a hasty peering around for danger. By maintaining a steady walk, Norman was able to keep pace with them. Only the sharp incline of the path caused him trouble. They were descending now, and Norman took the utmost care to keep his footing. A grazed elbow or stubbed toe wouldn't be the end of the world, but a fall could harm his young charge. He picked his way carefully down the path, holding his hands in front of him—not just for balance, but to protect the sleeping stoat in the sling on his chest.

The sun was setting when they finally saw the tree line. It cut a jagged silhouette across the orange sphere, like teeth gradually nibbling away at it as it descended. Duncan urged them to hurry, but they were all tired by now.

"C'mon, lads, let's not dawdle. There's dry beds and fresh victuals beyond those trees. Let's have at 'em before it's too dark, eh?"

There were a few weary grunts of agreement, but the stoats quickened their steps only briefly before falling back to the same exhausted plod. The party drew up tighter as the light faded. No one wanted to be out of earshot or eyesight of his companions as the night came on. In the dark of early night, they would not see the ravens until it was too late. Duncan peered anxiously at the sky more often now, and around at his men, gauging their strength and calculating their odds if they had to fight another squadron of ravens. Frequently his gaze fell on Norman, his sharp eyes darting over him, judging him before falling on the bundle around Norman's chest. Norman tried to look strong and dependable.

That last half hour before nightfall seemed to last forever. The stoats were accustomed to moving around in the dark, but Norman's eyes weren't quite so acute. He frequently stumbled on the rocky path, making a huge ruckus. His travelling companions glared back at him scoldingly, as if they could not believe he could be such a clumsy oaf, then motioning upward as if they were sure that his din would summon the blackwings.

When the sun itself finally disappeared into the jaws of the forest and only a few faint orange rays seeped up into the sky behind them, Duncan's party fell into a more constant bounding sprint. It was as if they could hear the wing beats of their enemies behind them. They forgot all caution and ran headlong for the trees. It was almost easier now for Norman, at a jogging pace. He lifted his feet higher, avoiding the ruts and boulders that had tripped him up when he walked, but he ran with one arm around the sling and the other in front of him. If he fell forward, he would rather break his arm than crush the little stoat.

He did not dare look back, but the sound of his own rushing blood in his ears sounded for all the world like the rustle of predatory birds at his back.

Norman picked out as his target a slender birch sapling at the edge of the forest. The pale gleam of its white bark was the only thing that stood out for him in the forest gloom. Upon reaching it, he grasped it tightly with his free arm and let his own momentum turn him around to face the direction from which he had come. The stoats scrambled in behind him. The closed bunch had broken up now, and each stoat was running at the best of his ability to the safety of tree cover. Only Duncan held up at the forest edge, urging the stragglers on, telling them how close they were to safety, reminding them of their brave deeds in the past and of their bold adventures to come.

Norman scanned the night sky and strained his ears, but there was no sign of a pursuit. He stood at that tree and counted the stoats as they rushed passed him. Duncan was the last. He slowed his pace and strode proudly into the forest on two feet, adjusting his sword hilt and Cavalier hat and nodding solemnly to Norman as he did so.

"That's all of them then?" Duncan asked.

Norman whispered, "Yes."

"And the boy? How's my boy?" the Prince asked, lowering his voice. Up close, the stoat's eyes and snout were more expressive. His bushy eyebrows were knitted close together, and his mouth twitched just slightly.

"Still asleep," Norman answered. He worried that the small animal might be slipping into unconsciousness. The boy's father bared a fang. It worried him too, but he took pains not to show it.

"Wise lad," he muttered gruffly. "Best we should all be asleep. Though where we'll find a stoat hole big enough for you, I don't know."

It was all right by Norman if they didn't. He didn't think he could sleep in a hole if he tried. Not too far into the woods, the stoats found a large oak tree whose roots had been undermined by some long-dried-up stream. Below the tangle of roots were more than enough hiding places for the stoats. Norman curled up on a sheet of canvas at the foot of the tree and covered himself with another one, placing the still sleeping Malcolm beside him on the inside, nearer the tree. Duncan posted two sentries, who were to change every three hours, but he stood the first watch himself.

They were still too close to the edge of the forest to risk a fire for warmth, but Norman hardly minded. He was exhausted. The fight and the long trek had been more exercise than he was used to. He felt it in his bones as soon as he lay down.

It should have been easy to fall asleep, despite the awkwardness of his bed, but the stillness finally allowed him to think about the strangeness of the surroundings and of the day's events. If this was not a dream, how did he get here, and how would he get back home? What were his parents doing now? Had they been looking for him all day? Had they called the police? The image of his mother crying at the kitchen table occurred to him—like a sudden, unpredictable memory. These thoughts, the thoughts that he had not let himself think all day, sent a shiver through him. He wrapped his arms around himself and pretended that it was the cold that made his body tremble.

The murmur of conversation from the resting stoats slowly died down, and all Norman could hear were the hoots and cracklings of the forest. He rolled onto his back and stared at the moon, careful not to crush the little stoat sleeping at his side. Only by imagining himself back in his own room could he coax himself to sleep. He had done the opposite so many times before, closed his eyes and imagined himself in a book with a forest or a castle just outside his closed eyelids. Tonight he closed his eyes and imagined himself in his own bed, imagined that if he opened them, the blinking amber lights of his computer would be there. He visualized a book laying splayed open on the bedside table next to his bed and pretended he could hear the indistinct ebb and flow of his parents' conversation downstairs.

Very gradually sleep overtook him, but not before, in a second of lucidity, he realized that falling asleep was as good a proof as any that he was not dreaming. You don't fall asleep in dreams.

The Woods

The friction of his dad's scruffy chin against his cheek woke Norman, irritating yet somehow comforting, the way he leaned in to give him a hug and whisper that it was time to get up. But the scrape against his cheek seemed more focused, perhaps softer, and just a little bit . . . wet. He opened his eyes with a start, and the stoat that had been licking his face jumped back too, emitting a little squeak of surprise. Neither could help breaking down into laughter that they'd managed to startle each other.

"You're awake," Norman said to the little stoat. His relief surprised him.

"And so are you, foignally," Malcolm teased.

Norman scoffed at the little animal's boldness. "*I* didn't sleep all yesterday afternoon. And I didn't get carried over the top of the mountain, either."

"I didn't sleep *all* afternoon," Malcolm protested, but not strenuously. He didn't say thank you in so many words, but there was plenty of gratitude in this friendly banter.

"How are you feeling?" Norman asked, inspecting his companion.

"Foighting fit," Malcolm replied, pulling himself up on two feet and thrusting out a proud white chest. Norman saw him wince as he did so.

"Your father will be relieved."

Malcolm acted as if he hadn't heard this last thing. "So I hear you beat the ravens off single-handed. Lifted a huge boulder over your head and crushed six of them in one blow."

Norman could tell he was joking. "They told you six, did they? It was eight, and not one less. Get it straight."

The two laughed again. Only the sound of Duncan's orders cut them short. "Aye, are you kits going to lie around gossiping all morning, or are you going to make ready to march?"

Malcolm stiffened at the sound of his father's voice.

"Ready, sir," he replied, in a low, subdued tone.

"And you, Norman Strong Arm," Duncan asked. "Do you hibernate like a bear as well as smell like one?"

Norman was taken aback by the insult. Duncan had said nothing to his son about his recovery, and had not shown any relief that the boy was awake. He was back to the gruff creature that Norman had read about in the first chapters. He thought of his own father, and how differently he would have reacted in such a situation. Perhaps stoats were different from human fathers, or perhaps warriors were just different from professors.

They were very soon ready to break camp. Norman rubbed his stiff arms and legs until they felt like they might work properly. The stoats had left him a large bowl of raspberries and blueberries, which he took thankfully and gulped down quickly. Duncan was impatient to get going. They were safer under the cover of the trees, but not totally safe. Ravens could move more quickly in the air than stoats could through the bushes, and even through the branches of the forest canopy a raven's eyes were sharp.

They moved hurriedly in single file along a narrow path that Norman never would have seen himself. After twenty minutes young Malcolm was already struggling to keep up the pace. He scurried forward as quickly as he could, but his foreleg was injured and forced him to limp. His breathing was laboured and wheezy, and whenever he thought no one was looking, he held his ribs and grimaced. Twice he refused a lift from Norman before he finally agreed to take a ride.

"I'll carry you later," the boy promised jokingly as he climbed wearily back into the sling.

Malcolm did not lie still for long. Now that his strength was returning, the young stoat found it impossible to stay still in the sling unless he was actually asleep. A short nap restored him. He fidgeted and tossed about for a while longer before poking his head out impatiently. He soon clambered onto Norman's shoulder and began chattering into his new friend's ear. Every now and then he yelled out "duck!" to warn Norman of an approaching branch that threatened to poke his eye out. The forest path was not made for humans, not even eleven-year-olds. While the stoats scampered relatively carelessly along the narrow path, Norman had to be constantly on the lookout for low-hanging branches and outcrops of roots. In between his cries of "duck" and "look out," Malcolm told Norman about his life among the river raiders.

"I've lived on boats all my life. I'd almost rather be on the water than on land. The best place in the wide world is up top in the sails. It's much like riding on your shoulder, 'cept smoother and safer. Riding with you is like riding out a storm clinging to a mast. You're lucky I have my sea legs, or else you'd have to catch me every few yards."

Norman struggled to keep up his end of the conversation. It somehow didn't seem right for the stoat to know about a world of school buses and summer camps. He kept his eye on the path ahead of him and let Malcolm do most of the talking. "Your mother doesn't mind you going up there in the rigging?" he asked him. "How about coming on this expedition with your father?" Norman's mother didn't even let him ride his bike without a helmet. He couldn't imagine her letting him climb a ship's mast, or take a sword and a bow and arrow into a battle with ravens.

"My mother died when I was young."

"I'm sorry," said Norman.

"River rats found our warren one night. They caught us in our sleep. They would have murdered us all if the fleet hadna returned. Father says he knew I was in trouble. He says he'll always know when I need him. The ships came into shore in time to drive the rats off, but not before they'd overrun the warren. Father slit their throats. I saw it with my own eyes, how he held them by the scruff of their necks and drew the knife across."

Norman thought of the raven he had killed the day before and felt a chill of horror go through his body.

"And your mother?" he asked.

Malcolm did not answer the question. "Since then, Father's kept me with him on the boats. He says that no one can protect me as well as he can. Says I'm safer with him in the midst of battle than home in bed with a hot-water bottle by myself."

"Do you think he's right?"

"Here is where I'm meant to be. He's all the family I have. We're keepers of a great dynasty, you know. My grandfather was the last of the Mustelid kings, a great warrior like my father."

"I know," said Norman, remembering the last stand of King Malcolm. "Your grandfather fought valiantly at Tista Kirk. No stoat was braver."

Malcolm seemed shocked that Norman knew the story of his grandfather. "It's true you're a seer then. Few creatures know the story of Tista Kirk. Fewer still know my own dad is King Malcolm's son. Amongst the marauders, only Rufus Singewhiskers, Simon Whiteclaw and Falk knew. The twenty that came with us are quickly learning. My father fears assassins. He said the wolves would send turncoat weasels to kill us if they ever found out about us."

Norman had read enough to know that Duncan was probably right.

"There's a great deal of killing in my family, a great deal of spilt blood. I sometimes wish it would end."

"What do you mean?" Norman asked. It was a curious sentiment for a stoat prince.

"I mean that there'll be a long war ahead of us. Many lads'll perish before it's won . . ." His resolve seemed to stiffen as he spoke. ". . . and I'll be at my father's side as I ought, a leader and a warrior."

"Not all stoats are warriors," Norman said, trying to rouse his friend from the gloomy mood that had descended upon him.

Malcolm snorted. "All the aloive ones are. Those that don't fight get slaughtered."

"What about your uncle, then?"

"Dead, like the rest of 'em," Malcolm muttered.

"No, he's not—he's alive," Norman said. "He escaped from Lochwarren too, just like your father, only he went to the Five Cities. He left Logorno a few days ago to meet your father."

"Logorno . . . ," Malcolm said in a low voice, almost a whisper. "And they say 'tis only a fairy tale."

"No, it's not a fairy tale. It's one of the five great cities. Your uncle Cuilean studied there and served as clerk to the Duke. He is a fine swordsman, but a scholar too. The Duke depends on him and delegates the judge's gavel to him when he is unable to attend court. You'll like your uncle. He's a good man."

"But not a warrior, you say?"

"In the Five Cities, he always wins the archery tournament."

"An arrow is a boy's weapon," Malcolm replied sulkily, but he argued like someone who wanted to be convinced otherwise.

Norman gave no second thought to relating everything he knew about Cuilean, though perhaps he should have. The boy listened eagerly, and it was only when they reached the end of their day's journey that Norman realized that he had done it again: he had changed the book. Malcolm wasn't meant to know about his uncle. The boy hadn't even been mentioned in the book as far as Norman had read, but almost certainly he wasn't meant to know about his uncle. His father had told Malcolm that Cuilean was dead. Was it a lie, or did Duncan believe his brother was dead? That must be part of the story. Probably he was supposed to find out at the end, when the brothers met again at Lochwarren. Norman was really messing this story up.

There was no use shutting up now. What was done was done: Malcolm knew about his uncle. Norman could hardly make him forget, so as they journeyed over the next few days, Norman and the young stoat traded stories about Undergrowth.

Once, and only once, Malcolm asked Norman about his own family. They were sitting down to an evening meal of nuts and berries. Norman scooped the last handful and smacked his lips triumphantly. The stoat shook his head and called him a pig, as if he wouldn't have taken the last handful just as quickly if he could.

"What about yer family then?" he said. "Are they all seers like yerself?"

Norman considered how he could describe his family to the young stoat. Would he be able to understand anything of this world of cars and homework and pesky sisters? He had only been away two days and already it seemed so far away. He had stopped hoping that sleep would return him. He knew that going back would take something else. But what? What could get him home? Maybe he had to get to the end of the book. That would surely do it, wouldn't it? Because if that didn't work, he hadn't the slightest clue how to get home.

Norman never answered his friend's question.

He fell asleep thinking of the new question that had replaced it in his mind. What if he never escaped the pages and forests of Undergrowth?

Plan of Attack

Pancakes. It took a few moments to identify the scent wafting up from the kitchen, but he had it now—pancakes. Mom was making pancakes, which was strange on a school day, when everything was such a rush. Usually that meant a bowl of cereal, or peanut butter toast. Maybe Mom was staying home today. Maybe she was flying out to a speaking engagement later in the day, and this was a farewell breakfast. Never mind. Her pancakes had never smelled so good. She made them from scratch, not out of a box, and there was no comparison. He'd go down to find a huge stack of them in the middle of the kitchen table, or else she'd have set a plate out for each of them and written messages with syrup in hearts or stars, or their names and initials, or "You Rock" or "Good Luck on Your Geometry Test." Only she couldn't have ever written that, could she? You couldn't drip all those words in syrup on a pancake. So why did he remember this? Why could he see it? It was like that trick your mind plays in a dream—you remember something that could never have happened in real life, but it seems so normal in your dreams. The strangest things seemed normal in your dreams, as if they had always been that way.

Norman's eyes snapped open. The forest was blurry beyond his sleep-encrusted eyes. He blinked them shut hard and opened them again slowly. No good. Sleep dust still clouded his vision of the undergrowth. It was impossible to tell if something was really moving out there or if it was just a dead eyelash on his own cornea. Closing his eyes again, he let himself awake more slowly. The disappointment of the missed pancakes sank in now—the disappointment of the missed bedroom, the missed kitchen, the missed mother. Did she even know he was gone? What were they thinking back there in the world outside the book? Did they think that he had been kidnapped or that he'd run away? Maybe they had begun to give up hope, and they were starting to pack his things away, his figurines and his computer games, his books. If they would only pick up the book he had been reading, they would see where he had gone. Norman longed for his mother and father to pick up *The Brothers of Lochwarren* and read him. Maybe he should cry out, so that if they were reading, they would know that he missed them and wanted to get out. They would read, "Mom, Dad, I'm here, help me!"

He never did cry out. It was absurd to think it would work, and the stoats would have been all over him for making so much noise. But it didn't stop him from thinking it and wanting to scream at the top of his lungs for help.

Duncan's company travelled through the highland forest for three days, descending slowly to the foothills below. It was tough going for Norman. The path didn't get any easier. Occasionally he would spot a clearing or a stretch of grassland through the trees, but he gave up suggesting that they leave the path. The stoats told him time and time again that they needed to stay under cover. Out in the open they'd be visible to any raven patrol. They had no doubt that the crows were looking for them—raven calls reverberated through the forest as the patrols called to each other.

More than once Duncan ordered them to ground and the stoats scrambled into holes that Norman would never have seen, while he did his best to blend into the leaves. This was easier after a few days as his pyjamas became filthier. Sky blue no longer, they were covered with dirt and grass stains, which made a natural form of camouflage. Norman knew he was in trouble if he ever got back home for laundry day.

The travelling made Norman grumpy. He could feel himself getting peevish. It was like being in the back of the car. He wanted to be home. He wanted to know how long it would be before they got where they were going. Only Malcolm made it easier. Wrapped around Norman's neck, he chattered incessantly, regaling Norman with stories of his life on the water, the grand future as a pirate king that he had planned but probably would have to give up now he'd found he was the last of the Mustelid dynasty. He was a happy little creature. Nothing seemed to bother him much. Not once did he complain about his injury or the difficulty of their journey. It made Norman feel silly for wanting to complain.

Norman was grateful for his company. When they stopped to rest, Malcolm didn't look for a hole like the others. He stayed outside and curled up with Norman. Duncan probably would have preferred that Malcolm sleep underground like the other stoats, but he did not protest. Each night, though, as he took the first watch, the warrior prince gave Norman the same look. Norman had lived with the stoats for only a few days, but he somehow knew that the sharp look in Duncan's glinting eyes was a warning: if anything happened to Malcolm, it was on his head.

On their third night in the forest, Norman was wakened by a faint whispering in his ear. He batted at his ear impatiently and grumbled, but the damage was done. He was awake now. He pulled the sleeping stoat beside him closer and tried to think of home, but the whispering restarted. It wasn't in his ear, he realized. It was some distance away. Norman had made his bed beside a hollow, moss-covered log. The speakers were at the other end of the log, whispering conspiratorially. They couldn't have known that Norman was listening.

"If it were up to me, I'd leave him lying there and be away with us. He's a foul-looking beast."

By now Norman recognized each of the stoats in the party, but this voice was new—new and not at all friendly.

"He has proven himself a friend, Whiteclaw. He saved my boy," Duncan answered.

"So I hear," the other man muttered gruffly. "Are ye sure it were no trick? He might 'a brought the crows upon you himself, so that he could act the hero. An old spy's trick—and I would know."

"It's possible," Duncan replied, "but I think not. He has the look of no spy. Who would send a spy such as him? Strong he may be, but he's noisy as a boar. There's no guile to him."

"An assassin, then," said the new voice.

"Na, I think not. I saw his face at the pass. He has no taste for killing."

The newcomer was skeptical. "Still . . ."

"Never you worry," Duncan reassured the unknown stoat. "He's watched at all times. He does us little harm now, and he could be of good use when we come to the mine."

"Aye?" grunted the other. "What use would that be, then?"

Duncan explained. "We'll need time to free the workers in the barracks."

"A matter of minutes. I've lads ready to move at the signal. It is all set up like you planned."

"Yeh, but it'll be a close thing. A diversion would give us more time."

"And you've a mind to use the beast for that?" the suspicious stranger asked, unconvinced.

"Aye, you'll have heard the ruckus he makes."

"Like an army of drunken rats," the stranger scoffed.

Duncan chuckled. "That's when he's trying to be quiet."

The newcomer laughed disdainfully, and then both were quiet. Duncan spoke no further of the plan.

"You'll not be forgetting the rest of the plan, will ye?" the other asked. "The ship broad enough to bear his load has never been built."

Duncan tutted. "I've not forgotten." His voice trailed off, as if he was considering an insoluble problem he'd tried to dismiss. "Even if the thing knows how to swim, he'd never squeeze his fat self through the gap. Our paths must part after Scalded Rock. I've not asked him to follow us to Lochwarren. We've fed him long enough. He can fend for himself."

Norman didn't sleep much the rest of the night. Hiking through the bush with a party of stoats was hard enough. He didn't know if he could survive on his own. The stoats had been feeding him. Without them he would be lost. He had to do everything he could to stay with them. It was more than just being lost in the woods—it was being lost in the book. He had to stay with the book's characters. If he was right, the only way to get out of the book was for the book to end. To have any hope of escaping, he had to stay with the plot. If he strayed away from the story, he had no idea what would happen.

It started raining just before daybreak. The trees offered some shelter, but not enough to keep him dry. By the time the stoats were ready to leave, he was thoroughly soaked. It made the trek all the more miserable. Today, Malcolm's continual chatter was more annoying than distracting.

"I ought to be better with a sword than I am," the little animal was saying, his cheerfulness undinted by the drizzle. The rain ran off his sleek brown fur as if he were wearing a raincoat. "I'm a dab hand with the bow, and I throw a mean dagger, but I ought to improve with the sword. I'll get Simon Whiteclaw to duel with me when we get a break."

Simon Whiteclaw was the stoat who had joined them in the night. From what Norman could tell—no one bothered to inform him—Simon was one of Duncan's chief henchmen. The mate of the *Hastewind* and Duncan's spy at Scalded Rock, he also appeared to be young Malcolm's bodyguard. He might be bad-tempered and unfriendly with everyone else, but he had all the time in the world for Malcolm. His opinion of Norman was clear. His eyes were rarely off him and there was no kindness in them. Doubtless the animal would be at Norman's throat if he made anything close to a threatening move toward the young stoat.

"Did you ever think you might be a soldier instead of a seer?"

"Huh?" Norman grunted. He'd stopped listening to his furry friend.

"Well, I'd be a soldier even if my dad wasn't," Malcolm continued. "Did you always want to be a seer? Is it your father's profession?"

"I guess so. He . . ." Norman struggled to describe what his father did. It was hard enough explaining it to his friends in real life, never mind to someone who captained a ship of pirate weasels and stoats. "He's a teacher. He works at a university."

"Ah, a university," the young animal answered, in the tone of someone who had heard of such things but had no idea what one was.

"But I haven't really thought of what I might do when I grow up. Maybe something with computers." Norman had forgotten who he was talking to.

"When you grow up? You mean to say you're not fully grown?"

"No. In ten years, maybe."

"Ten years? You're still a kit? By the Maker, you'll be huge then!" Malcolm's voice went high pitched with surprise. "And you're out of the nest? Isn't your mother looking for you? I'll bet when she finds you she won't be gentle picking you up by the scruff of the neck."

Norman chuckled. It was a funny image for Norman, imagining his mother trying to pick him up with her teeth by the scruff of the neck, like a mother cat. Simon Whiteclaw cast him an ugly look that cut the merriment short. They slogged on in silence for the rest of the day, Norman now preoccupied with thoughts of his mother. He'd been missing for days now. She would be angry, yes, but mostly she would be worried. His stomach tightened into a knot of guilt and despair as he imagined her pacing, crying, listening by a phone that would not ring.

At noon Duncan pulled them up at the edge of the woods. He alone strode out into the open, leaping quickly onto a tree stump and gazing at the rocky horizon. The forest gave way to scrub and stumps here. The hillside beyond them had been clear-cut. No tree was left, and the ground was brown and barren. Forest creatures didn't do this. A line of smoke rising over the hills gave Norman some idea who did. Behind the smoke was a flat grey expanse—the Obsidian Desert.

"What do you see, lad?" Duncan asked.

Malcolm had clambered up onto Norman's head to get a better view.

"Smoke, over the cliffs. Is it the mine?"

"Musts be," his father replied.

A branch beside Malcolm's shoulder twitched, and Simon Whiteclaw's voice added its agreement. "Aye, 'tis the Rock all right." The surly old creature spat in disgust and scrambled back down the tree.

Duncan remained motionless on the stump, until with an invisible gesture his sabre was unsheathed. Turning to face his men, he wielded the weapon boldly.

"Tomorrow," he growled emphatically, baring his sharp eyeteeth, "many more stoats will be free. Many more will raise their swords against the wolf occupiers. Tomorrow, it all begins."

Simon Whiteclaw disappeared again that afternoon, as noiselessly and unceremoniously as he had arrived. Norman tried to take some cheer from it, but knowing what little he did of the battle plans, it was difficult to be too cheerful. Tomorrow, after the battle, the stoats would abandon him. It was hard to see any way around it.

For once Malcolm seemed to understand that his friend was in no mood to talk, and he left him alone. Norman sat on a log and watched the young animal talking with his father. The boy was almost fully healed now, and Norman expected that he was trying to convince his father that he was strong enough to play his part in the next day's fight. As he watched them, he thought of how similar father and son were, both so fearless, both so sure of themselves. He wished that he felt half as confident. As he watched and considered, both father and son turned suddenly toward him. There was a distinct look of surprise on the older stoat's face. Norman had the impression that they had been talking about him. Uncomfortable with the thought and with the intensity of their sharp weasel eyes, Norman looked away.

Duncan came to Norman just after nightfall. He looked preoccupied, as if he had been wrestling with a decision and still wasn't sure what he'd decided. He stood by Norman for a minute before finally speaking.

"Can you read a map, lad?" he asked finally. He spoke in a subdued voice that was far from his normal commanding tone.

Norman nodded. Again the stoat was silent for a few moments before asking, "Is it true what the boy says, that you're only a kit, not even a juvenile?"

Norman wasn't sure how to answer. Duncan knew he was not an adult. He had told him his age when they met, but perhaps years meant something different to stoats and other animals.

"It's true that I'm not fully grown. I'm still a kid to my kind. I really shouldn't be away from home alone."

Duncan rubbed his sleek head as if trying to fathom this. "And so why are you out of the nest, then?"

Norman really didn't know what to say. "I'm trying to get back home, but I got lost."

"Well lost too, I imagine. There's none of your kind in these parts. Likely home is beyond one of the barriers—sea, snow or desert."

If this was a question, Norman ignored it. He merely said, "Yes."

The stoat's muzzle twitched, as if he was chewing on food as well as on a problem. "So a map would help, I imagine."

Norman found himself anxious to ease the animal's obvious discomfort with this conversation. "It might, yes—a map would help."

Duncan thought for yet another moment then appeared to suddenly make up his mind. "You might as well have this, then." He drew a piece of folded parchment from his cloak and held it out to Norman. Norman took it tentatively. "There are no giant lands on this chart, but perhaps this will give you some idea how to get back to your own folk."

Norman opened the parchment and peered at it intently. It was a very good map of this corner of Undergrowth.

"I'd take you with us, lad, but you'd sink one of our boats." There was real regret in his voice.

Norman was about to say that he could swim or walk beside the river, but he'd just found their location on the map. Duncan leapt beside him onto the log. The stoat pointed out Scalded Rock on the map with a short dagger. "We'll commandeer the mine's boats here tomorrow and head back toward Rivernest." His sword followed the snaking dark line of a river into the mountains. "Here the river goes straight through the mountains. There's hardly any daylight to be had through that gorge."

"The gap," Norman murmured, remembering what he'd heard whispered through a log the night before.

"Aye. The water tunnels right through the rock. Even if you could follow that far, you'd never squeeze through that channel."

Norman could see that this was true.

"But if you should not find your way home, the boy would be glad to see you again. When Lochwarren is ours again, you're welcome there. I dare say we could manage some accommodation. It'll be a few months yet, but if you see the red flag and my black ensign in the highland towers again, you'll know that Lochwarren is mine."

Norman was so relieved to hear he still had this option that he ignored Duncan's assumption that he was the heir.

"You should be on your path in the morning before the attack," Duncan continued. "You'll want to be well out of the way when the fighting starts."

"You don't want my help tomorrow?" Norman asked. "You don't want me to cause a diversion?"

Duncan regarded him sharply. "Aye, you are a seer, then . . . or a listener, perhaps. That was before I knew you were just a boy."

"Ah," said Norman, finally understanding. Malcolm had spoken to his father about it. "I wouldn't be in the battle. You'd want me away from it to cause a diversion."

"That was the idea," Duncan replied cautiously.

"Will the battle plan work without the diversion?" Norman asked.

Duncan stroked his furry chin and considered the question. "It can still work, but it would be a surer thing with a little time."

"I'd like to help, then," Norman said, surprised by his bravery. "For this." He held out the map. "And for your family."

Duncan regarded him curiously. "You're no warrior, Strong Arm, I see that. What's your interest in this fight?"

Norman didn't have to think before answering. "The stoats are the rightful kings of the highlands."

"Aye. So, seer, what do you know of this fight? Will I be King before it's over?"

"I'm sure that the stoats will win." Norman had read enough Undergrowth books to know that they usually ended well. "But it won't be easy, and I can't say who will be King."

"You can't?" Duncan murmured thoughtfully, perhaps skeptically.

Norman had noticed that Duncan didn't like to talk about his brother's claim to the throne. Young Malcolm had been surprised to learn that his uncle was alive. Norman wondered if anybody else knew.

"Well," said Duncan finally, affecting the cheerfulness of a good leader. "Since the seer predicts success in this fight, I don't see why he cannot help. Let me tell you what I would have you do, and once you've heard me out you can say whether you are still willing."

Scalded Rock Mine

At the edge of the woods above Scalded Rock, Norman watched and waited. The camp and the narrow trickle of water behind it seemed deserted. A battered and dull wolf flag swung desultorily from a flagpole. At the quay on the narrow river, three merchant ships bobbed in the shallow water. These were the only movements, until, as the sun emerged from behind the black sand of the Obsidian Desert, there was finally some sign of life in the camp. A long, high whistle sounded. Duncan had told him this was the signal for the change of shifts, and sure enough there was movement at the mine's mouth.

From this distance, Norman could make out only shapes. The taller ones would be foxes—guards and supervisors. They took up positions at the head and tail of a long, slow line of labourers trailing out of the mine. Thankfully, there was no sign of wolves. The three wolf overlords of the mine were off somewhere hunting, as Simon Whiteclaw had predicted.

Normally foxes would have nothing to do with wolves, but wolves were no miners, and these foxes extracted good profit from the partnership. The long line of small, bent figures hobbled after their fox masters, crawling as slowly out of the mine as the sun crawled into the sky. These were the stoat workers, rounded up and brought here to do the dirty work. They were the last of the generation that could remember a stoat king. They were the ones who had been too injured to flee or too stubborn to give up their homes. Even after the defeat at Tista Kirk and the fall of Castle Lochwarren, these proud farmers and hunters had stayed at their farmsteads vowing to fight for their homes to the last. This was their reward: enslavement, forced to work for their conquerors.

Norman watched their sluggish march toward the barracks and heard the clink of the chains that held their feet. They looked utterly defeated. His heart sank. These poor creatures were supposed to form the heart of Duncan's avenging army? Duncan was a great leader, but the fox overseers of Scalded Rock had worked their slaves to the brink of death. The thought stiffened Norman's resolve. All the more reason to rescue them, all the more reason to do what he had promised to do. Any minute now he would be called into action.

"Do you see them?" he whispered.

Malcolm, perched quietly on Norman's shoulder, took the tiny spyglass from his eye and shook his head. "If I could see them, then they wouldn't be doing their job. But they're in there, all right."

Norman felt a nervous churning in his stomach. It would all begin soon. For the umpteenth time he checked around him for his "weapons": the sheet of tin they had stolen from one of the mine's abandoned outbuildings and the wooden stick were both where they had been sixty seconds earlier, lying secure against the tree.

"I should be down there," Malcolm muttered between his teeth. "Not one of 'em is stealthier than me. I could be in that prison in a flash. Before they blinked, those guards 'd feel my dagger at their throats." This didn't sound like empty bravado. Malcolm was aching to be down there with the marauding party.

"Your father wanted you here with me. I tried the spyglass. It's too small for my eyes. He said you were the best lookout he had."

Malcolm did not reply but growled an angry, frustrated growl that exposed his long fangs. Perhaps he too suspected that his father had an ulterior motive for keeping him out of the fight.

Down below at the mine, the night shift had crossed the dusty square from the mouth of the mine to the compound that housed the barracks. The guards halted the column outside it. The long whistle sounded again, summoning the day shift to its drudgery. The animals that crawled from the barracks looked hardly more rested than the returning night shift. Norman wondered if they gave their returning friends any sign of what was going on inside the barracks. It was impossible for him to tell from this distance, but surely if Duncan's men had infiltrated the barracks there would be some sign of it. Surely the miners would walk taller knowing that today they would fight for their freedom. Their slow tramp across the square gave away nothing. Even over at the quay everything seemed quiet. The merchant ships floated calmly at anchor. There was no sign of the river pirates there either.

"What do you see?" he asked Malcolm anxiously.

Malcolm responded with his usual sarcasm. "I see stoats, you big oaf."

As the day shift trudged out of the compound and marched to the mine face, the night shift lined up at the doors to the three dormitory buildings. A fox at each door unshackled the exhausted miners. They looked like they were ready to drop. Norman prayed that they would find the energy to fight and run when the time came. He watched until the last stoat dragged himself inside and the barrack doors were bolted shut.

"Are they at the mine yet?" he asked Malcolm.

"The first stoats are just goin' in. Any minute now, it'll be time."

These next few minutes seemed to take forever. Norman didn't even know he was holding his breath until he finally had to exhale. Malcolm, nervous and fidgety on his shoulder, was too preoccupied to mock him.

"They're all in the tunnel now. Start yer count."

Norman counted the seconds under his breath, like he would in a schoolyard game. "One steamboat, two steamboat, three steamboat . . ."

At fifty steamboats, he bent down to pick up the rusty sheet of tin.

Malcolm was counting along with him now, though he surely had no idea what a steamboat might be—". . . fifty-eight steamboats, fifty-nine steamboats, sixty steamboats. Okay, it's time."

Norman took a deep breath and held the tin sheet up in one arm. He was too nervous to swing with all his strength, but even a light blow with the stick was enough to make a clang resound through the valley. Two fox guards scurried out of the barracks. They peered around but didn't spot Norman and Duncan in the trees.

"They've heard you," Malcolm twittered excitedly. "Don't stop now!"

So Norman hit the tin sheet again, harder this time, following it up with another and another in a steady beat. Thump, thump—bang; thump, thump—bang; thump, thump—bang; thump, thump—bang. This apparently was his most valuable skill for this battle: making noise.

More foxes had emerged from the mine buildings. They were pointing to the forest edge.

"You've got their attention now," Malcolm said eagerly. "The vermin are pouring out of the barracks."

"What about the mine?" Norman asked.

"Keep going," Malcolm urged, "and holler something. Don't your people have any war cries?"

Norman continued his rhythmic banging and shouted the only thing that seemed to go with drumming.

"We will, we will rock you!" he bellowed. "We will, we will rock you!"

Malcolm chuckled to himself. "You should see 'em now—they're all out of the mine. The boss seems to be trying to get them to form up in ranks. Good luck. Cowardly droolers. Who ever knew a fox that was up to a fair fight?"

Norman had now switched to a cheer his soccer team chanted before games: "We're number one, not two, not three, not four.

We're goin' to win, not lose, not tie the score. We're number one, number one. Let's go, Duncan!"

As if on cue, a great shout was heard down below. Norman looked down to see a great swarm of stoats rush from the mine. Within moments the stoats from the barracks were unleashed too. There were no shackles to be seen. Gates seemed to have been magically unlocked. The two parties rushed unimpeded toward the small huddled group of foxes. Now Norman could see Duncan at the head of the night shift, his sword held high. At the head of the day shift, he saw the distinctive markings of Simon Whiteclaw. The two groups converged on the cowering foxes like the sharp-toothed jaws of a single giant angry stoat.

The enslaved miners no longer looked beaten and weary. Only their weapons made them distinguishable from Duncan's rescue party. The workers held their picks above their heads as they charged. The rescuers brandished their swords. Both looked utterly fearsome. The foxes retreated slowly backward as the charge came.

Above them Norman continued through his meagre repertoire of war chants. "You've got to fight, for your right, to paaaarty!" he screamed. Malcolm seemed to take no notice of the words. He delighted in the effect. Though faced with an onslaught of vengeful stoats, the foxes made no move to flee to the woods. They knew the danger in front of them, but could only guess at what horde of fearsome beasts awaited them in the woods. Norman could see them eyeing the vast desert behind them as the best available escape route. Some of the more cowardly ran in this direction even before the stoats were on them. Duncan's archers sent a few arrows their way to hasten their flight.

"I'm gonna knock you out. Mama said knock you out!" Norman bellowed, so excited that he was just shouting whatever came into his head. He was gripping the stick so hard now that his hand was almost numb.

A great roar came up from the valley floor below. The two pincers of the stoat advance had closed on the retreating foxes. The long battle hisses of the stoats drowned out everything but the high-pitched yelps of wounded foxes. The mine guards put up a feeble fight, overwhelmed by the stoat numbers. But they knew exactly how much their captives had to be vengeful for, and they could not expect mercy from them now. Whenever a fox got a chance, he limped away from the melee. The attackers let them go. The goal of this battle was not bloodshed, but victory.

"Look," Malcolm shouted excitedly, pointing toward the ships still at anchor at the river dock. "The flag! The flag of the stoat kings flies again!"

This was the signal to disengage. Duncan's men had secured the boats. The time had come for them to make their escape. Duncan's men continued to take the fight to the foxes, while the miners disengaged and rushed in small groups to the boats. If the foxes noticed, they could do nothing. When the miners were all safely onboard, Duncan's men too began to slowly edge backward toward the river. A few more foxes took this opportunity to flee, but a few braver creatures now saw what was happening and fought back. Foxes who would not fight to keep their slaves suddenly found anger when the ships were threatened—ships laden with diamonds, their precious diamonds.

A trumpet clarion came from the boats.

"That's the signal. It's time," Norman said solemnly as he put down his makeshift cymbal and drumstick.

Malcolm was unusually silent.

"Come on, Malcolm. I'll carry you down to the edge of the valley. It will be a shorter distance for you to run."

The little stoat nodded silently. His intelligent little eyes looked moist and clouded. Norman tried to remember if he had ever heard of a stoat or weasel crying in the Undergrowth books. He knew that if Malcolm cried, he would not be able to hold back his own tears.

"I'll see you in Lochwarren soon," he tried bravely as he stepped slowly down the slope closer to the battlefield. "Your father has promised to build me a barn. We'll go swimming together in the loch, like we said."

"I still don't believe that creatures like you can swim," Malcolm answered, trying to cheer himself up with a joke, but neither of them laughed. They walked on in silence now until they were level with the battlefield.

"You better stop here," Malcolm warned. "You're to be well away before the foxes start their hunt."

"Goodbye, Malcolm," Norman said quietly, putting his friend down gently on the ground.

"Thank you, Norman Strong Arm," Malcolm said. Norman took three steps, then turned and saluted the boy. "Take care and keep to the map," Malcolm added, "and trust only stoat folk and their kin." It was the same advice his father had given.

"Look after yourself," Norman called. The stoat bobbed his head to nod and turned. In a flash he was bounding his way to the boats, skirting the battlefield. Within a few minutes he would be safely on board. Norman vowed to watch him until he was securely on deck.

From the boats another trumpet sounded, faster and more urgent than the first clarion. There was no plan for a second trumpet signal. Out in the open, on the stretch of desert between the woods and the river, Malcolm stopped and looked up. Something unexpected had happened. Norman peered around fruitlessly for the cause of the alarm. Out on the plain, Malcolm still stood frozen. Perhaps he understood the trumpet's code better than Norman. While Norman watched his friend's indecision, the cause for alarm finally became clear. Three dark shapes burst from the forest nearer the river. Too large, too fast to be foxes, they could only be . . . "Wolves," Norman gasped to himself. Instinctively he backed farther into the woods.

The remaining stoat fighters hastened their retreat. The wolves were tearing directly toward them, and the foxes, chastened by the appearance of their wolf masters, began to fight back more fiercely. The stoat skirmishers would make it to the boats in time. Already one ship had lifted anchor and was moving slowly down the river on the current. Those fighting the rearguard had but a little distance to run, and their retreat would be covered by archer fire from the mast tops. It was Malcolm who was in trouble.

The wolves' path to the boats intersected the young stoat's escape route. He was cut off. Norman could see him twist round, trying to decide whether to turn back to the forest or to continue toward the boats. Every second he hesitated made it worse. Another boat left the shore and followed the first downstream. All of Duncan's warriors were at the river's edge. Safety was only a leap away for them, but for Malcolm it was a full ten minutes' sprint. Any moment now the wolves would reach the last stoat swordsmen. Malcolm seemed to realize that if he had ever had an opportunity to make a dash for the boats, it was gone. He had made his decision, and was scampering quickly back to the forest edge. His best hope now was with Norman.

Norman waited, breathless, at the tree line, willing his little friend to move faster. One eye he kept on the last ship. The rest of the stoats were all on board now, but this last boat remained at the water's edge. One figure, surely Duncan himself, taunted the wolves from the prow, gaining Norman and Malcolm a little more time, creating his own diversion to finish this battle, just as Norman's had started it. At the bow too there was motion. Norman caught a glimpse of a white tail dipping below the water's surface. A few metres downstream, a matching snout appeared—Simon Whiteclaw.

Malcolm arrived at that moment. "You're not rid of me yet, Strong Arm. Let's get going," he gasped. Without a further word, they disappeared into the forest.

The Pursuit

They fled headlong through the forest. The branches that whipped Norman's face did not sting yet. All he felt was fear. He had not been afraid during either of the two battles he had participated in. Ravens and foxes didn't frighten him, even if they could hurl stones and swing swords, but the wolves were something different. Just the sight of them bounding out of the darkness had sent a shiver of terror through his bones. These were killers, eyes and ears alert to prey, teeth made for rending flesh, and legs that hurtled the beasts with ferocious speed. Norman could not outrun them, nor could he fight them. He would be torn to shreds.

This sort of terror was new to Norman. A few days ago he would have told anyone that wolves were an endangered species and an amazing animal. Back home on the living-room wall there was a picture of arctic wolves. Norman's mother had won it at a silent auction for a wildlife charity that reintroduced wolves back into their traditional territories. That was the world of another Norman. In this world, Norman knew that wolves were hunters—ruthless and implacable. He did not want to face them. It was the image of those cold, intelligent eyes from his own living-room wall that drove him on. It was as if they could see him running and knew that they would catch him. During all his panic, they were calm and assured of capturing their prey.

The forest grasped at him on every side, tearing his filthy pyjamas, stubbing his toes, aiming twigs at his eyes. Malcolm bounced his way between Norman's shoulder and the trees, scurrying off to scout ahead and then back to whisper breathless directions into Norman's ear. Norman doubted he had ever run as fast, even on the flat grass of the playground or the smooth tiles of the school gym. Malcolm's reconnaissance kept them clear of steep gullies, impassable cliffs and dense brush, but their path was still strewn with rocks and roots that tripped Norman's feet, sending him headlong in the dirt, bruising another rib, scraping another elbow. Malcolm encouraged him to his feet each time. There wasn't a moment to spare to check for cuts, to rub injuries or to make friendly jibes about human clumsiness. They were running for their lives.

The wolves hadn't seen them at the mine. If they had, Norman and Malcolm would be dead already. They were alive only because Duncan had fought on at the river's edge as long as he could and because the wolves had stayed to hear the story and punish the foxes who told it.

There was no use pursuing the fleeing boats down the river. They could harry the boats from the river's edge and expose themselves to stoat archers, but they could not stop the ships entering the gap and disappearing into the mountain canyons. The wolf hunters would hear about the disturbance in the woods that had started it all, and they would quickly pick up the scent of a human boy and his stoat companion. The pursuit would not be delayed. The wolves would be determined to find some creature, any creature, involved in the attack on their precious mine and to exact their revenge.

The sun was high in the sky when they stumbled, exhausted, into a small clearing. Neither boy nor stoat said a word, each sucking deep breaths of air into their starved lungs. They lay upon their backs in the grass beside each other, blinking up at the sun while their chests heaved. Norman patted Malcolm on the head kindly, hoping the gesture said everything he wanted say. He was glad that the little stoat was here with him. Somehow it made him braver. He could not have found a path through the woods without the animal's help, but he was proud of having done his part too, carrying Malcolm on his shoulders and doing the heavy running when Malcolm's injuries caught up with him. This pat on the head was supposed to say everything it meant to be a friend in a time of trouble. And he was sure that Malcolm's curious little stoat wink in return meant the same.

They had almost caught their breath when a gruff voice startled them to their feet.

"That's enough of a rest now."

Norman leapt to a shaky version of the guard stance he had learned in his white-belt karate class: feet planted and fists raised. Malcolm was at his shoulder, his bow drawn and an arrow nocked. They might have scared a party of marauding field mice or a couple of mole farmers, but it was hardly a show of force to cause a trio of wolf hunters any grave concern. Luckily it was not a wolf hunting party they turned to face.

"Ye couldna found a longer route?" Simon Whiteclaw asked. "Were ye aiming to put the fang beasts off your trail?"

The two friends had no reply to this. Malcolm put his bow down and returned the arrow to its quiver. Norman relaxed his shoulders and lowered his fists.

"You're not thinking of heading back the way ye came, are ye?" Whiteclaw asked, his voice making it clear what he thought of this plan. "The wolves will know that trail by now. They'll be waiting for you at the pass, I expect. The foul black birds will have let them know where to find you."

These accusations of incompetence were meant for Norman. There was scorn in every syllable.

"We're not going over the mountains," Norman shot back. "We're going to the Borders."

Malcolm gave Norman a quick sideways look. This was news to him. They hadn't discussed a destination. They had just run.

"The Borders, eh?" Simon asked with a sneer. "Well, you're taking a mighty curious route if that's where you're headin.'"

There was no answer for this.

"You'll set us right though, Whitemitts, won't you?" Malcolm affirmed brightly. He didn't care that they had been running the wrong way. His old friend and guardian was here. A human boy might be an amusing companion, but a seasoned tracker and fighter was handier in their current predicament. Even Norman could see that they were better off with the older stoat's guidance and protection. He just wished that Simon Whiteclaw didn't look at him that way.

"Shall we check the map?" Norman patted his chest pocket, where he'd safely stowed the tiny stoat chart. He was trying to be helpful. Whiteclaw only scoffed.

"Don't need no map. Just need a brain in yer 'ead." He reached into his pocket and pulled out two small chunks of bread. He tossed one to Malcolm, who caught it deftly and set upon it greedily. The older stoat seemed to think for a moment before tossing the second at Norman. It hit him in the chest, but Norman recovered to catch it before it hit the ground. It was a whole meal for a stoat but hardly even a snack for a human boy, yet he was grateful for it anyway. "Thank you," he said, before popping it in his mouth.

Simon Whiteclaw grunted and bounded off into the forest. It was not the direction that Norman would have taken.

Perhaps it was his imagination, but Norman was certain that the trail became less human-friendly now that Simon Whiteclaw was leading them. Complaining was useless. He was breathing raggedly already and words would only have wasted more breath. He did his best to absorb the trail's fury and keep up. It seemed to Norman, when he could spare a second to think of it, that they were heading vaguely downhill.

At midday they stopped for a bite to eat. It was literally a bite for Norman. He let the bread dissolve in his mouth so that he could savour it longer, but it did nothing to assuage his hunger. While the stoats chatted, he foraged for something else to eat. His days with the stoats had taught him a few things about staying alive in the woods. Not far from their rest spot he found a stand of blackberry bushes. The berries were plentiful, but the picking wasn't easy. Still, it was worth the stings and scratches. He ate as he harvested, stuffing the berries hungrily into his mouth. When he had nearly exhausted the bushes, he collected one last handful for his companions.

Simon Whiteclaw could not disguise his surprise when Norman held out his hand. His eyebrows furrowed suspiciously and he motioned Norman's hand away.

"Let the boy have them," he muttered ungratefully.

Malcolm winked his funny little animal wink and picked the berries one by one from Norman's open palm. Malcolm was fearless again now his guardian led the way.

"How far are the Borders?" he asked brightly.

"Three or four days to Edgeweir," Simon growled in a low voice, "if I were on my own." His whiskers twitched as he added, "It'll be a few more days with you lot."

Norman felt certain that Simon really meant with *him*.

Little Malcolm's cheerfulness was unaffected. "Ah, it'll be nice to spend a few days in the Borders. It's been months since I've seen the inside of a pie shop. Edgeweir is a biggish place, isn't it? It should have a pie shop or two. Norman, have you ever tried a spiced lingonberry pie? Well, you haven't lived. When we get to the Borders, we'll share the biggest lingonberry pie that can be bought."

"It's not a shopping trip we're on here, young pup," Simon scolded. "Edgeweir is no holiday town. It's a dangerous place. There's wolf spies aplenty in the Borders towns near the Wolflands. *If* we make it to Edgeweir, you'll be keeping out of sight, my son."

Simon cast a weary glance at Norman. No doubt he was wondering how a human boy could possibly be kept out of sight.

Malcolm chattered on undeterred. "At least we've outrun the wolves," he said brightly, licking blackberry juice from his paws.

Simon Whiteclaw harrumphed. "Ye think ye've outrun 'em, do ye? Don't you believe it. Wolf hunters won't let you go that easily. They're still out there sniffing us out. It's not like we didn't leave a trail."

With this dour pronouncement, he rose and shouldered his pack. "We've tarried too long," he declared. "Let's be off."

If it was possible, the terrain became rougher and the woods thicker when they resumed. The forest was a solid wall of pine needles and branches. Norman covered his head with his arms and used it as a battering ram, charging, sometimes just stumbling forward. Only Malcolm's merry chatter kept him on track. His eyes were useless in the dense woods.

Occasionally Simon tried half-heartedly to keep the young stoat quiet.

"Quit yer chatter, will ye," he ordered, finally losing his patience with his young ward. "Ye want the entire wolf horde to hear ye?"

At that moment, Norman came crashing through the forest behind them, snapping branches, crunching twigs and grunting.

"Are we stopping?" he huffed.

Norman couldn't see the older river raider roll his eyes.

It was the wolf howls that finally silenced the ebullient little stoat. Near dusk on their second day out from Scalded Rock, they heard the first one, a distant cry somewhere in a valley behind them. Nothing was said between the stoats and the human boy. They merely quickened their pace. They heard the howls intermittently through the night while they tried to sleep, and again the next morning—hollow, hungry cries from the valleys behind them. More often now one cry was answered by a second.

By noon on the third day it was impossible to deny that the wolf calls were getting closer. The fleeing stoats and boy did not stop to eat that day. Simon handed out what morsels he had left in his satchel and they consumed them on the trail. The ordeal was taking its toll on Norman. His entire body ached and he found his mind drifting, imagining that he was back home again. The terrain was smoother and the trees more sparse, so he could walk upright and unimpeded now, but they were moving faster to keep ahead of the wolves. The pace aggravated Malcolm's injuries and he had to be carried again. Norman didn't mind. The stoat hardly weighed anything, and he was happy to be of some use. It focused his mind, reminding him where he was and why.

A few hours after nightfall they stopped. If he had been alone, Simon would likely have carried on through the night, but he could see that both the human boy and his stoat ward could be pushed no further. It would be dangerous to keep going in such a state. He guided them to a half cave beneath an overhang of rock, completely concealed from the path—you would have to know it was there to find it. Norman threw himself down thankfully. For the second night in a row, there would be no fire. Norman rubbed his arms and legs as much for warmth as to smoothe out the bruises and aches. Even in the cold it was not long before he was asleep. His young friend curled up beside him for warmth and they were both asleep in no time.

The moon was high in the night sky when Simon Whiteclaw startled them awake.

"I'm taking yer bow," he told Malcolm in a whisper. The young stoat did not protest. "The three hunters have joined up again. They have our scent. I'm going to double back and see if I can't slow 'em down a bit."

He was gone before either Norman or Malcolm fully appreciated what he was saying. Rubbing the sleep from their eyes, they didn't speak for a long while, only listened to the forest. Soon enough they heard the high, hollow howl of the wolf call. The predators called in unison now, egging each other on, sensing that their prey was near. The closer the cries came, the harder it became for Malcolm and Norman to remain quiet and still. They fidgeted and looked for signs of nervousness in each other, each reassured that he wasn't the only one terrified of the wolves' approach.

"Do you think Simon's missed them?" Norman asked through his teeth when he could hold it in no longer.

The little stoat replied with assurance, "No chance—old Simon's the finest hunter in these woods. Didn't he sniff out the long snouts? They don't even know we're here yet."

Norman nodded, tried to believe this, but the image of the three wolf rangers coming ever closer tormented him.

"But how can he take them on alone?" he asked, breaking the silence again. "I mean, one stoat against three wolves. Isn't that . . ." He decided not to worry about insulting his friend. "Isn't that a mismatch?"

Malcolm didn't turn to look at Norman. As he answered, his sharp eyes remained focused on the forest darkness. "Simon'll pick his spot. He won't meet 'em on the ground. He'll stay up high, in the trees, and keep his distance. That's why he took the bow. Hand-to-hand, not even Simon is a match for a long snout. But wolves are no archers, nor are they climbers. As long as he's in the trees, he's as safe as houses."

Norman took a serious look at the woods around them and wondered whether they wouldn't be better up a tree themselves. But the next wolf howl froze his motions and thoughts. It had changed—closer and angrier now, mixed with growls. Neither boy nor stoat spoke as they listened. Both knew that Simon had sprung his ambush on the wolves. Each tried to imagine the progress of the battle from the sounds. The night became filled with fierce wolf cries, bitter barks and every now and then a high-pitched yelp of pain. Only wolf sounds were heard. Simon fought silently; so too would he succumb silently. If Simon fell in battle, there would be no howl of despair or pain. The boys would not know until it was too late.

The sounds of the skirmish may have lasted only a few minutes. Then a silence blew through the forest—no howls, no barks either of victory or of anguish. Could it have been that easy? Had Simon's arrows picked off all three of their pursuers? If it was that easy, Norman found himself thinking, why hadn't they ambushed the wolves sooner, rather than blundering madly through the woods? He kept this thought to himself. Even he knew it was too much to hope. Maybe he just didn't want to jinx it.

After that, the two were more silent than ever, waiting, either for the return of Simon victorious or for the wolf assassins to burst into the clearing and finish the pursuit for themselves. Norman had almost given up hope when they heard the rustle in the trees above them.

"Simon," Malcolm cried. His relief breathed through his voice. Norman felt it too: so the old warrior had done it.

His relief was short-lived. "Shh," Simon whispered as he came closer. "It's not over yet, boy. Get yerself up in the branches, now. Be quick about it."

Accustomed to obeying battle orders swiftly, the young stoat did not hesitate. He did not seem to think about where to go, leaping immediately into the tallest tree, a thick pine that overshadowed all the rest. He scampered up the trunk effortlessly, chattering as he moved. "Did you get any of them, Simon? Are you all right?"

"Got one," Simon huffed. "His running days are over. The others scarpered when they saw it was just me. They musta figured who you—" Simon Whitetail did not finish his answer. His breath was ragged. He must have run at full tilt through the forest canopy to reach them before the two remaining wolves did. "You, beast," he said when he had regained his breath, meaning Norman. "Can you climb?"

Norman eyed the stout pine that Malcolm had scaled. The lowest branches were too high for him to grasp from the ground, and he did not have a stoat's sharp claws to allow him to just scamper right up the trunk. No other nearby tree offered the same safety. Only a few straggly aspen saplings persevered in the shade of the big pine. Norman wasn't sure if any of them would hold his weight. Maybe if he looked farther away.

The deep belly howl of a wolf close by decided for him. His body was moving before his mind, hands grasping the likeliest of the nearby aspen saplings, feet scrambling beneath him, snapping twigs. The thin aspen swayed under his weight, swinging like a reed as he climbed higher, until it seemed it would bend right over and deposit him on the ground if he climbed any higher. Norman only hoped that he was high enough. He had no idea how high wolves could jump, or whether they could chop down a tree.

These visions tumbled through his head as the first wolf crept into the clearing. Norman saw only the bright yellow glow of its eyes and heard the low anticipatory growl. A second set of eyes soon appeared beside the first. They kept low to the ground but peered up. Knowing their prey, they scanned the trees and sniffed the air. How is it possible that they don't see me, Norman managed to wonder, but only for a second.

In another breath, the wolves leapt to action. All snarls and flashing teeth, they assailed the slim trunk of Norman's tree. The sapling lurched under their weight. Their front paws stretched up higher on the trunk and pushed again, and Norman looked down into the eyes of the animals that hunted him. A horrible, sickening fear overtook him as he gazed into the narrowing eyes. It was as if these eyes had always hunted him. He knew the jagged teeth beneath them, the salivating mouth and the meat-tasting breath. This was the big bad wolf of every kids' story. It knew him, knew his terror. Norman's legs went weak beneath him. He hardly felt his feet slip. He only felt himself falling. His hands knew better, grasping the trunk and arresting his fall, but the wolves saw what had happened and redoubled their assault. The big pink creature was afraid, and fear was a wolf's desire. Norman's feet dangled just beyond the wolves' reach now. He clung to the tree with his arms, but without a foothold he was sunk. It was only a matter of time before his strength gave way.

If you died in a book, Norman wondered, did you die in real life, or did you wake up again in your bed?

He did not hear the whoosh of the arrows. Nor did he hear the wounded yelp of the wolf. All he heard was the beating of his own heart, the sound of his terror. He was losing his grip, sliding slowly down the tree toward the gnashing jaws of the hunters below. But arrows were flying now. From high in the pine, Simon unleashed arrow after arrow at the wolves below.

When Norman finally hit the ground, only one wolf remained on its feet, but one wolf was enough. The arrows had stopped flying now, and there was an awful silence in the clearing as Norman shook off the fall and scrambled backward away from the dead wolf's arrow-riddled body. The remaining hunter crouched low and let out a murderous snarling growl as it slunk toward Norman. Its eyes gleamed cold and angry, imagining its vengeance. So utterly animal was its movement that its speech surprised Norman.

"So this is the fearsome beast of the forest?" The wolf's voice dripped with disdain. "Big you might be, but clumsy and soft. You'll make a good meal, you will. I will howl over your corpse tonight, and my murdered brothers will hear their vengeance in the spirit world."

Norman used his arms to crawl backward as far as he could.

"That's right, little piglet, squirm," the wolf snarled. "Try to wriggle away."

The wolf reared now on its hind legs, an extraordinary pose. He loomed over Norman. Even if Norman could have pulled himself to his feet now, the wolf would have been taller. The wolf now reached behind his back and pulled a long, wide weapon from his shoulder scabbard—the wolflaird's broadsword. Though Norman had read about this fearsome sword in a half dozen Undergrowth stories, he could not have imagined it to be so deadly looking. The wolf wielded it with two hands, his paws wrapped deftly around the heavy hilt. Twirling it slowly above his head, he stepped closer again to Norman. The sword cut the air, making a deep whoosh, whoosh like a helicopter blade, and then, suddenly, without warning, the point of it was at Norman's head. The tip of the blade rested on the bone of his forehead, sending a sharp pain through his skull like an ice-cream headache, but the wolf put no weight on it. He did not want it to be over yet.

"That's a look I know, little piglet. You'll be wanting to beg for your life right now."

Behind the wolf, a sudden movement caught Norman's eye, then a flash of glinting steel, and the wolf turned, surprised, as if stung by a wasp.

On a tree stump six feet behind the wolf stood Simon Whiteclaw, defiant, with sword drawn.

"Leave the child alone. Avenge yourself on me—if you can." Even on the stump the old warrior wasn't even half the height of the wolf. The wolf's broadsword's reach was three times that of the little stoat rapier.

"It was me who killed yer mates," Simon taunted. "I sent the arrows that rid this undergrowth of their filth. You're next."

This taunt was too much for the wolf hunter. He let out a mad howl as he lunged toward Simon, hurling himself and the heavy sword with full force at the defiant stoat. But Simon was too quick for him. He leapt gingerly from the stump to the branch of a nearby tree, from there to another, and while the wolf was still pulling the blade of his heavy sword from the stump where it had landed, Simon swept down on a slender whip of pine bough. The bough arced downward, behind the wolf, giving Simon the chance for a quick swish of his rapier. When the wolf turned again, holding a bleeding ear, Simon stood high in yet another tree.

"Try again, you lumbering oaf," he scoffed.

But the wolf wasn't going to play by Simon's rules. The next sweep of his great broadsword sliced the branch away from beneath the stoat, sending Simon tumbling to the ground. Norman stayed long enough to see the brave stoat warrior get to his feet, but then Malcolm was tugging at the collar of his pyjamas, urging him to follow.

They scrambled as noiselessly as they could through the undergrowth, with the sounds of blades swooshing and hacking at branches behind them. At the first clearing, Malcolm jumped onto Norman's shoulder and they ran through the open land. There was no use being stealthy anymore. The wolf had sniffed them well and could track them easily now. All they could do was get as far away as possible. If Simon somehow won, somehow managed to disable a wolf four times his size, then the old warrior would find them. If he could not, if even his wiles and sword skills weren't enough, then they were doomed. It would be the assassin who caught up with them, not the crusty old stoat warrior. They did not look back. They dared not. They could imagine the shape of their pursuer well enough.

Neither boy noticed when the sun rose behind them. They had reached a small stream before they realized that it was daylight. Norman, remembering something about bloodhounds and scents, stepped gingerly to the middle of the stream and, finding it no deeper than the middle of his calves, continued downstream. The little stoat on his shoulder whispered his hopeful approval—"Yes, we'll lose him like this."

Norman ran as long as he could through the stream. Gradually it widened and deepened. When it came to his knees, Norman waded back out, on the same side they had entered.

"Maybe the wolf will think we've crossed," he suggested.

They ran along the bank all day, as slowly the stream widened into a river. The ground beside it became softer, flatter, greener. Every minute that they ran, their hope grew. If the wolf had beaten Simon, he would have been upon them by now. But even this hope had a flip side: if Simon was victorious, surely he too would have caught up with them.

Early in the afternoon, the boys staggered to a halt. Norman threw himself to the ground, exhausted, in a grove of wild apple trees. Malcolm, better rested for his ride on Norman's shoulders, leapt to life and quickly collected an apple feast for the two of them. They ate wordlessly but not silently, scarfing the fruits noisily like wild animals.

"Perhaps he went in the opposite direction on purpose—to lead any others away from our trail," Norman said, out of the blue. They both had been having the same silent conversation. Each had been debating with himself, searching for a scenario in which Simon was still alive. Malcolm did not reply.

Three days was how long it took them to reach the borderlands, following the river out of the mountains into the region of free villages between the Wolflands and the domain of the city hares. The Borders lay on the other side of the river, but they had missed their chance to cross. At nightfall on the first day, they consulted the map and discovered that this was the very river that defined the edge of the Wolflands. By then, neither boy wanted to go back to the narrow point of the stream. There was nothing left but to follow the river until the first bridge.

They heard Edgeweir before they saw it. The rattle of cartwheels on cobblestones echoed down the river. The boys slowed their pace and approached quietly. Soon the chatter of animal voices joined the sound of the wooden wheels on the bridge stones. Traffic on the Edgeweir bridge was busy at this time of the day, as traders and gatherers hurried back to the shelter of homes and inns before nightfall.

Norman and Malcolm watched from the safety of the woods as the traffic dwindled. A trio of truffle-hunting pygmy boars trotted gleefully over the bridge while the sun set, singing hunting songs and chortling over their day's discoveries. They were followed soon after by a lone figure, hunched and moving slowly. A cowl covered his head, but as he crossed, the dusk light was enough to illuminate a fox's face—reminder enough that the Borders didn't guarantee safety. Wolves and foxes were tolerated in the Borders, and the wolf lords tolerated the rough independence of the border villages. The last creatures across the bridge were two badgers—warders, the Borders' police and defence force. It was their job to protect the citizenry of the Borders. Sturdy fighters and canny forest men, many of whom had spent their early career on the other side of the law, they were more feared than thanked.

Norman watched them lumber across, sharing a lit torch between them and muttering incomprehensibly. The boys' eyes followed the light down the road, waiting for the sound of their buckles and chain mail to jangle out of earshot.

An hour later, before the moon rose, Norman and Malcolm slipped across the bridge in darkness toward the shimmering evening windows of Edgeweir. Behind these glass panes, families ate hot dinners, and travelling companions supped together before retiring to more or less clean beds. Inviting though these warm windows shone, they were not for the boy and his stoat companion. It was not yet safe to show their faces, and might never be safe for Norman to show his. A young stoat might pass unrecognized among the market stalls and the inn tables of a Borders settlement, but a human boy would be a spectacle worth crowding round, a tale worth telling neighbour and stranger alike, until the rumour of him arrived in wolf ears. No, warm mead and warm beds would have to wait until they had reached lands safer than this.

Instead they spent the night a small cave in the woods behind the settlement. They covered themselves with leaves and huddled up together as they had for many nights before. Norman lay awake long after the little stoat was snoring quietly away in deep slumber. He felt safer tonight, if only a little, on this side of the river. He worried a bit less about being woken by the vengeance howls of pursuing wolves, but it left space in his mind to trouble over the other thing, the deeper concern that had haunted him since his arrival here in the world of Undergrowth. How many days ago was it now? He was losing track. This made it worse. He was beginning to worry—not just about how to get back, but about whether he could *ever* get back to his real home.

The Other Brother

Even fear made slow progress in waking Norman up. There was a noise out there outside his sleep, but he was so tired. It made him sick to even think of opening his eyes. He wanted to just call out, "Who's there?" But he knew he couldn't. It wasn't safe. There was no knowing what was lurking in the bushes, and something *was* lurking in the bushes. Norman was sure of it now. There was that movement when he first opened his eyes, and a slight rustling of leaves while he half fell back asleep, dismissing it as a bird or a squirrel. But you could not dismiss birds or squirrels. In Undergrowth, birds or squirrels could slit your throat. There was nothing for it but to wake up properly and rub the sleep out of his eyes. That would mean disturbing Malcolm, who was still snoring quietly and quickly in the crook of his elbow. Norman shifted his weight slowly, hoping to rouse his little friend gently. The whisper froze him where he lay.

"If you value your life, unhand that young stoat."

There was no need or desire to rub his eyes now. They were wide open, staring up into the branches of the oak tree that overhung their camp nest. There stood two stoats, perfectly still, their feet apart to brace themselves, their red cloaks swept over their shoulders and their bows drawn. Norman stared at the unwavering points of their arrows. There was no doubt about their intended target. If those arrows were loosed, Norman would never have to worry about wiping sleep from his eyes.

"No . . ." He wanted to add "it's not what it seems," but the stoats interrupted him.

"'No' what? You fancy an eyeful of arrow, do you?"

Norman gulped, and thought quickly before he said another word.

"I'm a friend of the stoats. This is Malcolm."

His captors were not so quick to respond this time. "A friend of the stoats indeed. Never a friend of your sort have I seen," the younger stoat on the left declared. His voice was even and unhurried, without a trace of fear or panic. He seemed confident that he would be able to dispatch Norman with little trouble.

The other stoat chipped in, "Some foul beast out of the North, are you? A mongrel monster, half bear, half wolf, perhaps?" Norman heard the impatience in his voice.

"No, I'm a man, a boy human. Ask Malcolm here."

Norman shifted again gently. It was as much as he dared to move, lest he provoke a reaction from the archers, but Malcolm only shifted in his sleep and smacked his lips as if enjoying a dream meal.

"Have you drugged the lad?" the lead stoat barked. "Is he poisoned?"

The older stoat squinted as if taking his final aim.

"No, I swear," Norman gasped, his voice breaking with desperation. "He's just tired. We've travelled a long way. Please just ask him. His name is Malcolm."

The lead archer seemed to think for a moment. His eyes never left Norman and his bow never wavered, but he let out a low whistle that rose and dipped, like a secret call. Duncan's scouts had used the same signal as they called to each other through the woods.

Malcolm's tiny ears pricked up instantly. He leapt upright and alert upon Norman's chest, into a stance ready for action, more awake already than Norman was even after five minutes staring down an arrow shaft. "What ho?" the boy stoat cried. His bright eyes immediately picked out the figures in the trees.

"Well, I never," Malcolm exclaimed, not startled but pleased. "I thought we'd be days before we found fellow stoat. Lower your arrows, lads. He may be an ugly beast, but he's *my* ugly beast. You'd like him in a fight. He can hurl huge crow-mangling boulders without the least strain, and he's only a boy yet."

But the archers remained immobile, not yet ready to believe that this huge, unheard-of creature was friend to stoat.

"What's your name, boy?" the young leader asked Malcolm. "Where do you hail from? Where are you heading?"

"I'm Malcolm. You can learn the rest when you put those arrows back in their quivers."

"Best you step away from the beast, boy. Perhaps you don't know the danger you are in." The arrows did not look like their next likely resting place was a quiver. "You say your name is Malcolm?"

Norman answered for him. "Yes, Malcolm," he said, with a calmness that belied his fear. "He is Malcolm, son of Duncan, son of Malcolm Sharp Sword, Lord of Lochwarren and last of the Mustelid kings."

Malcolm himself turned and gaped at Norman. True, they were in a spot, but they had agreed to conceal the young prince's identity.

"Malcolm," Norman continued, for he had recognized the red cloak and the gold emblem of a stoat guardant, "meet your uncle Cuilean. The other gentleman who would like to poke out my eye must be James."

It took a few more minutes of explanations for James and Cuilean to finally relent and lower their weapons. They settled down in the dell to hear the whole story, but not before James had been sent to the village below to fetch breakfast. Malcolm narrated their journey over a breakfast of muffins and warm raisin bread. It was the best meal Norman had enjoyed in Undergrowth. That morning he would not have traded it even for his mother's pancakes.

As the little stoat told the story, Cuilean's eyes darted occasionally to the boy human beside him for confirmation.

"Is it true?" he asked finally, when he heard the story of their attack on Scalded Rock. "You freed the prisoners at the mine?"

Norman only nodded, but Malcolm emphasized the totality of their victory: "And stole the season's treasure. There's enough there to buy three swords for every stoat who wants to take up arms with us."

Cuilean looked pensive and spoke lowly, as if to himself. "Yes, a great victory, a fine victory." Then, recovering his nobility, he patted his nephew on the shoulder. "I expect no less from your father. He was always meant to be a great warrior. I look forward to seeing him again and fighting alongside him."

Little Malcolm beamed with pride.

All morning they talked, telling each other their plans. Norman was mostly silent, correcting Malcolm when he exaggerated a little on his abilities as a seer or warrior. Cuilean regarded the human boy with curiosity rather than hostility now, but he addressed no questions directly to him, which was all right with Norman. He didn't really want to have to explain how he had read it all in a book.

James looked up, startled, when he heard the tale of Simon Whiteclaw's last battle.

"He was one of ours once," he murmured. "A captain in the Mustelid navy, before he went a-pirating. I always knew at heart he was a good man. He would have fought bravely."

It shouldn't have surprised Norman to see the three stoats cross themselves silently in Christian fashion, but it did.

"Your adventure at Scalded Rock obliges us to alter our own plans. We were heading that way ourselves," Cuilean said when the whole story of their attack and escape had been told. "We had a sneak attack planned, entering the highlands via the South Wolflands through Queen Millie's Pass. Queen Millie's Pass probably remains a secret, but with the fall of Scalded Rock, all South Wolflands will be roused. Your three wolf hunters will not be the last to follow your trail. Your ruse at the river where it emerges from the mountains makes it difficult for us. You were close to Queen Millie's Pass then, very close. You might have found it yourself, had it been on your map."

Norman withdrew the chart from inside his pyjamas, and laid it out for the stoats. "It only shows one pass on the western edge of the mountains." He pointed to the pass at the north end of the range, just above Scalded Rock.

"Winding Gap," said Cuilean. "You would have passed through it with Duncan. That is likely where you fought the ravens. No, no stoat would be so foolish as to mark Millie's Pass on a chart. The wolves may have our lands for the moment, but they will never have our secrets." He smiled and winked at his nephew.

"What will we do now, then?" the young stoat asked.

"We'll double back a little, trace the southern edge of the Glace Mountains and enter the highlands on one of the more travelled routes. These we'll have to put away." He indicated the red cloak that he wore around his shoulders. "We will have to travel in disguise again. The rats have had the run of these lands since the wolves moved in. They are no friend to stoats. Nor, I doubt, to hairless human boys," he added with a chuckle.

"And where are we heading?" Malcolm asked. "Where will we meet Father? In Rivernest?"

Cuilean became cagey, casting a quick glance at Norman. "There's no reason to decide at this moment. I have contacts in the highlands. We'll send out messengers. Your father has seized the initiative. We shall see what we can do to support him."

And that was all they would get out of him. Perhaps Cuilean had thought better about being totally candid with his nephew and the strange human beast. He did not mention their final destination, nor did he reveal the target of his own preempted surprise attack.

The sun was already high in the sky when they set off. James and Cuilean had made some muttered plans that they did not share with the boys. Norman didn't bother trying to find out. He knew already that he would have to earn Cuilean's trust, just as he had earned Duncan's. Mostly he was just relieved to have an adult about again, someone else to make the difficult decisions. They travelled through the forest once more, not seeing anyone. Norman walked alone while Malcolm chatted with his new-found uncle. It was late in the afternoon when they first spotted the plumes of blue-grey smoke rising from the chimneys of another border village.

"This is Tintern," announced Cuilean with a half smile. "I'm told it was once a pleasant place. James, can I ask you to escort young Malcolm to the Feather and Whistle? Try not to be seen, and order a meal up to our room. We shall keep out of sight as much as we can. Tell them the boy is ill. Mention bramble fever or something if anyone asks. That should keep the curious away. In the meantime, I'll find somewhere to hide our large friend here."

Malcolm protested. He did not want to be separated from his human friend, but Norman prevailed on him. "It will be good for you—a comfortable bed, a hot meal. You're not healed yet completely." It was the thought of hot mead and lingonberry pies that finally swayed him.

"I'll see if they have a few dozen extra pies for you, shall I?" the youngster joked as they parted company.

Cuilean and Norman walked in silence after this. An uneasy feeling filled Norman's gut as they walked. Maybe they were getting rid of him now. Travelling in disguise through the more populous parts of Undergrowth would not be easy. Cuilean wouldn't have ignored the problem. Maybe Norman would not have the opportunity to win the other brother's trust.

When Cuilean did speak, he was the gentle and thoughtful brother Norman had read about in the beginning of this book.

"Young Malcolm says that you have been carrying him for days."

"Yes," Norman answered sheepishly, "but he was no trouble. He's not very heavy."

"Still, you have been a good friend. I know what it means to have a good friend in a strange land. I thank you for that."

Norman did not know how to answer.

"And is it true that you are a seer?" Cuilean asked after another long silence.

Norman wondered what to answer. "I see certain things. Not everything, not everything I want."

"When we left Lochwarren," Cuilean began hesitantly, "our father gave us each a gift."

Norman nodded but said nothing.

"The gifts were messages. If I knew what gift, I would know better how to conduct this war."

Norman answered the unasked question. "I can't see what your gift was. And . . . I don't know which of you two is meant to be King."

Cuilean laughed, as if relieved. "You are wise for your size," he said cheerfully. "There is a saying in the Five Cities, 'Big of skull, small of thought.' You prove it wrong."

He stopped at the crest of the hill and nodded toward the valley below.

"We are here now," the stoat announced cheerfully.

The Abbey

They had reached the top of a small hill. Below, in a deep green valley, lay the largest building Norman had seen in Undergrowth. Built of massive grey stone, it was buttressed, ornate, clearly the work of many years and hundreds of hands. It was about the size of a school portable.

"Tintern Abbey," Cuilean declared. "The last and finest of the Canid monasteries."

Fine though it might have once been, Norman could see as they descended the slope that Tintern Abbey was in bad repair. Only the church itself had any roof left, and only half of that. Thick wooden beams stuck out like ribs where the slate stopped. No windows or doors remained. The late afternoon sunlight streamed right through the tall gaps in the stonework where the stained glass should have been. It had clearly been this way for some time—a heavy curtain of ivy draped over one wall, and the abbey floor was carpeted with thick green moss.

"Was it destroyed, or did they never finish it?" Norman asked. Even he could see how much work it must have been for the animals of Undergrowth. It was impressive and at the same time disappointing.

"A little of both," Cuilean replied. "They finished the roof, perhaps a hundred years ago now, but then the building stopped. The fox kings of Louwth needed the money for their wars."

Norman tried to remember his history of Undergrowth. "The Christianized foxes who ruled the hill country after the crusade of Ferrix?"

"Yes," Cuilean nodded in confirmation. "Ferrix and his descendants ruled here for two hundred and fifty years. For two hundred of them they were at war. In the last days, they had no time for building churches. Their strongholds and city walls needed the attention of the masons."

"I never understood who was against who in these wars," Norman said.

"Better historians than you or I have had the same problem," Cuilean replied. "Often it was the foxes against themselves, the grandsons and great-grandsons of Ferrix squabbling over the right to rule, the right to be paid tribute. If not that, it was the desert wolves to the west or the rats."

"Who rules here now, then? Why didn't they ever finish the abbey?"

"No one rules here now. It suits everyone. Each village has its own council, its own clique of bullies. No one is powerful enough to restore the old citadels, and no one cares for the churches. It suits all the nations that surround it that none of their enemies controls what we now call the Borders."

They had arrived at the abbey. Norman had a strange sense of dizziness. It was as if he was trapped between scales. The abbey was the closest thing to human scale that he had seen here in Undergrowth, and yet it was too small to be what it was meant to be: colossal and awe-inspiring.

Now that they were beside it, Norman saw a smaller building behind the great church, in full repair and apparently occupied. A thin curl of smoke rose lazily from its chimney.

"Stay here," Cuilean ordered, "out of sight of the Abbot's house. I must have a word."

Norman sat in the lengthening shadow of the church while

Cuilean had his word. He had never found it strange that Undergrowth's history had so many parallels to human history, with its medieval wars and habits, its cathedrals and crusades. It was a book, after all. The person who wrote it knew about all those things. But it was different when you were *in* the book, when it was a real world. If Undergrowth existed like this, without a person writing it, it was peculiar, suspicious even, that the animals had villages, cities and countries like human civilizations. It was weird that they spoke English or any human language, bizarre that they were Christian. As he waited for Cuilean to return, he wondered what sort of animal their Christ was. Did they all imagine the same one, or did foxes imagine a fox Christ and rabbits a rabbit Christ? Norman didn't go to church and his family wasn't particularly religious, but he felt guilty thinking this question.

"By the Maker, you've brought us a strange one, you have, Prince." This was a new voice, the voice of the Abbot. "You made it sound like a hairless bear or a woodwitch, but I think I know what this is. Not for nothing is Tintern the home of this earth's finest bestiary."

The fox abbot stood and appraised Norman as if he had seen dozens of his sort. On his hind legs, the Abbot stood more than three feet tall. He might have been four, if his shoulders weren't bent and his snout didn't stick forward like an old man's. Was he an old man? His fur was grey, but that might have been his natural colour. His voice was raspy and thin, but that too might have been his natural fox bark.

"Aye, we'll look after him for a night or two," he said. "Your father kept the roof over our community's head for long enough. We can't begrudge you the half roof of our abbey, and it will be needed tonight all right. We'll have a rainstorm for sure."

Norman and Cuilean looked up at the clear evening sky. No cloud justified the Abbot's prediction, but neither boy nor stoat bothered to contradict him.

"We'll find something in the larder for a beast of his ilk," the

Abbott continued. "Luckily it's been a good harvest and we've had little need to send succour to the poor."

While the fox and Cuilean made plans for him as if he wasn't there, Norman wondered why the Abbot looked familiar. He couldn't put his finger on it. Something about his face, which looked, well, arrogant and knowing. It wasn't as if Norman had seen a lot of foxes up close in his life, and he didn't pretend to know anything about fox physiognomy, but if that slight curl of the snout exposing one canine on the left side had been a human mouth, you would have called it a sneer. And if a human raised the hair above one eye, like the whiskers sprouted from around the white patches of the Abbot's glinting eye, you'd think he was trying to let you know he was in on some secret.

Cuilean did not linger at the abbey. Explaining that he had to get back to his friend in the village, he turned to Norman and bowed slightly.

"I will take my leave now. Know that you have my gratitude for your services to my family. I look forward to hearing more of your tales and your strange wisdom, but I must go for now. The Abbot has offered you the shelter of the abbey and has promised to bring you an evening meal. You will be safer here than anywhere else I can imagine in the Borders."

Norman thanked him quietly. The stoat nodded again and tossed his cloak over his shoulders. "We shall see you in the morning," he called as he strode away.

Norman crawled into the abbey through the arched main entrance, like a dog crawling into a kennel. There was plenty of room inside for him to lie down or sit up, but not enough to stand. The roof was tall enough, but the cathedral's internal vaults and beams cluttered what would have been his head space. Yet the moss that covered the abbey's granite floor was better than any bed he'd had yet in Undergrowth, and even half a roof was enough to shelter him from the Abbot's promised rainstorm. As he lay there on the moss watching the last rays of sun disappear between the ribs of the roof's unfinished side, he had time to wrack his brains over who the fox abbot resembled, but not long enough to come up with an answer.

Stars were just beginning to glint into life between the roof beams when the Abbot reappeared. He carried a torch, which lit his face mysteriously.

"I've brought you some supper," he said in his raspy voice. He seemed out of breath. "I've carried it myself, as I daren't let the young monks see you yet. I'm a wily physician, but even I've no remedy for eyes popping out of your head."

"Your name is Norman?" the Abbot asked, heaving a wrapped package to the floor. Norman's nostrils came alive as the Abbot unwrapped the package and the scent of warm apple pies wafted upward.

"Norman, North Man, Man from the North . . . That makes some sense with the bestiary here." He nodded to the pies, indicating that Norman should help himself. Norman didn't need a second invitation.

The Abbot had taken a small leather-bound book from inside his cloak and was reading out loud. "The *man beast,* called by the wood ducks *Hewn Man* and to which the black bears give the epithet *Smaller Giant,* dwelleth in the North beyond the mountains and beyond the ice seas. Borne of an egg, like a salamander or snake, its skin is thin and pinkish even as an adult, so that the man must cover itself with the skin of other animals. Weak and unable to care for itself long after its infancy, the man requires the protection of its sire and dam for many years, and unprotected man kids are often devoured by older animals in their pack."

Norman gulped down a bite of apple pie quickly enough to exclaim, "That's not true!"

The fox winked his whiskered eye and grinned. "It could be."

There seemed little point arguing with him.

"I won't go further," the Abbot said. "I think it's conclusive enough. You are a man. It says your skull is thick and obdurate, harder than any stone, and that though you are large, your thinking apparatus is smaller than a vole's."

Norman shrugged. He didn't have to react to the fox's goading. It was better to eat in silence.

The abbot fox leaned in closer. The torch between them made the fox's gleeful whiskers shine. He really did look familiar—there was something about the supercilious way he curled his snout or the unnatural shaggy tuft of hair falling over his glinting eyes. And there was something else strange about the Abbot's face. Norman noticed that a circular hole had been gouged out of one of the fox's perky triangular ears.

"What happened to your ear?" Norman asked.

"Hunting accident," he replied. "Beast was hunting me, and I let it get too close with its arrow." The fox winked again. "Cuilean says you can read. Is he wrong? If a beast with a brain the size of a vole's could be taught to read, a fox could make a fortune selling it to a travelling circus."

"I can read," Norman answered sullenly. "And my brain is not the size of a vole's." He held out his hand to take the book before he fully considered whether the Abbot would really sell him to a circus.

The Abbot did not hand him the bestiary. Instead, he reached inside his cloak again and withdrew a different book. Norman wondered if it was some trick, whether the book might be written in some strange animal language rather than English, just to make a fool of him. He took it reluctantly, eyeing the fox suspiciously as he drew it from his hands. It was a small book in human terms, no bigger than his palm. It reminded him of the tiny white bible that his godfather had given him for his christening. He opened it carefully to a random page in the middle. The pages were smooth and almost unmanageably thin for his big human fingers. To his relief, he saw that the lettering was decipherable. The book was handwritten in calligraphy, like the medieval texts Norman's father had shown him at the university, but it was in the alphabet that Norman knew. The language was English, and after a few sentences it became easier to read. He read it out loud to spite the annoying abbot.

That night while the boy slept on the bed of thick moss, the rain fell around him with a hushing sound that reminded him of his mother. Even as he dreamt, he wondered what they were doing back there in his home, whether they missed him, whether they were looking desperately for him. But he needn't have worried. He was asleep there too, as he was asleep here. Perhaps his mother was just waking now, a coffee pot filled and beginning to steam. His father, somewhere, was slapping a clock radio, reprimanding it, not very gently, for waking him so rudely . . .

Coffee pots? Clock radios? Norman looked up sharply at the fox, who raised both eyebrows now in a gesture that rolled his eyes as if to say, "Don't ask me."

"I know where I've seen you before . . . the library . . ." Norman managed to murmur only this before a strange and unconquerable need for sleep overtook him. Wasn't it always like this when you stayed up to read in bed? The good bit was always just a few pages away, and though you sat up reading long past the time when lights should have been out, you always nodded off just at the wrong time.

At Home Everything Is Not Normal

There was shouting somewhere down below, and the scent of coffee and of toast burning. Someone was calling Norman's name. Malcolm and Cuilean must be back. Probably they'd already had breakfast and had brought him some of the famous lingonberry pies that Malcolm had raved about. Norman wasn't ready to get up just yet. He rolled over to face the wall of his cathedral, but it was too late now. He was awake. His eyes opened slowly and focused on his soccer medals dangling from the bookshelf. His team had won the league two years ago, and he'd won the most improved award.

Again, someone called his name from downstairs. "Norman, I won't tell you again. It's time to get up."

Of course she'll tell me again, Norman thought. Mom will keep telling me again until I do get up.

"Wait a minute . . . ," he muttered aloud to himself, sitting straight up in bed and looking around. It was true. He was in bed. Was it all a dream, then? The *Brothers of Lochwarren* lay open face down among the crumpled bedsheets beside him. This was his room. That was his mother calling up from downstairs. No talking ferrets were about, and it was apparently a school day. But just a dream?

He looked down at his hands. They were filthy, smeared with pine sap, moss stains and forest dirt. Swivelling his feet over the side of the bed, he caught a shocking glimpse of his other extremities. They were quite literally black. They dangled beneath the ragged cuffs of his pyjamas, which were no model of cleanliness themselves.

Norman scrambled to the bathroom as his mother shouted up again, "Are you out of bed yet, Norman?" In the bathroom mirror he assessed the rest of the damage. His hair was matted and ragged, his face and arms were covered in scratches and every area of exposed skin was smeared with grime. His pyjamas were in tatters, beyond rescuing. He looked like a cartoon representation of Robinson Crusoe. His mother would kill him if she saw him like this. He had a good excuse—but he couldn't imagine ever having the courage to tell his mother he'd been busy helping restore the stoat dynasty in the highlands of Undergrowth.

His days in the forest with Malcolm had trained him to know when to act and when to think. He could consider explanations and wonder how it all had happened later. Now was the time to act. He turned the shower on as hot as he dared and left his tattered pyjamas in a pile on the floor. Using the hardest sponge he could find, he scrubbed his skin with the same determination and sense of urgency as he'd felt days before while the wolves pursued him through the forest. It was time for dire measures. He even resorted to shampoo and hair conditioner on his tangled and pine-tar-clumped mop.

When he was done, he could almost run a comb through his hair, but all his scrubbing had done was reveal the scratches and cuts along his arms and legs. His feet, in fact, appeared unchanged. The dirt had actually stained them, so that he looked like he was wearing black socks. Long sleeves and jeans might cover most of this, but there was one long scratch that ran from below his eye to his cheek that he could never cover. He'd have to find an explanation for that.

"Norman, I appreciate you having a shower without being asked. This is a huge advancement, but I wish you could have made this great leap forward on a day when you weren't running so late." His mother's voice was just outside the door.

"Nearly ready," he mumbled back through a mouthful of toothpaste. He hadn't realized how awful his breath had turned during his week with the animals. When his mother's footsteps sounded again on the stairs, Norman slipped out of the bathroom and smuggling his shredded pyjamas back to his room. He dressed quickly, pulling on the clothes that covered the most skin. It was late fall. He could get away with a turtleneck. He was stuffing the bundle of rags that were his pyjamas under a pile of toys when he felt something in their inside pocket.

Trembling fingers unfolded the smooth brown patch of material to reveal the dark outlines of Undergrowth's geography. "Duncan's map," he muttered to himself. "I *knew* it happened"—as if the scratches, bruises and stained feet weren't enough to prove that he'd actually been to Undergrowth. Still acting instinctively and moving with animal speed, he slipped Duncan's map into *The Brothers of Lochwarren* as a bookmark and bolted downstairs.

Norman had almost managed to gulp down a bowl of wheat squares when his mother noticed the scratch. "Norman, what on earth have you done to your face?"

"The cat. I was playing with it last night in bed, and it scratched me."

Norman's father came into the room at that moment. Aethelred had been bought to appease Dora after the death of Moggy, but it showed no interest in children and was mostly his dad's cat. It spent its days snoozing beside the computer when Norman's dad worked at home in his study, and curled up any spot of sunlight if no other source of warmth could be found.

"You must have been tormenting him, then," his father said.

Norman blushed, feeling guilty for accusing the cat. He regarded the animal with new interest after having spent a few days with its furry brethren. "It was an accident," he said. "He didn't mean to do it."

It was all Norman could do to keep himself awake through the school day. He hadn't realized how exhausting his adventure in the wilds of Undergrowth had been. Now, when he had time to rest and think about it, he was amazed that he'd been able to do it. Just last year he had tried out for the cross-country running team and had been useless. He'd had to stop and suck wind before everyone else. It was amazing what being chased by angry wolves did for your athletic performance.

Back at school, Norman unleashed his new agility in gym class as he dodged balls like never before, if only because he knew how much it would hurt to take a ball to any part of his bruised body. He actually fell asleep on the bus going home, waking only when Dora shouted his name and the whole bus erupted into laughter. He dragged himself off the bus, up the driveway and up to bed, where he collapsed, exhausted. He dozed off again there for twenty minutes, dreaming he was back in Undergrowth.

He fully expected to wake up in Undergrowth again. That was how it had worked last time. He had simply fallen asleep and arrived there. He'd come home the same way, by falling asleep, but there must be more to it. There had to be some other trick, something to do with the book. Where was that book, anyway? He groped through the pile of sheets and blankets that he'd twisted around him in his slumber. Not there.

Reluctantly Norman climbed out of bed again. If possible, his joints felt stiffer and his muscles more sore than they had that morning. He pulled the bedclothes off the bed and shook them, but no book fell out. It must have fallen under the bed. Norman winced as he knelt down and reached under. His arm slid back and forth but managed only to plough up a field of dust bunnies and cat fur. He flattened himself on the floor and peered under the bed. There, in the corner against the wall, was the dark outline of a book fallen face down on the floor. Unable to reach it from this side, he climbed up again and reached down between the wall and the bed, his fingers groping for the fallen book. When they finally grasped it, he yanked it out fast, like one of those weirdos on TV catching poisonous snakes or wombats, as if it might get away if he wasn't quick enough.

Aha, he thought triumphantly to himself as he fell back on the bed. At least now I can find out what happened. He sighed, and brought his captive prey to his eyes—*The Grey-Haired Monocolist*? So that's where that had gone. A few weeks ago he had searched franticly for this book. It was overdue at the school library, and he was gathering the courage to declare it lost. It didn't matter so much to him now. He would have gladly traded it for *The Brothers of Lochwarren*.

He searched his entire room, going as far as transporting the clothes from heaps beside the dresser to a heap in the laundry room and borrowing some strange instrument called a broom to sweep the entire floor, but *The Brothers* was not to be found. The more he searched, the more frustrated he became, and the more he felt the need to blame somebody else.

He stormed over to Dora's room. Without knocking, he swung the door open. His sister, who was lying on the floor playing some game, turned around startled, holding a plush stuffed unicorn in one hand and a painted silver wand in the other.

"You're supposed to knock," she complained.

Norman knocked.

"What do you want?" she asked.

"I'm looking for my book," Norman said.

"So?" Dora began waving her painted wand in circles and whispering annoyingly.

"Have you seen it?" he asked accusingly.

"Nope."

"You don't even know which book I'm looking for." Norman ground his teeth, getting more agitated by the second.

"I haven't seen any of them."

Norman couldn't let it go. He had looked everywhere. Somebody else must be responsible. "Have you been in my room?"

"No." Her defensive tone gave her away as much as the movement of her body, as if to hide something behind her.

Norman took two steps forward and Dora moved again, still trying to hide something. "You *have* been in my room," he muttered. "Give me back my book."

Dora squealed. "I don't have your book!"

Norman was close enough now to see what she was trying to hide: a regiment of Spivitski Skirmishers, fully assembled but half painted. Norman needed to buy two more colours of paint to finish them. They stood in formation now, on the floor behind his sister, surrounded by stuffed animals.

Norman erupted. "I told you not to touch anything in my room! Those are fragile. You could break them!"

"I was being careful with them. I was only playing. It's not like *you* ever play with them."

"That's because they aren't finished. Now give them back. And my book too."

They were both screaming at the top of their lungs now.

"I don't have your stupid book," Dora shrieked.

"Like I believe you," Norman scoffed.

Neither noticed that their mother was at the door. "What on earth is going on in here?" she asked, in a level just higher than her normal, calm voice.

Dora and Norman answered together.

"She's been taking my stuff without asking—"

"He butted in here, without knocking, and he's wrecking my game, because he's mad that everyone laughed at him on the bus—"

Their mother sorted it out in her usual efficient manner, by reminding them of their chores. Dora was sent to clean the cat litter, Norman to sort the recycling. He was only just allowed to rescue the regiment of Spivitski Skirmishers from the clutches of Nodlow the yellow dino and Sushi the Siamese cat.

Norman was folding cardboard boxes vehemently when his mother came to him in the garage.

"What book are you looking for?" Meg Jesper-Vilnius enquired calmly.

Norman didn't answer immediately, but his need to find the

book overcame his resentment. "It's one of my Undergrowth books, *The Brothers of Lochwarren*."

"The new one?" his mother asked.

Norman nodded. It sometimes surprised him that his mother listened and knew things like this.

"Well, you've obviously looked in your room, and your sister promises she hasn't had it, so it's best that you sleep on it. It's amazing how sleep can help your mind solve problems. You look like you could use a good night's sleep."

Norman hated how his mother always gave sensible advice that he didn't want to hear. He could tell her a few new things now about the power of sleep.

Surprisingly, after supper and homework and a little TV that night, Norman did sleep, as soundly and as deeply as he ever had. And once again he woke up in his own bed. Undergrowth seemed farther away this morning. He hadn't even dreamed of it. Dressing slowly and brushing his teeth, he did his best not to imagine what Malcolm was doing now. It was no use wondering if he safer with his uncle or whether Cuilean's path to Lochwarren was just as dangerous. His mother was right: sometimes solutions to problems did come to you in your sleep, but this was because you let them sneak up on you. You had to try not to think about them.

Trying not to think about something is a nearly impossible thing. By reminding himself not to think about his book, Norman only made himself think about it more. Where had he left it? Had he just lost it, or had his excursion into the book done something to the book itself? Maybe it was impossible to read a book once you've been in it. If you were making up the laws of the universe, this would be a plausible one. If only there was someone he could ask—perhaps that librarian, the one whose double was a fox abbot in Undergrowth. Once Norman's mind had started wandering, only the most extreme intervention could bring him back. Perhaps only Dora could accomplish this. She came screaming down the stairs while Norman was slurping his cereal.

"Mom, Dad, look what he did. He wrecked my book. He wrecked it!" There was nothing like a hysterical accusation to bring your mind back to the breakfast table.

Standing by the coffee machine at the counter, Norman's father raised his head from his mug.

"Calm down, Dora. What's happened?" Edward Vilnius asked wearily.

"He wrecked my book. He ripped it . . ."

Norman's dad knew him a little better than this. "I hardly think, Dora, that Norman would—"

Dora continued to sniffle and rage. "He did. He found the most important page and ripped it out. He wrecked it."

Startled, Norman dropped his spoon.

"Did you see Norman rip your book?" his father asked, taking a calming sip of coffee.

"No, but he's mad at me 'cause he lost his book, and he doesn't want anybody else to be able to read."

"Dora, that's just silly. Are you sure your gerbil didn't just eat it, like it did your science project?" At this Dora actually stamped her feet. Her father should have known better than to make a joke about it.

Dora completely lost it. "You all hate me. You don't want me to read. You only want *him* to read."

Their father took a deep gulp of coffee before continuing. "I'm sorry, Dora. I didn't mean to tease you. Let's take a look at the book. Which page is missing?"

Norman couldn't resist taking a look for himself. Dora held the book open, as if it was proof in itself of Norman's guilt. Sure enough, the book went from page 78 to 81. A whole page was missing.

"Hmmm," their father mused. "You know, Dora, they don't make books like they used to. See this glue here on the spine? That's called 'perfect binding,' but it's not perfect at all."

Edward Vilnius knew more about books than they ever cared to hear, especially Dora at this moment, but Norman took up the idea. He had a queasy feeling in his stomach. This was a little too coincidental, and he very much preferred a logical explanation.

"It's true, Dora," he said. "I had a book that lost pages like that. They just came unglued. Yours probably came from the bookstore like that. I had to go to the library to read the missing pages."

"That sounds like an excellent idea." Norman's mother had appeared again, to be sensible and cheerful.

His father had reached the end of his coffee, and perhaps his patience. "I'm sure Spiny would be happy to take you to the library this evening after school, so that you can read your missing page."

"Happy" wasn't quite the right word.

There was no one at the front desk when they walked into the library. Norman went to the catalogue computer and looked up the title of Dora's book—*The Gypsy's Secret: Fortune's Foal.*

How lame, Norman thought, as the listing came up. There were twelve copies of the book in the city library's various branches. Twelve copies—that was crazy. He looked closer at the listing. Their branch alone had two copies. One was signed in. He jotted down the catalogue number and hurried to the shelves. The sooner he got this over with, the better. Five minutes of scanning book spines later, he found the right shelf. He needn't have bothered. Dora was sitting on the floor beneath it, book in hand.

"You knew where it was?" Norman said, exasperated.

"Of course. I've read eight books by this author already," Dora replied smugly.

"Is the page there?" he asked, worried that Dora's missing page problem might become as complicated as his own.

"Of course it's here," she snapped testily. "Stop interrupting me. I'm trying to read it."

"Fine by me," Norman muttered and wandered away. "I'll see you outside."

As he detoured by the front desk to throw away the catalogue slip, a too-familiar voice made him jump.

"Hey, Book Boy, you're back."

Behind the counter stood the strange librarian. He was dressed in black again, his hair was spiked high now, and he'd added a streak of purple.

"Yes, I'm back." Norman eyed him suspiciously, searching the teenager's pale face for the resemblance to the fox abbot he'd met in Undergrowth. Now that he saw him again, Norman wasn't sure. It had been dark that night under the arches of the ruined church, and Norman had been so tired.

"Yes, I'm back," he repeated, " . . . thanks to you." It came out somewhere between a statement and a question.

"I'm touched," the librarian said flatly. "You should come for the books, though."

Norman laughed a false, nervous "hah" and tried again. "You know what I mean, in Undergrowth." He sounded less than confident.

The pale librarian stretched his face, as if mildly amused, and passed a pencil through the hole in his ear.

Norman could not stop himself from pushing for an answer. "Did you do something to my sister's book too?"

The librarian smiled indulgently. "You're a crazy little kid, aren't you? You should read less and sleep more."

"Isn't sleeping what caused all this?" Norman replied.

The librarian looked the other way and typed something on the computer, as if he didn't have time for this. Under his breath, he muttered, "That's funny. I thought it was eating that caused all this."

"What did you say?" Norman gasped incredulously.

The librarian made another wide-eyed "I don't know what you're talking about" face.

Norman felt a tug at his elbow. "Come on, Norman. Let's go," Dora whispered at his side. It was such a quiet voice that Norman had to look down to make sure it really was his sister.

"What's wrong?" he asked. Dora looked like she had been crying. "Is everything okay?"

"Let's just go home," she repeated.

"Is this the sister?" the librarian asked, leaning over the counter to look down on her. No one answered him. "Pony troubles?" he asked Dora, his forehead furrowed in mock seriousness. "I feel your pain. I've been there."

Norman opened his mouth to say something, but nothing came out. What could he say that didn't sound crazy? Dora tugged again at his sleeve. "I want to go now." She really did sound upset. He led her outside slowly. As he opened the door, he looked over his shoulder at the librarian, who winked just like the abbot back in Undergrowth. He would have to deal with this later.

Dora was strangely silent as they walked. They were nearly home when Norman finally spoke.

"What's the matter, Dora?" he asked, trying to sound as brotherly as he could.

"Nothing," she replied sullenly.

Norman took a deep breath. He didn't even have to pretend to be concerned. "What happened at the library?"

"It's the book," she said, not capable of keeping up her silence. "It's all wrong. The book's wrong. They killed Serendipity. That can't happen."

"What do you mean? Who killed Serendipity?"

"The gypsies," Dora sniffed, trying not to cry.

Norman tried to be calm, but inside his own throat was constricting with panic. "It's only a story, Dora. Sometimes bad things happen in books."

"Not in *this* book," she insisted.

"How do you know?"

"Because it didn't happen the first five times I read it!" Dora glared at him as if he was the idiot.

Norman stared back incredulously. "You mean you are having a fit over a book you've already read . . ." Then what she was saying hit him. "But it's changed, it's different now?"

Dora just nodded, curling her lower lip to stop it trembling.

Norman didn't like the sound of this. He had no idea how to console his sister. He decided to try to distract her by his usual method of being really, really annoying.

"What is this dumb book about, anyway?"

"It's about a girl and her horse, only it's not just a horse. It's a special horse."

"A special horse, like one with wings?" He said, intentionally picking a fight.

"Not special like that," Dora insisted. "It's a therapy horse. It helps people."

"Yeah, by giving them rides places."

"No, it helps them when they are upset or not right in the head," she explained.

"Who needs a horse for that? That's dumb."

"I'll tell you what's dumb," Dora countered. "Sword-fighting hamsters are dumb."

"No way . . . you just don't get it. Undergrowth is about—" Norman stopped there. How could he explain to Dora that it was more than a book, that it was all real and that he'd seen and felt it?

"Anyway," Norman said, "you shouldn't worry about it. This is probably just a new version of the book. They do that sometimes when they make a movie. They change it, you know, to make it exciting. You should keep reading and see how it turns out. I'll bet you everything is okay in the end."

"I don't want to read it anymore." Dora's voice was so small and pitiful, even a brother couldn't ignore it.

They arrived at their front doorstep. Norman put his hand on the door handle and turned to Dora. "Do you want me to read it and tell you what happens?"

She didn't answer him then, but that night as he was lying in bed, he heard shuffling outside his room, and a skinny paperback was slid beneath the door.

Fortune's Foal

Having to read a girl's book was embarrassing even if no one else knew about it. Ponies, fairies and unicorns had no place in real stories. If the unicorns wore battle armour and had sharpened obsidian blades attached to their horns, and the fairies swarmed in squadrons like aerial ninjas, maybe . . . but that was unlikely. He braced himself for a sickening set of slumber parties and horse shows and sparkly rainbow-riding white unicorns. It took a dozen pages or so to realize it wasn't that bad. It wasn't great, but it wasn't awful either.

Amelie Saint-Saens was the heroine of *Fortune's Foal.* She lived on a farm with her father, Georges, who was the local vet. From what Norman could tell, Amelie's mother had died in a horse-riding accident when Amelie was very young. Georges Saint-Saens was a withdrawn man who rarely spoke. After Amelie's mother's death, he had sold all her horses and had forbidden Amelie to ride.

Fortune's Foal began with a new birth at the Saint-Saens farm. One of the neighbour's mares had been brought to the Saint-Saens barn to foal. It was expected to be a difficult birth, and the owners wanted the vet to be right there when the horse went into labour. For Amelie, though, there was something special about this particular mare, a big and elegant chestnut. Her name was Fortune, and she had been Amelie's mother's horse. Fortune was the one horse Georges Saint-Saens could not bear to see sent far away. She had gone to the neighbours, the Ventnors, as a sort of exile. The Ventnors planned to breed her, and Georges Saint-Saens was to take a half share of the profits.

Amelie often accompanied her father on his rounds and had seen several foals born, but the men had barred her from the barn when she tried to join them this time. The foal was tangled in its umbilical cord and wasn't dropping. Even from the house, Amelie could hear the mare's painful sighs through her open window. If Georges Saint-Saens hadn't been such skilled vet, neither foal nor mare would likely have survived. As it was, only the foal made it through the night. The mare was not young. The birthing took a lot out of her, and she had lost a lot of blood. For a while it looked like the foal might not make it either, but the men had spent the night in the barn keeping the newborn warm and fed. By morning Amelie was allowed to come and see the new foal.

They called the foal Serendipity, in part from his dam's name, but also because it seemed to be luck that Fortune had been sent to a neighbour when the rest of the stable had been sold off to strangers. Serendipity rose and stood on four wobbly legs when Amelie entered the stable. He sniffed the air curiously, wrinkling his nose and snorting. They had brought in an old Shetland pony to keep the foal company. The pony moved in between the foal and the girl to protect her new charge, but the young colt's curiosity was not so easily deterred. They played a shuffling game of peek-a-boo from behind the grey pony's back until the pony gave up and Amelie was giggling uncontrollably.

It was obvious that Serendipity was going to be Amelie's summer project. Like her mother, Amelie had always loved horses. No matter how her father tried to keep her away from them, she was drawn to them. And this horse was special. Amelie could tell just by looking at him, the way his bold brown eyes met hers and returned her gaze so constantly. He knew her too. It was like finding your best friend.

Amelie looked after Serendipity for weeks, feeding him, encouraging him to test his wobbly legs and watching him grow into a frisky and fearless little colt. This was a bitter sweetness. Every day that the colt grew stronger was another day closer to the one when he would be sent away. Amelie was desperately attached to Serendipity and would have done anything to keep him. She knew it was impossible, and she didn't dare ask her father, but it didn't stop her wishing it.

Perhaps it was only her anxiety over losing Serendipity, but Amelie was having trouble sleeping. Three nights in a row she was awakened after midnight by the sound of strange animal calls—a low hoot or growl that she did not recognize. Each night she stood at her open window and tried to pick out the animal in the darkness, but every time she went to the window, the noise halted, as if the animal had spotted her. Only once did she hear anything further, and that was just a bit of rustling in the long hay behind the stables. It could have been a raccoon, or maybe even the wind swirling through the long grass.

In town at the grocery store that week, Amelie overheard a strange conversation. A talkative lady who always seemed to be at the cash register was rattling on to the clerk about gypsies. They were on their way through again this year, she announced in her busybody's voice. Better lock up your chickens and hide the jewellery. You know what happened last year. Amelie couldn't help scoffing. She didn't think that there really were any gypsies hereabouts. Amelie had only ever heard of gypsies in movies about carnivals and soothsayers. Her father had some classical music that he called "gypsy music." He played it so loud sometimes that it upset the animals outside. She hated dad's gypsy music almost as much as the animals did. It jangled and screeched and made you nervous inside, but it seemed to make her dad very happy, so she never complained about it.

For Norman, all this talk about gypsies and bad classical music was almost as annoying as the music was supposed to be. Norman's dad had a few intolerable CDs himself, so Norman could sympathize.

The town gossip about gypsies reminded Amelie of something else. Several times that summer she had seen a young girl playing by the riverbank near the horse meadow. She looked only eight or nine, but she always appeared to be alone. This seemed so unusual to Amelie that she had twice approached the girl to see if she was all right. Each time Amelie had tried to speak to her, the girl had run away. The first time she had run right into the bush on the other side of the river, fleeing as if she were being chased. The second time, though, the strange girl had stopped at the top of the opposite riverbank and stared back at Amelie. Her nut brown face had shown no fear, and her dark eyes had glistened with curiosity. The two girls stared at each other silently from opposite sides of the river until Amelie called across, "What's your name?" The younger girl did not answer, just held her stare a moment longer before slipping into the woods and disappearing.

Amelie dreamed of the girl that night, dreamed about gypsies and about her horse Serendipity. In her dreams, he was already *her* horse, and each time the animal sounds outside woke her, she was saddened to realize that in reality, this would almost certainly never happen.

The whole farm was awakened that morning by the shouts of the farmhands in the stables. The new foal was gone. Amelie bolted from her bed, unsure whether the shouts she'd heard were in her dream or not. Her foal gone? Serendipity? The entire household had congregated down at the stables. The stablehands formed an impenetrable barrier between Amelie and the foal's stall.

"Let me through," she cried. "Let me see." But the men did not budge. Georges Saint-Saens turned and shook his head solemnly at her.

"Somebody call the police," he barked, turning his back again to Amelie. A stablehand rushed off immediately to do as ordered.

"There's so much blood," somebody whispered.

"Surely the poor thing couldn't survive that."

"Who would do such a thing?"

"It's sick."

"I'll bet you it's those gypsies. They've been sneaking around folks' farms all week."

"This must be one of their rituals. I can't wait until Sheriff Wilkyn gets his hands on those greasy scumbags."

It was driving Amelie crazy. What had happened in that stall that had outraged them all so much? Finally she squeezed her way through. An arm grabbed her, but it was too late. She stood there gaping at the scene in the stall. Blood was everywhere, soaked into the hay, splashed on the boards of the stall. Vomit surged into her mouth. She rushed blindly from the stable out to the cruel grey morning.

Norman stopped reading. Even he could see that this didn't belong. It might happen in one of his mother's creepy murder thrillers, but gruesome murders didn't happen in a little girls' horse book. Small wonder his sister didn't want to read any farther. Norman wasn't sure he wanted to continue himself. This had to have something to do with his Undergrowth book, and the missing page. Had Dora eaten a page of her own book, he wondered? Was it a contagious disease, a mania that caused the entire household to start eating their books? What if Dora had fallen into her book the way that Norman had fallen into his? Once he'd got this idea into his head, he couldn't get it out. What if Dora was there now with those horse-murdering gypsies? Norman got up and tiptoed to his sister's room. She was lying there asleep, twisted in blankets, snoring just slightly. Is that what Norman had looked like while he was in Undergrowth? He crept closer to her bedside and listened to her breathing. She seemed genuinely restful. It was hard to imagine that she was really in a land where people killed horses and knocked kids unconscious with shovels. Well, maybe not too hard to imagine. Norman shook his sister's shoulder.

"Wha . . . whasamatter?" Dora rolled over, opened her eyes momentarily and gazed at him sleepily, before her lids snapped shut again.

"What are you dreaming about?" Norman asked in an anxious whisper.

Dora grumbled something incomprehensible. He repeated the question. "What are you dreaming about?"

Dora groaned, and answered slowly, in a barely discernable mumble, "Candy."

Norman felt as foolish as he did relieved. Had he really believed that his sister had been transported into a book? He was beginning to wonder whether it had actually happened to him. As he climbed into his bed, the red LEDs on his alarm clock flashed exactly 2:00.

"I better get to sleep," he told himself. He wouldn't admit it to himself, but he was a little too creeped out to keep reading in the dark.

Don't Mind Me. I'm Just the Reader.

The tickle of something inside his nostril finally woke him up. He sniffed and snorted without opening his eyes. It smelled musty, like the basement or a hamster cage. Had he sleepwalked to the basement perhaps? I've got to stop staying up all night, Norman thought. It was two o'clock when I put Dora's book down last night. I don't even remember getting out of bed this morning. That's how bad it's getting. Maybe if I just open my eyes slowly and don't yawn, no one will notice I fell asleep again.

He did open them slowly, keeping his head leaned against the wall. It became clear what had been tickling his nose: straw. He was lying in straw. He knew exactly what had happened. He wanted to pretend he didn't, but he knew exactly.

"Tell me I'm not in my pyjamas, tell me I'm not wearing pyjamas," he muttered to himself. It might be acceptable among rodents, but real people, even fictional ones, thought it was weird if you went out in your pyjamas. He let out a sigh of relief. There was something to be said for falling asleep with your clothes on. He stood up cautiously, brushing the straw from his jeans and T-shirt. He was in a barn. He was pretty sure he knew which barn, too. Sun was streaming in through the only window in the stall, illuminating the loose bits of dust and straw floating in the air. It was morning, sunrise, in Dora's stupid horse book.

He had to stand on tiptoes to see out the window. He could see the farmhouse from here. It was exactly as he imagined it, a big two-storey house of red brick. A white porch was wrapped around it, and a copper weather vane turned slowly and silently on the highest of its steeply pitched roofs. A neatly raked path led from the house to the barn, and the grass on either side was a uniform shade of bright emerald green. Everything in this book was flawless. No weeds grew on the gravel paths. Nothing seemed dirty. It was as if every piece of wood, every fence rail, every barn board had been freshly painted that morning. Norman had been to a real farm and knew they were never like this.

The smart thing would have been to walk up to the house, introduce himself somehow to Amelie and try to explain why he was here and how he could help. The trouble was he had no idea why he was here and what he could do to help. He had to think of a story for Amelie. He couldn't just say, "Don't mind me, I'm just the reader. I'm here to help."

Instead, Norman told himself he just needed some time to think and do a little investigation. Maybe he could figure out what the gypsies had done with the horse. It was a little girls' book, after all—how hard would it be to solve the mystery?

The horse barn was just as perfect as the rest of the farm. The door hinges didn't even squeak when he pushed his stall door open. This is what little girls like Dora imagined farms should be like, clean and fresh, smelling more like wildflowers than horse manure. It was probably just as well. From what Norman remembered, the smell of horse manure wasn't all that pleasant.

All this clean, tidy perfection made the scene in the last stall all the more disgusting. The stench struck Norman between the eyes as he opened the stall door. It was dark and oppressive, a bit like vomit, a bit like incense in the church his grandmother sometimes took him to. It made his stomach churn and his head spin. He had to grab the railing to make sure he didn't faint. He'd seen a little too much killing for a kid his age, Norman thought.

When he'd caught his breath, he raised his head and took another look. It looked as grim as it smelled. The blood had dried now, staining the straw a sickly brown colour, like an old cola stain. It was everywhere. Georges Saint-Saens was right: there was no way the horse could have survived all that. But why? Why would anyone do that?

Norman had a couple of theories. Most likely it didn't have anything to do with this book at all. The missing page had disturbed the story, and things were happening that shouldn't happen, things that didn't belong in *Fortune's Foal* at all, just like they had in Undergrowth. If this was true, then it was Norman's fault. The missing page from *The Brothers of Lochwarren* had started a chain reaction. It had infected Dora's book and changed it too. But maybe this could be fixed. Despite his intervention, the stoat rebellion in Undergrowth seemed to be going pretty much as planned. By introducing Malcolm to his uncle, Norman might have actually made things better . . . maybe. So maybe he just had to do the same sort of thing here. He had to fix things. But how could he fix a murdered horse?

Obviously, he had to find out who killed the horse. He had to put *that* right at least. And he had to find this Amelie girl another horse. That would fix things, wouldn't it? He wished he'd asked Dora who might have done it, who Amelie's enemies were, who her father's enemies were. It was probably the gypsies, but maybe that was too obvious. Norman would have to talk to Amelie carefully, see what she knew. Together they'd figure it out. But he had to get to her alone first. He had to find a way to explain to her.

"It's those goddamned gypsies. Those filthy horse butchers better not let me catch them."

Norman turned around, startled. He had heard lots of worse swearing in real life, but this was pretty harsh for one of Dora's horsey novels. It was one of the stablehands. He spat on the ground to punctuate his threat to the unseen, long-gone gypsies.

"Why would they do something like this, anyway?" Norman asked. Without waiting for an answer, he introduced himself. "I'm

Norman, Amelie's cousin," he declared quickly, very much to his own surprise.

He might as well have said that he was Zorba from the planet Omega 3 for all the stablehand seemed to care. He just nodded, as if he already knew.

"Who knows what those savages do? Most likely they carved it up for those filthy sausages they try to sell out at the farmers' market." He came closer and whispered knowingly, "Though some say it's all part of some satanic gypsy sacrifice."

"Satanic gypsy sacrifice?" Norman didn't do a very good job of disguising his incredulity, but the stablehand didn't seem to notice.

"They say those gypsies do all sorts of mischief, devil worship and all that. Usually it's just chickens and pigs they steal. Must be something awful big to call for the murdering of a horse."

Norman nodded vaguely, as if agreeing. His eye was caught by a mark on the outside of the stall door. It was new and deep. Five deep gashes had been gouged into the greying wood, exposing the fresh yellow wood beneath.

"What are these?" he asked.

"Gypsy signs, probably," the stablehand said, as if he was an expert on all these things. They didn't look like any kind of sign to Norman. They looked like claw marks, as if some huge cat had been stretching and sharpening its claws on the door.

"Last year the Greenlys over on the other side of the river found a gypsy ritual site near their farm," the farmhand continued. "A bunch of burned animals laid out on a big slab of rock—squirrels, rabbits, skunks even. And they'd made one of their secret gypsy signs on the grass with the ashes."

Norman made a grossed-out kind of face. Not that he really believed any of this, but it seemed to be the reaction that was expected of him. He didn't really know anything about gypsies. His only reference was a novel study his class had done on *The Painted Wagon,* and that had been mostly about prejudice and racism. Maybe there was more than one kind of gypsy.

"If the gypsy signs are secret, then how would you recognize them in the ashes?" Norman asked distractedly. It was hard to keep his eyes off the horrible scene in the horse stall. He couldn't stop his mind from speculating about those long scratches on the door.

"Well, none of us normal folks would do that," the stablehand answered, as if it was obvious, "so they must have been gypsy signs."

Norman turned to see if maybe he was joking, but the stablehand stared back, nodding and rocking slightly on his pitchfork, like someone delivering the cold, hard facts.

"I guess you're right." It seemed easier just to agree.

Maybe Norman hadn't been completely believable. The stablehand raised his chin as if to say "so long" and continued down the long aisle of the horse barn. Norman said, "See ya," quietly, as he strode away.

The stablehand's story didn't really make sense. Norman didn't believe it, but it was another creepy thought to consider. Devil worshipping and animal sacrifices would be a pretty bad thing to appear in a book for eight-year-old girls, and Norman didn't like the idea that he might be responsible for their introduction. There seemed little more to discover in the horse stall. The book had described it accurately. It was an ugly and disgusting scene, but there weren't any obvious clues. Even the scratches could be nothing—somebody accidentally scraping the door with a farm tool. If this had been one of the detective books that Norman had been into last summer, he would have spotted some clue in the straw, a foreign cigarette butt or a button or some broken piece of jewellery that the police had missed. No such luck. It wasn't that kind of book. Even so, he thought he might as well take a look outside the barn to see if he could see anything peculiar.

Around the back of the barn, something very peculiar did in fact appear. Most of the farm was covered with almost perfect lawn—the sort you see on professional baseball fields and in front of houses in expensive subdivisions. The horses around this farm must trot around in slippers, Norman thought, because they never seemed to tear up the turf with their hooves. Here at the back of the barn, though, was a patch of torn-up ground. A muddy trail led from a locked side door across a meadow toward a line of trees. Norman followed it slowly away from the barn, looking all the while for that telltale cigarette butt or the perfect shoe print. He tried not to get too excited. Surely the local sheriff had already followed this trail and extracted whatever clues there were to be had. It was that obvious. It was exactly the sort of trail that evil horse-murdering forces from outside the book would make when they snuck into a horse barn. The trail led to a wide clump of dense bush and trees, beyond which Norman could see nothing.

Norman had reached the edge of the field when he heard voices behind him. He turned to see a group of people following the same trail from the barn, too far away yet for him to recognize any of them. Norman returned his attention to the muddy trail. After the trees the field gave way to a sharp incline. About six feet below was a wide, fast-moving river. A boat was tied up to a tree by the banks. Not a small boat, either, but a long, narrow wooden boat—a barge, that was what they called them, a gaudily painted orange and green river barge.

The voices behind him were clearer now. He could just make out what they were saying.

"Are you sure he said he was my cousin—not a friend, someone from summer camp?" It was a girl's voice: Amelie. This was not good. This was not good at all. What on earth could he tell them? Norman turned around slowly to watch the little group of people coming toward him. He could make out Amelie, her father and the rumour-mongering stablehand from the barn. Norman raised his hand in a friendly greeting. Maybe if he just caught Amelie's eye and looked honest, she would go along with his story. Maybe there was a code word he could use to tip her off—something about her mother's accident, maybe.

A sound below on the river drew Norman's attention. There were people down there, too. Keeping one eye on the group approaching across the field, he edged closer to the river. Steadying himself against a low branch, he peered over the bank, but the branch was springy rather than solid, bending under his weight and casting him forward. The sandy bank subsided beneath his feet and he began to slide slowly down the steep slope. Norman crouched, nearly sitting down on the loose ground to keep his balance as he slid. He grasped at the scrub to slow his descent, but his impression was that the voice more than any action on his part stopped his movement.

"Stop, boy. Don't move." It was a thick foreign voice. A short, swarthy man stood on the riverbank, a small girl at his side. The girl's eyes were big and brown as they stared at Norman, stared as if he were a magical creature or something fearsome and mythical. Did she know? Did she somehow guess what he was? He could hardly ask the question, because the man beside her had his shotgun pointed at Norman's head.

"Get down on the ground. Put your hands over your ears," he ordered gruffly. Norman just stared, dumbfounded. His assailant seemed to look right through him, as if Norman was too insignificant to look directly in the eye. Without looking away, the man whispered urgently to the girl at his side, "Leni, get back on the boat." Though his voice was firm and insistent, neither Norman nor the girl obeyed. Norman began to edge closer to him and the girl just stood rooted on the spot, staring.

Another gypsy leapt from the boat, making a splash in the water behind them. He held no gun, but the screwed-up squint of his eyes and the curl of his mouth as he glared at Norman were just as threatening. "Come *now,* Leni," he muttered through gritted teeth. "In the boat."

While they hesitated, Norman acted. It was a new instinct, this impulse to fight and to anger, something young Malcolm had helped him find inside. Norman been coiled there all that time, tightening his muscles and storing the energy. While the gypsies hesitated on the riverbank, he uncoiled all that energy and leapt at the man's knees. His shoulder hit the man's shin, sending a shiver of pain down Norman's left side. He couldn't tell if it was him who growled or the man with the gun. The next sound was the harsh, ear-hammering blast of the gun going off.

Norman rolled and looked up to see if anyone had been hit. What he saw on the riverbank paralyzed him for a moment. Halfway down the bank, only a few feet behind where Norman had been standing moments ago, was a shape that didn't belong here. The wolf's bright yellow eyes narrowed as it fixed Norman in its sights. The grey beast lowered itself, the ragged fur on its neck rising with its shoulder blades, the creature coiling to jump and pounce as Norman had. Its lunge would be far more deadly.

A voice at the top of the embankment caught the predator's attention, and its vicious head snapped sideways to locate its source. Amelie and her father had arrived. The girl looked pale and tired. She had her arms crossed in front of her, wrapped around her skinny chest as if to keep herself warm. She walked close to her father, almost leaning on him. George Saint-Saens stepped in front of his daughter protectively. All of them stared down incredulously at the scene below: Norman and the three gypsies strewn in a haphazard pile on the riverbank, and the haggard wolf ready to pounce. The armed man rose to one knee and aimed his shotgun again.

The wolf, trapped between the two groups, seethed and snarled. Turning its vicious head back to Norman, it let out that deep, hateful growl Norman had heard in Undergrowth, the last time he felt sure he was about to be killed. "Interloper," it hissed, baring all its brown-stained fangs. Norman was momentarily stunned. Had anybody else heard it?

At that moment the wolf turned, bolting up the bank toward Amelie and her father. They took an instinctive step backward, unintentionally giving the wolf time and space to lunge. Norman watched in horror as the beast leapt through the air at Amelie, who raised her arms to protect herself. The wolf's momentum carried him though her, knocking the girl to the ground. The ragged claws that had targeted her face raked deep gashes through her light cotton shirt and into her forearms.

There were screams, followed by more gunshots than Norman could count. When he recovered his wits, his first impulse was to scramble back up the bank to where Amelie had fallen. The realization had sunk in now: He had caused all this. He had brought the wolves here. They had escaped from Undergrowth and were still hunting him.

A strong arm wrapped itself around Norman's chest and pulled him backward. He felt himself tumbling down the embankment again. Above him was just a tangle of tree branches and flashes of bright blue sky. A hand covered his mouth as he tried to scream in protest. His cry came out muffled and unclear. He struggled to break free, but his captors' arms held him fast. There were more arms than two here. There must be several attackers—and not kids, either: big, hairy, muscular ones.

They dragged him along the riverbank away from the farm. Behind them they heard Georges Saint-Saens shouting at them to stop, but the shouts were getting farther away. In his mind's eye, all Norman could see was the bright white of Amelie's blouse and the deep, awful red of new blood. Norman's captors shifted their load. Ahead of him Norman glimpsed the orange hull of the river barge. They were loading him onto the boat. As they lifted him over the gunwales, he made one final effort to escape, kicking out his legs and twisting his upper body simultaneously. There was a grunt of pain, not his own, and he suddenly felt that he was falling. There was no time to judge whether his manoeuvre was successful. A sudden sharp surge of pain shot up from the back of his skull. His vision started to blur, and he felt like vomiting. It felt like he was falling into a deep grey well. Perhaps he was drowning, he thought, before it all went black.

Among the Gypsies

Norman woke to the same sick feeling in his stomach. There had been no dreams, no slow coming back to wakefulness, no expectation of breakfast and home.

"I'm not dead, then," he said aloud, attempting to rise on one arm. The movement made his world lurch. His stomach started to heave, and he managed to kneel in order to be sick. They were dry heaves mostly—not a stream of sick, but a thin yellow stream of drool at the end that tasted like acid. When it was over, he stayed in the same position for a while with his eyes closed, just glad that the nausea had stopped. Taking the advice of his mother's yoga tapes, he took deep breaths through his nose—breathe in, breathe out. It seemed to work. He felt less dizzy, less like throwing up again.

Cautiously now he opened his eyes. They did not need to adjust to the light. Wherever he was, it was almost as dark as it had been behind his eyelids. Shifting his weight slowly, he edged away from the pool of half vomit he had created for himself and sat up, pulling his knees up to his chest. He didn't feel well enough to stand yet. It was just as well. The room he was in was small—not just narrow, but low. If he stood up straight, he would knock his head on one of the wooden beams that crossed the ceiling. Just the thought of it sent a shot of heat through his skull from the point where he'd been hit.

Tentatively he reached a hand up to the spot. It was not hard to find. A little crust of scab had started to form on the sharp lump at the back of his skull. He didn't dare do more than brush it with his fingers. He just knew how much it would hurt if he pressed on it.

"You're not dead, then." Funny how he had just been thinking the same thing. It was a girl's voice, thin and scornful. She sat so still there in the corner that Norman might not have noticed her if she hadn't spoken.

"Lucky for you. You could have killed me." His own voice sounded whiny and weak. He said nothing more, hoping that in a few minutes he'd feel strong enough to sound angry.

It was the girl called Leni. She peered at him from the corner, where she was seated like him on the wooden planked floor, knees to her chest, but her head was held higher and her dark eyes were more vigilant. It was as if they glinted in the dark. She looked maybe a year or two younger than him. She had that superior look of kids who had older brothers or sisters and thought they knew so much more than other kids because of it. She dressed pretty normally for a gypsy, if that's what she was—jeans, a flowery blouse. Her black hair was straight and cut short like a boy's.

"You don't belong here."

How did she know? What did she know? Did she know that he had come from outside of the book?

"That's no reason to kidnap me and knock me out."

The girl always seemed to wait a few seconds before answering, as if she might not answer at all if she didn't feel like it.

"That's your own fault," she said finally. "You shouldn't have wriggled so much when they were bringing you onto the barge. You made Feliz and Varnat lose their grip. They couldn't stop you banging your head on the gunwale."

Norman harrumphed softly. It was a plausible story, but it didn't make him happier. They shouldn't have been trying to abduct him anyway.

"Well, what would *you* do if strangers tried to grab you and kidnap you?" he said.

"You don't belong here," she repeated flatly. "And you let the wolf get away."

Norman looked down, further deflated. Somehow he had hoped that they had managed to kill the beast. They sat together in silence some more, eyeing each other suspiciously. Norman burned to say something that would bother her, get any kind of reaction out of her.

"I guess I don't belong here. Who would want to belong here—with a bunch of murderers?"

The girl didn't even smile.

"What did you do with the body?" Norman continued. "Did you slaughter him? Did you sacrifice him in one of your creepy gypsy ceremonies?"

There was just a hint of reaction, maybe an angry squint of those dark eyes.

"The foal had a name, you know," he continued. "His name was Serendipity. His mother died giving birth to him, and he nearly didn't survive, and now you've killed him."

But the girl had regained any composure that she had lost. Maybe he had only imagined that he'd made her uncomfortable.

"Jeez," he muttered, mostly to himself now. "What kind of evil witch murders a baby horse?"

Had he been looking, he would have seen that these last few words had more effect on the girl than anything he'd said before. Her eyes widened then blinked reflexively, and she had to stop herself from jumping up immediately. Norman didn't hear the gulp before she finally did stand up.

"Stay here," she said. "I'll bring you some water and food."

Stay here? It wasn't as if he had a choice. He watched the girl climb a ladder up to a trap door in the ceiling. When it opened, he heard the sounds of the barge crew navigating the boat, and of the river water slapping against the hull.

It seemed like hours before the deck hatch reopened. It was the creak that woke him, not the light. A cloudy night sky hovered above the hatch. Norman remembered finally that you aren't supposed to fall asleep when you have a concussion. A little late now, he guessed.

"Come on up, we're eating," the girl called down from the deck, not bothering to descend.

Norman stood up carefully and eased himself up the ladder. The deck was cluttered with small animals, loose and in cages—ducks, geese, hens, a small piglet tied up to a mooring—but there were no humans on deck. They were all ashore. Norman heard them before he saw them, the sound of laughing voices beyond the trees on the bank, more voices than would fit on a single boat. There were several boats tied up at the shore, all of same size and proportion: narrow river barges—houseboats, really—just big enough to squeeze in a single gypsy family and their possessions. The girl was standing alone on the bank. "Come on. I'm hungry, even if you aren't," she said peevishly.

Norman thought for a moment about making a run for it. The girl wouldn't be able to stop him. If she shouted, the gypsies beyond the trees would come running, but he'd have a decent head start. He would run as fast as he could for five minutes and then hide. That was his best chance. The gypsies would give up searching for him sooner or later, and he could make his way back down the river to . . . to what? The farm? They might want to see him back there, but not for the reasons he wanted. Amelie and her father knew that Norman had lied when he had introduced himself as her cousin, and they probably suspected he had something to do with the murder of the horse. Amelie wouldn't believe him if he told her he was trying to help now, even if he managed to let her know that he knew her story. But that was not the real reason he did not run. He had not forgotten that there was still at least one wolf out there in this forest.

"Are you coming or not?"

This girl was worse than his sister.

"I'm coming. Hold your horses."

The gypsy girl gave him a nasty look.

Maybe this was the best place for him in this story. The gypsies were responsible for what had happened to the foal. They had messed this book up. The best way to set the story straight might be to stick with them and try to figure out exactly why they had done such an awful thing. Besides, he really was hungry.

He followed the girl up along the bank toward the voices. Lanterns hung from the trees around a small clearing. In the centre of this clearing, a dozen men and women were seated around a campfire, eating and chatting. A similar number of small children gambolled around or, in the case of the smallest, lay on blankets dozing by the fire. One of the men played a strange, slow song on a violin, and every now and then a voice piped up with an accompanying song. Norman didn't recognize the language or the tune, but it seemed like the only possible tune that could be played in this clearing in this part of the book. It had such a sad, kind feeling to it that it made him wonder how such people were capable of something as barbarous as butchering a horse. Maybe it was out of character for them, too. Maybe their story was also messed up.

Only a few faces looked over at him as Norman took his seat at a break in the circle around the fire. Either these gypsies weren't very good captors or they knew that they could recapture him easily if he bothered to escape. Their eyes focused on each other, not on him, continuing conversations uninterrupted by Norman's arrival, telling jokes, singing and scolding children between bites of their evening meal. The main portion of that meal was being roasted over the fire—two or three small animals skewered on sticks and suspended over the flames. The girl removed one of the sticks, examined it and offered it to Norman. Norman wasn't used to seeing his supper as animals. When he ate meat it usually came in a box from the freezer, prepared and shaped beyond recognition. He couldn't help wrinkling his nose as the girl waved the charred animal on a stick in front of him.

"No, thanks, I'm a vegetarian."

"Huh?" she asked.

"I'm a vegetarian. I don't eat meat." He'd just decided that.

"It's good. Feliz caught it just today, a nice fat *ulven*."

Norman shook his head. He had no idea what an *ulven* was, but whatever it was, he was sure he wasn't going to eat it. The girl seemed to think that he just didn't want to eat strange meat. She tried to explain what the meat was, miming some sort of forest creature, making claws with her hands and gnashing her teeth.

"No, thanks," said Norman, more sure than ever. "My best friend is a stoat."

The girl blinked her bright black eyes and stared silently at him for a moment. Norman was pleased that he'd said something to surprise her. It made him feel less vulnerable. She stuck the empty end of the stick in the ground and got up. Norman eyed the charred animal waving on a stick uneasily until she returned with a plate of bread and roasted vegetables.

"Here you go, veggie boy."

Norman was too hungry to think about whether this was meant as an insult. He dug into the food without a further word. The few words that passed between them while they ate were hers. The gypsies around the fire were all relatives of some sort. Big Feliz and Varnat were her cousins. Aunts tended the fire. Uncles played the accordion and violin.

"That's my father there." With her charred stick, Leni pointed to the largest of the men laughing in the firelight. Norman recognized him as the gypsy who had pointed the shotgun at him—or at the wolf, as it turned out. "He's our chief. He makes the final decisions and settles all the disputes. Of all the men, he knows the river best." This last thing seemed to be his greatest claim to fame above all the others.

Norman filled himself with roasted vegetables and soaked in the warmth of the fire. He was beginning to feel almost safe. At least the wolves of Undergrowth couldn't get at him here—could they?

"Which one is your mother?" Norman asked.

Leni didn't answer immediately. When she did her voice was lower and constricted.

"My mother died a long time ago."

Norman looked over at the girl. She did not return his glance. Her eyes were fixed on the flames.

"She died when I was born. I never knew her," she continued in a flat voice.

Lost for something to say into the silence that followed, Norman thought of Amelie. "My friend lost his mother too," he said, thinking of young Malcolm back in Undergrowth.

"You mean *her* mother," Leni corrected. Norman looked at her blankly for a moment before he realized that she meant Amelie. He hadn't thought of that. Strange, that both girls in this book had lost their mothers, just like Malcolm. He still wasn't sure if Leni and the gypsies belonged in this book. Maybe the loss of their mothers was the line that got crossed. Maybe in some great universal library Leni's book sat cover to cover with *Fortune's Foal* and *The Brothers of Lochwarren* on the shelf of books about children with no mothers.

"She looked after the horse that was murdered." Norman had said it without thinking, really just musing aloud, trying to puzzle out the connections in this book and why such a horrible thing had happened. "She was looking after Serendipity. She knew he was special."

"She didn't know how special," Leni muttered darkly, perhaps to herself. She leapt up and drove her roasting stick firmly back into the ground.

"Are you finished eating?" she asked, her voice strained. Was she angry or upset? Norman indicated his almost empty plate.

"It'll be my father dealing with you," she announced summarily. Before Norman could reply, she had skulked off to the other side of the fire.

Norman watched her silhouette explain it all to her father and the other men, waving her arms as she talked. What an idiot, he thought. I shouldn't have told her anything. She's spilling it all to her father now, the little spy. He mopped up the vegetable juice from his plate with the last of the bread and strained to watch Leni and her father. Even if they had been speaking English, Norman couldn't have deciphered a word. They were too far away. He would have to wait to be dealt with.

It was much later when the men came to his side of the fire. He'd heard enough gypsy songs by then to imagine that he understood the words. There'd been more than enough time to think about escaping and to decide that it was no use. The big man, Leni's father, approached him slowly. He hardly seemed to go around the fire. It looked more like he just stepped over it. The upward motion he made with his chin clearly meant that Norman should get up. Norman did so without questioning. In the same way, he followed the big man into the forest. He rubbed the lump on his head nervously as he tripped along the path. Once or twice he looked behind him, regretting that he hadn't attempted an escape earlier. The outlines of Feliz and Varnat behind him in the shadows of the path assured him that he'd missed his opportunity. They were watching him closely now. His only hope, he realized, was Leni. Could something he had said have moved her? Maybe she had persuaded the gypsies not to murder him. If he was lucky, maybe they'd just leave him tied up in the forest.

The forest path closed in on them as they drew deeper into the woods. It reminded him unnervingly of the pine forests of Undergrowth and of his flight from the wolves. Was it too much to hope that the stoats would appear in the trees now, springing an ambush on the gypsies? How many arrows from Malcolm's bow would it take to bring Leni's father down? He had to stop himself thinking like this. This was a different forest, a different book.

The path widened suddenly to a small clearing. Strange how bright it seemed now that the full moon's light shone down into the circular space carved out of the forest. It was like a little stage, or the spot under a desk lamp. Norman actually gasped as he drew up to the clearing and saw what was standing there in the middle, tethered to a tree and not happy about it, feet pawing the ground, shaking his head furiously as if trying to shake off a swarm of bees rather than just his halter.

"Serendipity." Norman spoke the foal's name in a relieved whisper.

The foal raised its head and snorted. A cloud of steam rose from his warm nostrils into the cool night air. Norman had a strong urge to touch the horse, to stroke its mane or rub its lively little ears, but as he took a step forward he saw the look in the horse's eyes, a look of wildness. They glared and twitched in a furious panic. The book hadn't said anything about this rage in the horse's eyes or the twitching anger in his limbs. Serendipity had been a calm, playful foal. The gypsies had done this to him. There was no blood, no obvious wound, but they had done something.

"We are no horse murderers." It was the first time Leni's father had spoken, but his voice was as brusque as Norman had imagined.

No, not horse murderers, just horse thieves, Norman thought to himself.

"The blood you saw was wolf's blood. We tracked it to the barn and arrived in time—" He stopped before continuing. "Just in time."

"Why?" Norman asked. "Why did you take the foal?"

Leni's father continued answering questions Norman hadn't asked rather than the one he had.

"The farmers talk bravely, but they are cowards. Their imaginations run away with them. They imagine horrible fates for themselves if they were ever to really find us. They don't know the forests nearly as well as their grandfathers did, nor the river. They think of it as a single path, not the tangle that it is. Roads have made them stupid. They even call us 'gypsies' now."

Norman took a good look at the man's leathery face, his curly black hair, his bushy eyebrows. What did gypsies look like, anyway? "You aren't gypsies?" he asked, confused.

"No more than their football teams are Seminoles."

Norman didn't get this answer. "What do you mean?"

Again Leni's father had his own questions. "Why did you lead the hunters here?" he asked. "What do the wolves want from you?"

Norman shrugged and blinked. What do you tell a character in one book about events in another? It wasn't as if he understood what was going on between the books either.

Leni's father looked disgusted by his intransigence. "Tell me what you know about the foal."

This could be an opportunity as well as an interrogation, couldn't it? They were showing him the foal, and they hadn't killed him yet. Why not take these as positive signs? If he told them everything he knew, maybe they'd trust him.

"The foal's mother—her dam, I mean—used to belong to the Saint-Saens," he said.

"The Frenchman and his daughter?" the gypsy asked.

"Yes. The dam was called Fortune. She was Amelie's mother's horse."

"Amelie is the girl?"

Norman nodded. "Fortune was sent away after Amelie's mother died. Amelie hasn't seen her since. Now she has her own foal, but . . ." Norman was surprised to hear himself choking up. So much death in this book, and so different from the death in his Undergrowth books—not the death of warriors in battle, but the death of mothers. Norman's unfinished sentence hung in the air.

An angry snort from the foal finally broke the silence. As he pawed the ground furiously now, there was torment in his eyes, perhaps anger, but even Norman could see a deep weariness too.

"You know the foal is special?" Leni's father asked. He did not look at Norman. He looked directly into the horse's eyes. The horse seemed unable to avert its eyes. It batted its giant eyelids but did not look away.

Norman nodded, but the gypsy was still not looking at him. He had moved so close to the horse that they were breathing each other's air. The man put one hand behind the horse's ear, and gently stroked. Serendipity's ragged breathing began to slow, and his restless feet merely twitched rather than stamped.

Leni's father pulled the horse's head to his own, placing his cheek alongside Serendipity's face. Norman saw the gypsy's mouth move but could hear no words. Whatever he was saying wasn't just a few words. It was as though he was telling the horse a story, a wonderful secret that kept him rapt and still. Norman just watched as the gypsy settled the little colt's nerves this way. When Leni's father finally pulled away, the foal no longer struggled with his halter. He lowered himself slowly to the ground and laid his heavy head down on the grass, as if all along all he had wanted to do was sleep.

Norman suddenly recalled what Dora said about Serendipity. She'd called him a "therapy horse." That wasn't the right word. The back of the book said something about equine-assisted therapy, how horses could help troubled people. But how was this horse supposed to help disturbed humans? It looked just the opposite to Norman—Serendipity was the one who needed therapy.

"This horse is special. He can help people," Norman said, breaking the silence created by the horse's slumber.

Leni's father turned quickly to face Norman. "You can see this?" There was a note of curiosity in his voice for the first time.

"I can't *see* it," Norman replied.

"Well then how can you know?" the gypsy asked suspiciously.

"I just know," Norman said hesitantly. "I read it in a book, that he can help heal people."

"A prophecy?"

"Sort of," Norman murmured.

"We have our stories about this, about horses with this gift. You can see how deeply he feels . . ." Leni's father's voice drifted off as he gazed at the fitfully sleeping foal.

Norman was emboldened enough to ask his own questions. "What is wrong with Serendipity?"

The gypsy's head snapped back to Norman, his eyebrows raised fiercely as if questioning Norman's right to ask this question, but now that Norman had begun asking, he could not stop. "Why does he look like that? Why is he so . . . so freaked out? And what did you say to him to make him go to sleep like that?"

Leni's father turned and answered sharply. "The wolves did that to him. A horse is a noble creature, a valiant creature. It comes into this world without fear and should grow up that way, but the wolves have undone that. You and those wolves have reminded him of his blood memories—of the wilderness, of the hunt, of being prey."

Norman was too stunned to answer. He knew the gypsy was right. Serendipity had been a calm foal. The wolves in his stall had unleashed some wildness. He understood how it was possible—how facing one of these creatures opened up a gusher of panic inside you, made you want to run until you couldn't feel your legs. He understood too well.

"Where are you taking him?" Norman asked quietly, even meekly now. There was no answer to this question, but he tried another. "What do you want with me?"

The gypsy turned stern and confident again.

"You do not belong here. The lore keepers thought you might have led the wolves to the foal. They worried that they did your bidding, but even I can see now that you are incapable of such things. Those beasts would not follow you."

Norman had half a mind to tell him a little bit about underestimation. Maybe he'd think differently if he knew that Norman was the veteran of three battles in Undergrowth. But then again, maybe not.

"You have to return the foal to Amelie," Norman said. "Amelie knows the foal is special. She can protect him." Norman had decided that the gypsies weren't completely evil. They really did seem to want to protect the foal. Another inspiration struck him.

"You said that your people have stories, right, about special horses, horses that can help people, right?"

Leni's father nodded but appeared not to listen. He was staring at Serendipity, who was shifting and twitching in his sleep.

"They can help people who are hurt, not just physically, but inside?" Norman continued.

"So the stories say."

"The girl, Amelie, needs that sort of help. She needs Serendipity."

The gypsy turned to him suddenly. "The French girl at the farm?" he asked. He didn't need to wait for an answer. "She doesn't need any help."

"Yes, she does." Norman couldn't hear how his voice was rising in urgency. "Didn't you see how she looked on the riverbank? She needs this horse. It's the only connection she has to her mother."

Leni's father stood up and walked to the other side of the foal, his face turned away from Norman. He stroked his goatee fretfully. "It's the horse that needs help now. It needs protection. It needs its own healing."

"Maybe Serendipity and Amelie can help each other," Norman ventured, then added more boldly, "Serendipity's mother used to belong to Amelie's mother. I guess that sort of makes them family. That's why they need each other."

Leni's father turned to him sharply. "Don't tell me what this horse needs," he shot back. "It certainly doesn't need those things you brought at its throat. Those weren't normal beasts. I know that. They may not be your creatures, but you know more about them than you are saying."

This silenced Norman completely. He and Leni's father just stood there staring at the fretful horse in the dark. They were silent so long, Norman wondered if he was supposed to go back to the fire.

"So this girl Amelie is your friend?" the gypsy asked suddenly.

Norman answered warily, "Not really."

"But she would vouch for you, if we asked her."

"She doesn't really know me," Norman admitted reluctantly.

The gypsy knitted his bushy eyebrows together in a suspicion-filled frown. "Then how do you know so much about her and her horse? Perhaps you are a spy after all, in league with those beasts."

Norman heard his voice break as he answered, "I'm *not* a spy." He wanted to glare back defiantly, but the exhaustion and frustration had him close to tears.

"Then how do you know all this?" the gypsy pressed angrily.

Norman fought the tremor in his voice. What could he say? How could he explain? The truth would probably do, he figured. It was no less strange than anything else in this book.

"I came from—"

"Don't tell us where you are from," the gypsy commanded sharply. "That's not what I asked. We don't want to know. It is not something that we should know. Coming here is *your* transgression. Don't make us any part of it."

So much for the truth.

"We know the French girl doesn't know you," the man continued. "We saw her face on the riverbank. There was no recognition in her face. There was suspicion. How do you know about her?"

"I read it in a book. Maybe it was a prophecy after all."

"So where is this book now?" Leni's father asked skeptically.

"I lost it," Norman said sheepishly.

"Naturally," the gypsy replied, full of sarcasm. He stared at the horse for a long minute, watching him stomp and fret, before turning back to Norman. "Tell us about the mother."

"She was killed in a riding accident when Amelie was small. Her father hasn't let Amelie near horses since, but she needs Serendipity now, and he needs her. Together they are going to do something special."

"Your book of prophecies tells you this too, does it?" He was mocking Norman now.

Norman didn't answer, and the gypsy for once didn't press. He stared past Norman at the restless horse, seemingly deep in thought. Then, without warning, he was all action again, a decision seemingly made.

"Feliz, Varnat," the gypsy called, sternly. "Bring the horse. It is time to go."

The two men stepped out of the forest where they had been waiting, silent and unseen. Feliz took the foal's tether and tugged him to his feet. Varnat did the same with Norman's shirt. Norman chastised himself as they walked back down the path. Why had he said so much? Why had he been so trusting? As they picked their way through the woods back to the moored barges at the dock, Norman cursed himself silently. He would keep his mouth shut from now on. But it was probably too late. He'd probably told him more than he needed to know.

The Gypsies' Talent

As the little flotilla of barges sailed deeper and deeper into the forest, the river split again and again into smaller branches. The channels became increasingly narrow through the day. More often now Feliz, Varnat and the other men had to jump out to manipulate the boats into some side channel. The channel mouths were well hidden by stands of reeds and low-hanging willows. If you didn't know they were there, you would never have found them.

A mist hung over the river like a ceiling. The sun was just a yellow blur above it. Norman felt as if the whole world was closing in. They moved slowly along the winding water paths, and time seemed to slow down with them. Norman sat on the deck and sulked, feeling sorry for himself. Every hour that passed took them farther away from the farm and made it less likely that Amelie and her friends would find him and the gypsies. They did not even suspect that Serendipity was still alive and that they could save him. These thoughts seemed to make the gloomy mist descend lower and the hisses and barks of the creatures skulking in the weeds and on the muddy banks seem more ominous.

The eerie animal calls didn't seem to bother Leni. She sang cheerfully to herself all day and, whether she knew it or not, responded to the occasional animal call with an imitative reply. They had left Norman on the same boat with Leni. Though released from the hold and allowed the freedom of the deck, he was no less a prisoner. His prison was just a few metres wider and longer. The marshland was forbidding enough to dispel any thought of escape. He would have no chance of finding his way out of this maze of backwaters, riverlets and soggy islets. Who knew what was skulking about onshore or lurking patiently beneath the surface of the iron grey water?

Boredom, more than anything else, broke his silence. You could stare at ripples in the water and wonder what the gypsies were up to for only so long before you started to drive yourself crazy. Yesterday it had been simple. They had killed the pony and they had to be found. Now it was more complicated. They hadn't killed the foal, but they had stolen it. Did that still make them the enemy? Were they really trying to protect the horse, or was that just a ruse?

Everything he had thought from the start was wrong. The attack in the stable had been his own fault. He had somehow unleashed the wolves from Undergrowth. He had let them into Amelie's world and made this horrible mess, and since his arrival he'd only made things worse. He was doing nothing to help in the pages of Dora's book. It made him wonder if he knew what was best after all. He wanted to make it right and do everything he could to get Amelie her horse back, but when he thought of the look of manic terror in the horse's eyes and his own role in it, he wondered if he should just stay out of it.

To distract himself from these circular thoughts, Norman rose and shuffled carefully to the other side of the boat, where Leni sat cross-legged, concentrating on something in her lap. She tried not to let him see at first, pulling her arms close to her body to hide something. Norman could tell it was a notebook of some sort. Maybe it was her journal. Maybe that's why she was so embarrassed.

"C'mon, let me see," he persisted. "What am I going to do? Who am I going to tell?"

Reluctantly Leni lowered her arms, holding the spiral notebook open flat on her lap. Norman was surprised to see she actually blushed, but more surprised to see that what she had been doing in her book was not writing a journal or drawing pictures of flowers or some other girly pastime. Across the page were dozens of arithmetic problems.

"They're probably all wrong," she muttered, making an excuse before he even said anything. "Feliz doesn't have any time to teach me."

"No," Norman assured her quietly, "they look pretty good."

He scanned the rows of jagged numbers she had written. "The addition and subtraction are all right. It's just the multiplication and division that need work."

It seemed to Norman that no one had actually ever taught Leni arithmetic, and that she was trying to figure it out herself. She seemed to know that multiplication made things bigger and division made them smaller, but not to know exactly how. It reminded him of Dora: she always wanted to figure things out for herself and hated when Norman gave her the answer. To be honest, he was never very much concerned with teaching Dora anything, just proving that he was smarter. With Leni, he softened his voice and pointed to the first multiplication problem she had set herself: five times five.

"You'll probably get it right away if you think of it in real terms, like if five people each have five apples, then how ma—"

"Twenty-five," Leni answered quickly, before Norman could finish the question. "I get it now," she insisted, shushing him as she raced back through her multiplications and set down the correct answers. It was the same with the division. As soon as Norman taught her the rule, she got it immediately and applied it to her questions.

"Okay, now you make some for me," she demanded, impatiently handing Norman the notebook and pencil.

She wasn't all that different from Dora, Norman realized. She seemed to look up to him, even if she hated to show it, and Norman was feeling too guilty to dismiss her offhand as he might normally do his sister. He spent the rest of the day making tests for Leni. She dangled her feet over the side of the boat and chattered while he wrote math questions.

"Will the French girl miss her horse?" she asked.

"I guess so." As if he too was preoccupied with the math, Norman's reply was bored and brusque, the way he would answer Dora. It was just the right tone to keep Leni talking.

"Can't she get another one?"

Norman paid more attention now. If he could convince Leni that the horse should be returned, maybe she would convince her father. "Probably not," he said, pretending it no longer mattered. "This horse was special. It . . ." He tried to sound disinterested, but really he was thinking of the right way to express it. "He connects her to her mother somehow."

Norman handed over the sheet of math questions. "Here," he said, "try these."

He became bored with the arithmetic long before she did, so he taught her some geometry, and gave her some tests on determining the circumference and area of various shapes. She loved that too and kept asking for harder and harder ones.

"You must be pretty good at school," he told her finally. "You're better than a lot of the kids in my class."

Leni's face brightened at the compliment, then clouded. "There are no schools on the river," she muttered, then added more bitterly, "I have to go make dinner now." She paused, handing the notebook to Norman before heading down below to the galley. "Make some really hard ones this time."

While Leni made dinner, Norman filled a page with word problems—trains going in different directions, how to measure water in buckets, the hardest things he could remember from math challenges and tests. When he had finished setting the test, he could still hear Leni banging pots in the galley. It hardly seemed right that a kid Dora's age should be making dinner by herself, but all the adults were busy with the boats. The flotilla seemed smaller than yesterday, and the gypsies who remained were in constant motion, poling the boats forward when they could, jumping off and pulling with ropes when they had to. No words were ever exchanged. Everyone seemed to know what was needed and went about it in a furious silence. Wherever they were going, they wanted to get there quickly and quietly.

Norman thought he might as well as lend Leni a hand. He felt guilty sitting there on the deck while everyone else laboured. Besides, he was developing an appetite for gypsy vegetarian soup. Leni had decided he was harmless and let him use a sharp kitchen knife to chop up carrots while she added them to a boiling pot on the gas hob. It reminded him again of the almost total lack of adult supervision. He hadn't seen Leni's father since the previous night's conversation. Feliz and Varnat seemed to be the only men in the whole flotilla.

"Where is everybody else?" Norman asked. "There were more people last night at the feast."

"They've gone to hunt the other wolf," Leni answered in a low voice.

"Oh," Norman said. He had reminded her why she didn't like him. He thought of the look of terror in Amelie's eyes and her bright red blood on the white cotton of her sleeve. "I should be with them," he said, sounding braver than he felt.

"No, you shouldn't," the little girl said firmly.

That was the end of that conversation.

For the rest of the day they followed some invisible gypsy path through the twists and bends of the river. At one point Norman felt sure that they had hit a dead end. The channels had become so shallow that everyone had to get out in order to float the boats over them. This was the only time that Norman ever saw Serendipity. To lighten the load on the boat, Feliz and Varnat led the foal off the deck onto the shore. The horse looked healthy and unharmed but was still skittish. Even untethered on an island hillock, he pranced nervously, as if afraid to touch the ground. His eyes rolled wildly and his head bucked every time his wide nostrils caught some scent on the breeze. Could he smell the wolves? Norman wondered. Just the thought of it made him imagine that he could smell them himself.

Leni followed her cousins onto the island. Norman watched her bring the horse an armful of wild apples. Serendipity at first refused to look at her, but the little girl seemed to be whispering something as she approached. The horse backed away, more slowly with every step. Finally he turned his head and looked into Leni's eyes. They held each other's gaze for a moment as Leni continued to speak. Then the horse bowed his big head and ate from her hands, calm again for a while. She too seemed to have that gift of her father's for calming the horse. As long as Leni stood with him and whispered, he seemed fine, his legs still, his nostrils not flared, his eyes quiet, but it would not last. You could tell that he was on the edge of panic, ready to burst at any moment. Though Serendipity seemed to trust his new owners, there was something new in him. Leni's father was right. The wolves had uncovered a deep wildness in him.

As he stood on the bank with one eye on the foal grazing nearby, the other on the boats, Norman realized the trick that the gypsies were playing. There was another channel parallel to the one they now travelled. The waterway beyond was much wider than any they had seen for days. Climbing the little rise of muddy land that separated the two channels, he saw a full, wide river, like the one they had left—exactly like the one they had left, in fact. They were on a narrow island in the middle of the river.

Gradually, Norman recognized the hills, and the church spire poking up behind them. They weren't far from the Saint-Saens farm—he had seen that same white church spire from the barn. The gypsies had doubled back and were going in the opposite direction. If the farmers were still looking for the horse murderers, they would be looking the wrong way.

It dawned on Norman suddenly that he could make a run for it. He could find the farm from here. He could swim the distance from the island to the shore easily. He cast his head around furtively to see if the gypsies were still occupied with the foal. The sharp black eyes of Varnat stared back at him from lower down the embankment. They knew. Long before Norman had realized, his captors had known this was his best chance to escape.

Norman leaned against a tree trunk and looked out toward the river beyond. A path followed the riverbank on the other side of the little island. In the dried mud, Norman could see dozens of hoof prints. These could be the searchers' horses. This trail might even lead right the farm. But if so, it was no use to him. He couldn't outswim or outrun Varnat. Norman slid his hands into the back pockets of his jeans and looked out at the river, trying to look casual but taking careful note of the direction of the spire. It might be important later. A landmark would help.

Norman had been out of sight too long. His keepers would suspect something. He scrambled back up the bank to the crest between the two channels.

Varnat met him there.

"What were you doing down there?" he asked, accusingly.

Norman scrunched up his face and looked at him as if offended. "Going to the bathroom. Do you mind?"

Varnat didn't answer. As Norman brushed past, the gypsy stayed on the edge of the ridge looking down at the river.

Norman's Test

Soon after leaving the island, Leni's family's barge split off from the rest of the flotilla, taking a small, slow-moving branch of the river while the rest of the boats continued in the main channel. Only Varnat, Leni and her father remained on the boat with Norman. Norman watched disconsolately as the other barges disappeared. That would be the last he'd see of the foal, he thought. He had missed his opportunity. Back there on the island he had been so close to the Saint-Saens farm—he should have just made a run for it.

No one seemed to take much notice of Norman's mood. He sat at the bow of the boat, ignored by Varnat and by Leni's father, who busied themselves with navigating the narrow stream. Only Leni paid him any attention, and it was not welcome. She nagged him for more "homework," as she called the math problems he created for her. He did so reluctantly and slowly, so that she had lots of time to prattle on about her twisted dream of what it would be like to live in a real house and go to school. Amelie had no idea how lucky she was, she said. Leni told him that she had been watching Amelie for weeks. Leni was sure "the French girl," as Leni called her, had seen her too, and was convinced that the two would be friends. Norman had finally had enough when Leni's idle prattle became totally ridiculous.

"Do you think that she'd let me stay with them?" she asked idly. "I could help look after the horses and go to school with the French girl."

Norman actually snorted. How could she be so silly? "Are you crazy? You stole her horse. Of course she won't let you stay with her." While she stared back in disbelief, he tried to think of something even more spiteful. "When they arrest your father for horse theft, you'll probably have to live in a juvenile delinquent's institution and go to school there."

The gypsy girl's eyes widened only momentarily before hardening. She didn't say a word, just rose and turned away, disappearing down into the galley. Norman was a little shocked at his own cruelty, or that his cruelty could be so effective. It wasn't like he meant it. Dora would have known he didn't mean it. She would have just done something else equally as annoying back. Leni's leaving like that without retaliating almost made him regret having said it.

He was still angry with her for taking it so badly when the clouds rolled in, obscuring the descending sun. Norman hoped it wouldn't rain. He didn't like the thought of having to take refuge below with Leni. The clouds accelerated the setting of the sun. It was almost completely dark when the boat came to rest beside a dock. In the gloom of the evening, Norman could just make out the source of an odd sloshing and creaking sound: a rickety wooden water wheel, just upstream from the dock, where the stream was blocked by a ramshackle dam. Beyond it the stream was clogged with rocks and broken logs. So they had reached the end of the road. Norman watched the gypsies tie up the barge, but did not offer to help. They knew how to ask. But when they all began to wander off down a path into the woods behind the dock, he was quick to jump from the boat and follow them.

The path ended at a small wooden shack. Surrounded by ferns and tucked underneath the boughs of ancient trees, it would have been impossible to pick out of the forest had its two windows not been lit from inside by the warm yellow glow of a fire or oil lamps.

As they approached, a small figure emerged and stopped silhouetted in the doorway.

"Aida," Leni cried, rushing up to the old woman who emerged in the dim light. The girl wrapped her skinny arms around the woman's apron.

"Wild one," the old woman said affectionately. "Come in. Let's see what strange thing you've brought me this time." The old crone held the door for Leni to enter. Her father and Varnat followed her, kissing the old woman affectionately and respectfully on each cheek before ducking inside.

Norman drew near but hesitated before stepping past the old woman.

"Tut, tut, tut," she muttered, shaking her grey-haired head. "You are a strange one. Strange—strange indeed. You had better come in."

Norman ducked past and smiled feebly. Inside, the three gypsies were already seated by the fire. They stopped chatting as he entered and turned to stare, watching not him, but the old woman's reaction to him. The way that Aida bustled around him, looking him up and down, you'd think she was buying him at a garage sale. Norman wanted to just yell "What?" but there was something about this house, this silence, that he didn't dare to break.

"Well, well, well. I'm not sure what to do with you," Aida clucked. She looked genuinely bemused, like she was seeing something that she'd only ever heard of in books. "Likely there's only one thing for it." She turned and began rummaging through a small wooden chest in the corner of her little hut. It was an unimpressive little chest—battered, painted and repainted in the same gaudy purples, greens and oranges as the gypsy barges. Even its brass latches were painted over with a few thick coats. The old lady stuck her tongue out, curled it up toward her nose and rolled her eyes ridiculously as she reached deeper into the chest. She even, at one point, stomped a boot in frustration on the planked floor. Had it been anyone else, Norman would have suggested that she remove some things from the chest, but he wasn't about to speak up and call attention to himself.

"Aha, there it is," Aida announced triumphantly. Her blue-veined hand emerged clutching a small book. It was bound in red cloth and appeared to have no title on either the spine or the front cover. "I got it. This," she declared, pausing to peer down her nose at Norman with a half-open eye, "was given to me by the *second* strangest creature I've ever met. Now, then, what would work?" she asked herself as she thumbed the pages. She squinted and moved the book back and forth to bring it into focus, reading at a few spots, tutting impatiently to herself, then continuing further. Finally she seemed to find the passage that she was looking for. "Yes, this should do the trick. Come on, then," she said, waving everyone over to the kitchen table.

Norman stepped forward to take his test. Varnat, Leni and her father huddled around the table to watch. If it was just a book, Norman thought, he was fine. If it was some sort of riddle or a puzzle, he could handle it. But the old woman did not hand the book to him. Instead she turned and held it open in front of Varnat. She kept her back to Norman and held her body in such as way as to shield the book from him. She obviously did not want him to see, and he thought it best not to try.

"Can you read what's written here?" she asked Varnat. The big gypsy blinked and looked confused. He bit his lip, squinted and concentrated, then looked up blankly as if requesting help from the others.

"Do as the lore keeper says," Leni's father urged him.

Varnat stared some more and shook his head. He avoided the old lady's inscrutable eyes and tried to hand it back.

Aida wouldn't take it from his hands. "How about you, wild one, can you read it?" she asked Leni.

Leni snatched the red book from her dumbfounded cousin, glanced at it, then brought it closer to her face. "There nothing in it, just blank paper," she said with surprise and handed it to Aida disdainfully.

The old woman turned finally to Norman, holding the book open on the table so everyone could see it.

"How about you, boy?" she said slyly. "Can you read it?"

Norman glanced quickly at the open page then looked up again suddenly into the eyes of the old woman, a frown across his forehead. The page wasn't blank at all. It was covered with small uneven type. The woman's eyes gave him no answer. "Well, can you read it?"

Norman moved closer, put his hand on the page and read silently to himself.

Amelie stood silently by the beech tree. Was it possible that the little girl didn't see her? Or was it that she saw her and didn't care anymore—that her curiosity had finally overcome her fear? Amelie took a step from out behind the beech tree. The gypsy girl must surely see her now, yet still she didn't run. Their eyes met momentarily, but the younger girl averted them shyly and glanced behind her, perhaps pondering another quick escape.

"What's your name?" Amelie asked as gently as she could.

The gypsy girl looked up again but didn't answer immediately. She peered down at her dusty shoes and whispered in the quietest of voices.

"I can talk to your horse."

Amelie grasped a branch and lowered herself a few steps down the embankment. "You can what?" she asked gently.

The younger girl raised her head and called out more boldly, "I can talk to your horse. I can teach you, too."

Amelie wanted to reply that it was not her horse, that it would never, despite her desperate wish for it, be her horse. "My name is Amelie," she said instead. "What's your name?"

"My name is Leni. I can talk to your horse. I saw what happened with the snake, how he got spooked. I can teach you—"

There was such a look of desperate earnestness in this strange little girl's eyes. Amelie had tried for months to speak with Leni, and now she had finally stayed instead of turning to flee. But how did Leni know about the snake, about Serendipity getting spooked? And what did she mean by "talking" to a horse?

Amelie smiled broadly at the young girl, flashing her bright white teeth, and brushed her long bangs out of her squinting eyes. She did not ask Leni how she knew about the snake. She did not ask her where she came from.

"Would you like to come and see him? His name is Serendipity," she said, as if this was the most natural thing to do. Still holding the branch with one hand, she offered the other to Leni. The gypsy girl waited for just one more moment, then all her reserve burst like water from a balloon, and with a wide, eager grin on her face, she scrambled nimbly up the riverbank.

The old woman interrupted his reading. "Well, can you read it?" she snapped. Norman peered into her face. Could she give him a clue? Her face told him nothing, nor did Leni's. Had Leni really not seen her name there on the page? Was he really the only one who could see the writing in this book? It was *Fortune's Foal,* the real *Fortune's Foal,* the version Dora had read and knew by heart. So Leni and Amelie were supposed to meet on the riverbank. They were supposed to be friends. Leni was supposed to teach her the gypsy trick of horse whispering, and there definitely weren't supposed to be wolves in the barn. Norman was shocked to see just how much he had messed up this book. If Leni *had* been able to read that page, she would surely not have been able to hide her surprise.

"Well . . . ," Aida repeated. Something in her voice was like a warning. Norman stared intently at her for a further clue.

"No," he said slowly, hesitantly. "There's nothing there. It's completely blank."

The old woman raised both eyebrows, her eye twitching momentarily. Was that a wink? Norman was sure that it was. "This will be for you, then," she said. With a surprisingly quick movement of her hand, she tugged at the open page. It came away with sharp ripping sound, like the sound of a bandage being removed.

Handing the page to Norman, she said, "You obviously know how to dispose of this. Mind you chose the right time, and *bon appétit.*"

With that, she snapped the book shut and returned it to the box. Norman stood staring at the page—the page that was supposed to be blank but clearly wasn't. The old crone's words were just sinking in. Had she really just said "*bon appétit*"?

Aida interrupted his ruminations. "All right, then, I've had enough of you. Get out of here." She put the red book away in her bag and shooed them all away with her hands. Varnat and Leni were already at the door. Norman was still staring incredulously. The old woman stared right back and gave him her final piece of advice.

"I don't think you know what you've gotten yourself into, boy." She tutted and shook her head. "There's many a weird in these wide worlds, but yours is perhaps the deepest. *I* wouldn't trust a feather such as you with it, but it's your weird now, so I'll bid you good luck. You'll surely have need of more than your share of it."

Maybe Norman's face reacted to this unintended insult. The thought that he was in over his head had occurred to him more and more. The old lady's face shifted—maybe not softened, but perhaps the many frown wrinkles relaxed just slightly.

"Never mind," she said. "What's written is written, and what's ripped is ripped. Just mind your grammar. And look after those girls."

It was perhaps the kindest thing she could have said. Only afterward, when he played it back in his memory, was he surprised by that last part. She had said "girls." Look after the "girls." She meant Leni and Amelie, of course. She wanted him to do something to help Amelie. But Norman couldn't help thinking of Dora, too.

Convincing Amelie

If he'd reflected on it, he would have realized that it had been too easy. The gypsies had doubled back beyond the Saint-Saens farm. They had stopped so close that he had better bearings than he really had the right to expect. He knew exactly which way to go. There were no twists in the river here, nothing like the descent into the swamps and mazy channels of the first day. Though he had heard his heart pound as the lifted the hatch and had cursed his ungainly feet as they thudded along the dock, there was no noise or light from the boat or from Aida's hut—no evidence at all of any pursuit.

The farm was still a half day's hungry walk away, but his greatest worry had been finding a bridge across the river. One presented itself about an hour before he came alongside the farm. He crossed it sneakily, vaguely afraid that there might be an APB out on him or someone from the sheriff's office, but he saw no one. The first people he saw were the farmhands taking the tractor out of the barn and hitching up a plough. They were already far away in some distant field. Norman could barely hear the sound of the engine rumbling as he sat hidden in a clearing watching the farmhouse.

A mix of emotions churned in Norman's stomach when he first saw Amelie emerge from the house. There was relief—whatever the wolf had done, it wasn't too bad. Amelie was up and about, walking. But there was anger, too, that this had been allowed to happen. Why did she have to come down to the riverbank at that time? Why didn't the gypsy just explain what he was doing when he pointed that gun? Underneath all this, he hardly admitted to himself, was something else. He didn't want to admit who really was to blame.

Norman watched from the river's edge as Amelie made her way from the farmhouse to the barn. Now that she was closer, he could see that her left arm was in a sling. The churning in his stomach took a painful turn. Amelie was tall for her age, and the way she walked, you could mistake her for an adult. In the book she was fourteen, but she looked older to Norman. She walked with her head up, her long brown hair pulled back in a ponytail. If the wolves had left marks on her body, it hadn't made her afraid. She glanced only once toward the brush where Norman was hiding, and if she was checking for wolves, it wasn't with a fearful look, but with a look of defiance.

She was heading to the barn, perhaps to mourn the foal that wasn't even supposed to be hers. When Norman thought of this, he was seized by the compulsion to run right over there and tell her that Serendipity was alive and that everything would be okay. But something stopped him. It wasn't just caution. Though he told himself he had to wait another to see if anyone was following her, that was not his only reason for hesitating. The sling reminded him that everything was *not* okay. Serendipity was safe for now, but spooked, really spooked. Amelie might not have been frightened by the wolves, but the little foal was terrified. You could see it in his eyes and the way he shook his head and pawed the ground. Not even the gypsies could calm him completely. At least one wolf was still out there, too. And Norman had unleashed it all.

He waited another ten minutes before taking a tentative step toward the barn. He still had no idea what he was going to say to her, how he was going to convince her. Why should she listen to a word he said? What would stop her from calling immediately for her father or for the police?

His hand hesitated on the barn door. Should he knock? The barn was so silent, he felt he couldn't disturb it. Instead he slid the door open slightly. It creaked ominously.

"Amelie?" he whispered hoarsely, poking his head experimentally into the barn. After the bright morning sun, the darkness of the barn took some time for his eyes to adjust to. Perhaps he should have waited a few more moments before stepping forward and calling out her name again. Perhaps he would have seen her standing still and tall beside the door with the shovel in her hand.

The shovel came down hard between his shoulders, knocking him to the floor. It didn't knock him out, but Norman saw stars for a moment, and it took his breath away. When he recovered it, the first thing out of his mouth was "ow." It seemed like a stupid thing to say, but he was a little stunned, and he couldn't think of anything else. He rubbed the spot on the back of his head and blinked his eyes up at Amelie, who stood in the barn doorway, one hand on the barn door, the other holding the shovel.

The shovel wavered slightly in her hand. Norman could tell she was gripping it tightly to control her shaking. Her blue eyes peered at him fiercely.

"You're lucky I didn't hit you hard," she told him. Her voice was low and bitter and it too shook a little bit as if she was trying to control it by gripping it tightly.

A wave of anger shot out from the burning spot between Norman's shoulders. She'd hit him hard enough. He fought not to say what he was thinking or feeling. Amelie kept staring, sizing him up and deciding he wasn't much.

"You're not so brave when you don't have your dog with you, are you?" she taunted.

Norman took a moment to understand what she was saying. All of he could think to say in reply was, "It's not my dog."

She seemed to think about this. "The gypsies'?" she asked, not giving any indication that she really believed him.

"It's nobody's dog," Norman stammered, wishing he could get up from his knees and talk to her on almost even terms. "It's not even a dog. It's a wolf."

Amelie took a step forward and huffed in disbelief. "There haven't been wolves around here for fifty years." The way she said it like that, you could tell that she'd been told this recently, had been reassured in exactly these words. She rubbed her wounded arm instinctively at the thought of it.

"Are you okay?" he asked sheepishly. He knew it sounded lame.

Amelie's nose turned up in scorn, as if he wasn't allowed to care about this. "Your dog nearly killed me. I have to have rabies shots now. It's a huge needle. I have to have seven shots."

Norman, who hated needles almost as much as he now hated wolves, could only repeat, lamely, "It's not my dog."

The only good thing so far was that Amelie had not called for help. She had no need to yet. She could trap him here in the barn, and Norman had no desire to take his chances with the shovel again.

"Listen, Amelie, there's something about the horse, about Serendipity—"

She wouldn't let him finish. Her calm snapped, and she stepped forward, shaking the blade of the shovel furiously in his face. "Don't you say anything about my horse. Don't you dare!" she threatened. A strand of her dark hair came loose from its elastic and fell across her eyes and she lifted her hand to sweep it back.

With all his heart Norman wanted to leap up now. It was a moment of advantage. She was off balance, and the shovel leaned loosely in the crook of her elbow. He could just tackle her at the knees. But that was the last thing he needed now—he needed her to listen. Stupid girl, couldn't she see that he wasn't the bad guy?

"He's not dead." He tried to say it as kindly as he could, but it came out angrily between his teeth.

"I'm going to get the police," she said, not listening or not wanting to listen. "They'll want to know why you lied about being my cousin."

Norman ignored her threat and repeated, "Amelie, believe me, he's not dead."

"Stop talking," Amelie cried. "Stop talking about my horse!" Her voice was shrill and broken.

"I swear to God, Amelie, he's not dead. You have to believe me," Norman pleaded. How was it when you told people that they had to believe you, you just sounded like a liar?

"Stop," she shrieked, "talking!" That shout must have been heard up at the house, Norman thought. He did what she said, watching her as she stepped from foot to foot in the doorway. She was trying to make a decision.

"Who are you?" she finally asked. "No lies." She shook the shovel as a warning.

"My name's Norman."

"Why are you here?"

He told her the story he had concocted on the way here. It sounded almost as ridiculous as the truth. He had run away from home a few weeks ago, he told her. He hated his family. The lie made him feel like a traitor. It hurt Norman to say it because he really wanted to be back home right now, but that is what he told her. He hated his mom and his dad, and they hated him, so he had run away to join the gypsies. He had been living in the woods near the farm, because he knew the gypsies came through the waterways near here. It was a crazy story, and it made Norman sound like an idiot.

All Amelie said was, "You don't *join* the gypsies. You join a circus, but you have to be born a gypsy."

Norman smiled weakly.

"Was it them?" she asked finally, her voice dropping in volume and register. "Did they do this to Serendipity?"

Norman shook his head vehemently. "It wasn't the gypsies. They were trying to help." Amelie looked at him as if this was the least unbelievable thing he had said. "They were following the wolves," he continued. "They knew that the wolves didn't belong here. They knew the wolves would probably attack some sheep or cow or something, and they were trying to stop them. Somehow the wolves got into the barn." Norman went on breathlessly. "They got into Serendipity's stall. They would have killed him, but the gypsies stopped them. There were two wolves. The gypsies killed one right there, but the other got away."

"The blood?" Amelie asked, her voice stretched and cracking.

"Wolf blood," said Norman. "Serendipity doesn't even have a scratch on him."

"You've seen him?" she asked. There was so much hope in her voice that Norman only wanted to tell her good things.

"He's . . ." Norman hesitated. "He's fine." He knew that Serendipity was not fine. Serendipity was a world away from fine, but this was too much to explain now.

Amelie didn't notice his pause. She was wanted to believe now. She wanted the foal to be alive. "Where is he? Take me to him."

"The gypsies have him. They're keeping him safe at their camp in the swamp."

"Why? Why would they take him? Is he their hostage? Do they expect an award or something?"

"It's not like that. They just didn't think he was safe here, not with one wolf still around."

Amelie stared at him and appeared to be taking all this in. She bit her lower lip and furrowed her brow as if searching for the answer to a difficult question. Her grip on the shovel was looser now, and Norman felt his head was in much less danger of being smashed in than it had been moments ago.

"Stay here," she said finally. She turned and closed the barn door, taking the shovel with her, leaving Norman in the dark. That had gone just about as well as it could have, he thought. Amelie wasn't an especially good listener and she really didn't need to swipe Norman across the back with a shovel, but at least she was listening now. He might just convince her to come with him and make this all right. As he sat there in the dark, though, he couldn't help but worry about what he had not said, about the change that had overcome the foal, the terror that could be seen deep in his eyes.

Wolf Bait

It would have been so much easier if Amelie had just listened to him. They needed to go back to Aida's little house in the woods. The old lady knew something. She had told him to look after the girls. Aida knew somehow that Leni and Amelie belonged in the same story. She would help Norman put everything back together—that's what she had sent him to do. The longer he thought about it, the more convinced he was of this mission.

Amelie had other ideas, though, and apparently only Amelie's ideas counted. As long as the horse was alive, she was following the horse. She didn't trust anyone to return Serendipity: she was going to take him back herself. There was no use telling Amelie that the gypsies knew the woods and swamps around here better than she ever would, and that they had been hiding from better trackers than her for years. There was no use telling Amelie anything.

They followed the river, deeper and deeper into the woods. It must have been roughly the same path that the gypsies had taken when they kidnapped him, or at least Norman thought it might be. It looked familiar, at least. The waterways wound in the same mazy paths. The trees overhung the banks in the same tangle. The same chirps and croaks and buzzes swirled around them as they trudged along, and Norman listened. Norman listened hard, waiting for a sound of a creature much more fearsome than the croaking and buzzing things. He had not forgotten that at least one wolf was still loose.

As they strode ahead deeper into the swamp, Norman lagged behind, vigilance and resentment combining to slow his steps. Their feet sank into the mud with each step now, and even Amelie was starting to look like she was having second thoughts about the path they had taken. Reaching a higher point above the mud, she put her knapsack down and rested against a tree. When Norman caught up with her, he was so angry he could hardly look at her.

He leaned against another tree some way away from her, letting out an exasperated sigh as he settled down, and drew the page of *Fortune's Foal* from his back pocket to remind himself why he was here. Staring at it, he was suddenly tempted to just eat it now and get out of this stupid book. What did he care if this pushy girl got her horse back? But Aida's admonition to look after the girls echoed in his ears.

"Staring at it won't make words appear," Amelie teased. Somehow she had snuck up behind him to see what he was reading. But it was the same for her as it was for Leni. Neither of them could see what was written on that page. They couldn't read their own story. Only Norman could see it. Only he could see that Leni and Amelie were supposed to meet, that even without the wolves, Serendipity would have been spooked and would have needed this crazy gypsy-talking trick.

He was dying to explain this all to Amelie, to show her that he really did know more than she did. It was killing him to keep it to himself. But had made a deal with the old woman. That's what Aida's test had been about. Somehow the old woman knew he came from outside the book. She had needed to know she could trust him to keep it to himself. In exchange, she had given him a way home. The page was the key, and he had a pretty good idea how to use it. The only thing that troubled him was how Aida knew. She'd received the book from a visitor, someone who was "the second strangest creature" she had ever met. Could it be someone from Undergrowth—the fox abbot, perhaps? Surely he would count as the *strangest* person anyone had ever met. It was a problem beyond solving. He just wanted to find the stupid horse and get out of Amelie's life.

So he kept his mouth shut and smiled blankly at Amelie. She could say what he wanted about his obsession with this blank of piece of paper, and he'd just have to take it. Frankly, this story was all a little unfathomable to him too. He understood that Amelie wanted to get her horse back, but it was, after all, still just a horse. It wasn't like it was her best friend or something. Yet that's the way she talked about it—like the horse was a person, like they had made all these plans together. It almost made Norman think that Amelie was a little crazy. He just kept reminding himself that she was written that way and that the book meant the horse to be more than a just a horse.

"What's so special about this horse?" he asked finally. "Why do you want it so badly? Wouldn't a fully grown horse be better, so you could ride it?"

Amelie's mouth dropped, as if he'd just questioned whether it was right to love your mother or to love pizza.

"He's not just any horse. He's special. I can see it in his eyes. He knows me. We have a . . ." She paused before finishing. "We have a bond."

Norman really, really wanted to understand this, but there was something he wasn't getting. He thought for a moment before asking, "Is it because your mom rode horses?"

Amelie glared at him, glared as if she really hated him at this moment, as if he had no right to know this about her mother. "Why do *you* care?" she returned. "He's not your horse. He's not your friend. Why are you here at all?"

Norman's response died on his tongue. He'd noticed a little quiver in Amelie's voice, and her eyes seemed awfully red.

"I guess it doesn't matter why I'm here," he said. "I'm just trying to help. I'm sorry about the wolf . . . I didn't mean for it to attack you. I didn't know it was there." His voice strained as he desperately tried to make her believe him. "I did come back to help you, though, didn't I? You have to give me credit for that."

"I don't have to give you credit for anything. You haven't done anything to help. If it were up to you, we'd be walking straight back to some gypsy hideout in the woods."

"You don't understand. I don't think the gypsies are bad . . . and they don't like being called 'gypsies,' by the way—they are trying to help."

"Like *you* are trying to help?" she scoffed. "Tell them no, thank you. None of you understand anything."

"Listen," Norman protested, "the old woman's hut is in that direction, upstream." He pointed over his shoulder in the direction from which they had come.

Amelie answered without turning. "I already told you that it's obviously a trap. What don't you get about that?" It was the sort of half answer Norman's father gave him when he really didn't want to think up a complete one. It bugged him when his dad did it. But what was Amelie—two, three years older than him? That was infuriating.

"What I don't *get,*" he hissed through his teeth, "is why it's so obviously a trap. Maybe if you let me help, we could find another solution besides getting lost in this stupid swamp."

This time Amelie did stop. She turned and declared haughtily, "Frankly, I find it a little strange that this intrepid explorer and friend to the gypsies doesn't know his way through this harmless little bit of marshland."

Norman felt the heat rise to his ears. He was sure they must be visibly red now. If Amelie only knew what he *did* know—that she was only a character in a book, and that he knew about her mother and her real horse and what she was supposed to learn from the gypsies. He was dying to tell her and to see that know-it-all look wiped off her face. But deep down he knew that this was wrong, and that no matter how annoying Amelie was, he should never really tell her she was just a made-up person in a book.

Serendipity's Rescue

Norman trailed Amelie, silent and sullen, his eyes hardly lifting higher than his blistered feet. Late in the day now, Amelie was charging on ahead. She hardly spoke to him. The longer they went without finding any sign of Serendipity and the gypsies, the more emotional she became.

Norman had stopped pestering her to turn around and go in the direction he's suggested. He'd long ago given up on the hope of changing her mind and his advice was starting to bother her more than he intended, but if they were competing to see who could annoy each other, Amelie was holding her own. She looked back now and asked condescendingly, "Can you please keep up?"

He could hardly tell her that there was a point to his lagging behind. He was listening, watching, trying to be the protector that Aida had asked him to be.

"Why?" he retorted. "We're going the wrong way anyway."

"If we're going the wrong way," she spat back, "you are welcome to turn around." There was a desperate tone to her replies now as they pushed on through their exhaustion and Amelie became less sure of her decision.

"You'd probably drown, and I'd get blamed for that too," Norman said. Perhaps he was pushing it.

Amelie halted and glared back at him, arms on her hips. Her mouth opened momentarily, but the reply did not come. Perhaps she, like Norman, realized that this was getting them nowhere. She allowed herself one exasperated sigh before turning and continuing. It was different from all the other exasperated sighs he had heard all day, less angry, more tired-sounding.

She took only three or four steps before she stopped again. But this time it was like her legs just gave way on her, as if she had lost the ability to force them forward. She slumped to the ground like a marionette with slackened strings. Norman rushed forward, wondering if she'd passed out.

"Amelie?" he asked tentatively. When she did not answer he tried again. "Are you okay?"

Amelie pulled her knees into her chest and rested her forehead on them. Norman could not see her face. All he could hear was her shallow, quick breathing.

"Are you okay? Is it your arm?" he asked. The thick bandage on her arm was soaked with sweat.

"Just go away, will you," her muffled voice begged from beneath her arms.

"I can't," he replied, shocked by the weakness of her voice. "I have to help you."

"You can't help me. No one can help me." She sounded younger to Norman. She sounded like Dora when she completely lost it.

"I'm trying," he told her earnestly. It was all he could think to say.

She sobbed in reply, "It doesn't matter."

"We can still find him. Come on, let's try to find Aida's cottage." Norman knew she was hiding her face so he wouldn't see her tears.

"It doesn't matter. It doesn't matter what you do or what I do. I lose everything. Everything that I care about is taken away from me. Serendipity's not coming back either."

Norman knew what else she had lost, but knowing was not enough. He had no idea what to do to fix this. He took a deep breath and surveyed their surroundings. Maybe he should take her home now, but they were so lost.

As he gazed at the river, he was gripped by a strange sense of déjà vu. It wasn't enough to say that the surroundings looked familiar. They had looked familiar since they had left the farm, because the landscape was all the same around here. It was all muddy streams, clogged with cattails and purple loosestrife, occasionally opening up to a wider passage of water with overhanging willows. Every now and then, the ground rose up high enough to support a tight clump of upright trees. It was on one of these little hillocks of dry land that they rested. And one of these islands looked very familiar to Norman—a real island, a long, needle-shaped ridge in the middle of a wide passage of river.

"I know where we are," he said, his excitement growing as he spoke. "I know where we are now, Amelie!"

Amelie looked up and swept her hair out of her eyes with a dirty finger, leaving a dark smear of soil on her forehead. She blinked and focused her bleary red eyes. When she spoke, her voice had regained its annoying authority.

"Yes, that's Thin Island." You couldn't tell this girl anything. "Father takes me fishing there."

"So we're near your house," Norman said, relieved. "We're not lost."

"We were never lost," she said firmly, rising shakily to her feet.

Norman wasn't sure he agreed. "This is one of the places that they let Serendipity off to eat." He wasn't sure why he said it, whether it was to try to cheer her up or just to tell her something she didn't know. Amelie didn't reply. She didn't even nod or shake her head. She just winced slightly, ducked her head and took a few tentative steps down the riverbank toward the island. Norman followed silently.

Whether or not Amelie wanted to admit it, they had been lost. It didn't matter that now they knew where they were—it was obviously an accident. They had walked in a huge circle. Norman was familiar with this sensation too. Only this time he didn't need Simon Whiteclaw to point it out for him.

Norman, for once, wasn't going to press his argument. He preferred bossy Amelie to the crumpled, defeated Amelie he had just seen. Ahead, at the river's edge, Amelie had stopped and was listening intently.

"Shhhh," she whispered, suddenly excited. "Can you hear that?" Her eyes grew wide and she stared at Norman for confirmation.

"What?" Norman said nervously. "I can't hear anything." He peered into the brush, thinking of the wolf again.

"Shh," Amelie said breathlessly. "Listen." Her voice was almost cracking.

All Norman could hear was the sound of the water, the bugs and now the wind that was picking up and rustling the trees. He shrugged and glanced over at Amelie. She looked different. Norman couldn't tell whether it was weariness or excitement or despair. She bit her lower lip and fidgeted with her sling.

"Did you hear a horse?" she asked him.

"But I don't hear any—" A high-pitched whinny interrupted him. Now he did hear something.

"It's him," Amelie declared, quickening her pace and rushing toward the water. "It's him right? It has to be him!" Now she needed his reassurance—his opinion suddenly mattered. "Come on," Amelie commanded. "I know where there is a boat."

Tied up and hidden among the trailing branches of a weeping willow was a small red fibreglass canoe that had seen better days. Its sides were bleached pink from the sun, and a brown sludge of muddy water filled its hull. Norman might have preferred to skip ahead to the inevitable and just swim out to the little island, but Amelie as usual was having none of it.

She untied the canoe quickly, grabbed one oar and thrust the other at Norman. He took it warily. He had a premonition, and he was right. If they were a bad team on foot, they were disastrous in a canoe. Amelie tried her best to steer, but Norman always seemed to be paddling on the wrong side. It wasn't that Norman didn't know what he was doing, and it wasn't that he couldn't work with a girl. His mom always sat at the back and steered on camping trips. It was just Amelie.

All this was forgotten when they reached the island. Amelie rushed ahead and let Norman tie up the canoe. He expected her to have the long-lost foal in her arms by the time he caught up with her. Instead, she just stood there in the open at one end of the narrow clearing. Norman slowed as he approached her, unsure of what to do or say. Amelie seemed to sway a little with the grass in the breeze. Both hands covered her mouth, as if, if she let them fall away, she would be incapable of suppressing a howl or screech.

"What happened to him?" she asked hoarsely when Norman finally arrived at her side.

Norman couldn't bring himself to answer her.

"What did they do to him?" she asked more forcefully.

At the other end of the island the little foal snorted and raged. Jumping from side to side, stomping the ground, feinting from left to right with his head, he seemed to be doing battle with some imaginary enemy. Norman could picture the shape of this imaginary foe all too well.

When Amelie finally turned to Norman, the look in her eyes was as wild as that of the foal. "What did they do?" she shrieked. There was a manic sound to her voice, as if she too was about to start flailing out wildly.

"They didn't do anything," Norman answered firmly, but his voice dropped to add, "It was the wolves. The wolves freaked him out. He was trapped in the stall with them." If Amelie had been paying attention, she would have heard the guilt in his voice, but she was already running across the field toward the foal. Serendipity lifted his head in recognition but did not dash across the clearing to meet her. Instead he began to snort and buck even more wildly. He gave up the battle with the imaginary demon and began to canter in a tight circle. Amelie stood right in his path to stop him, but the little foal would not look at her. His giant eyes rolled back into his head, exposing the whites. His nostrils flared and his hooves beat the ground again. The sound of Amelie's voice seemed to help a little, but his breathing was still ragged and loud.

"What have they done, poor thing?" she sobbed, stroking the foal's long neck. Serendipity backed up slightly, but did not pull away when she tried a second time to touch his mane. All Amelie could do was keep repeating the question, "What have they done?" Her voice was more and more despairing as she failed to calm the horse. She wanted to reach both arms and throw them around the horse's neck, but the foal could not tolerate it. Every time she pulled closer and raised the second hand, he balked. The lightest of caresses with the just the tips of Amelie's fingers was about as much as he could take. Amelie stayed there like that for the longest time. She made no other sound. She did not sob, but when Norman dared to look up at her face, her cheeks were wet with tears.

The easiest thing would have been to fetch help from the farm. Norman offered to stay with the foal while Amelie brought help, but she would not hear of it. She was not leaving Serendipity now. Norman had stopped reminding her that it wasn't her horse. On top of everything else, this would have been too much.

"Well, you don't expect to put a horse in a canoe, do you?" She was too upset to rise to his joking challenge.

"You take the canoe." She was still sniffing and blinking to stifle her tears, but her voice had regained its presumptuous tone. "I'll swim across with Serendipity."

Norman shook his head in disbelief. "If the horse can swim across, it doesn't need you with it." She glared at him for a moment and was about to disagree but stopped herself. She didn't actually say "you're right" or even nod, but she saw that it was true.

She coaxed the foal to the side of the island closest to the river shore. Here the water was only a half dozen metres wide, and shallow. Serendipity would be able to touch the bottom most of the way across. Amelie took the canoe back to the riverbank, while Norman stayed with the foal. Once she reached the other side, Amelie clapped her hands together and called to the little horse.

Serendipity may have been afraid of imaginary wolves, but he had no problem with water. With the encouragement of the lightest tap on the haunches from Norman, he bounded into the water like a kid at the beach. On the other side, Amelie continued to clap and coax, her face brightening as the horse pushed powerfully through the water, responding to her calls. It was strange to see him so calm and powerful in the water when he was so skittish and hesitant on land. Stranger still was how much lighter Norman felt, seeing Amelie so happy to have the horse back.

Serendipity emerged from water on the other side, shaking the water from his mane with playful glee. They would be all right, Norman told himself. The horse would get over his scare. Amelie would convince her father to let her keep him. That's what *Fortune's Foal* was all about. It wasn't about battles and swords. It wasn't even much about kidnapping. It was about girls being reunited with their horses. Crazy as it sounded, Norman almost understood it.

That's why what happened next was so terrible. It had no place in this book.

The dark shape on the riverbank behind Amelie shattered Norman's dawning understanding of *Fortune's Foal.* The hunter was even more haggard than the last time. His grey hair was matted and tangled with burrs. One eye was almost closed shut from a cut just above it. He looked lean and angry and desperate, and he was looking directly across the water at Norman. For a moment Norman thought only of himself, glad that he was separated from the wolf by the narrow flow of water. But he regretted his cowardice immediately. Amelie and Serendipity were completely exposed, and now Norman was powerless to help them. All he could do was watch. He opened his mouth to warn Amelie. Even this was hard, because by shouting he was again destroying her happiness. She was wearing a white blouse, just like the other day. It was grubby and torn from their trek through the swamp, but Norman imagined it blossoming red again with blood.

His warning shout never came. The wolf spoke first. He didn't growl or seethe or crouch. He stood tall and upright, confident that his moment of revenge had come. He looked directly across the narrow channel at Norman and barked his promise: "I'll have you next."

Amelie must have heard, but what she heard, or what she thought she heard, Norman would never know. Horse and girl turned and shrieked in horror at the wolf that loomed above them. Serendipity let out a crazed high-pitched whinny. The sound of his terror spoke for the three of them. Norman would always remember a silence that followed the echo of this shriek, but perhaps that was just a way for his memory to try to capture and arrest the moment.

The next sound was of shots, three of them in quick succession. When he looked again, the wolf was lying limp and lifeless on the ridge and the gypsies were emerging from the trees. Varnat and Feliz came first, approaching the beast cautiously to see if they had done the job. They were standing with their boots on the wolf's thin belly when Leni and her father appeared from the trees and motioned for Amelie to join them.

Homecomings

"You used us as bait," Norman said, realizing and articulating this slowly. "You knew the wolf would follow me." He shook his head in disbelief. "You used me as bait."

Varnat shrugged and pulled a blank face, as if he knew nothing about it or didn't see what was wrong with the idea. He and Feliz had quickly dragged the wolf's carcass away. Norman didn't want to look at it. He didn't want it turning its eyes to him and speaking again. He wanted to believe it was dead, and surely the gypsies would make sure of that.

Only Varnat, Feliz and Leni had accompanied them to the farm. Leni held Serendipity by a ragged rope halter. The horse was as frightened and skittish as ever, dancing around from side to side as if what he wanted most in the world was to bolt like lightning across the field away from all of them, but the little gypsy girl had held firm, occasionally whispering something into the horse's twitching ear. Norman couldn't hear a thing she said, but he saw the horse's ear rotate forward to focus on her words. Amelie had watched, fascinated, a hint of jealousy on her face as she watched the younger girl handle her horse.

This animosity had not lasted long. Late in the day now, after supper and explanations at the Saint-Saens farm, Amelie and Leni were chatting casually like old friends. Amelie's initial distrust had evaporated somewhere on that long trip home. Norman wasn't included in this new friendship. Typical girls, he thought to himself. They're almost all right when they're alone, but get them in a group and they're all just as self-involved and cliquey.

Still, it was painful for Norman to watch them now in the paddock. Amelie clearly wanted to coddle and mother the frightened colt like she had when he was born, but Serendipity would allow only the most fleeting of touches. In the first chapters of *Fortune's Foal,* Amelie had been able to look deeply into the horse's eyes and feel as though he understood her. Norman had thought this was sappy at the time. Such a connection now seemed impossible. Serendipity couldn't hold any of their stares; his eyes darted away nervously every time they tried. Even Leni, to whom he seemed to listen so intently when she whispered whatever she whispered into his ears, couldn't get him to make eye contact.

Leni was teaching Amelie a few words in the language of the travellers. The older girl watched intently as Leni enunciated the words. After a few repetitions, Amelie mouthed the shape of the words silently along with Leni, then repeated them quietly out loud. Leni's face brimmed with joy as she spoke, leaning in closer to her older friend, delighted to be on equal footing with the girl she had watched for so long from the riverbank. When Amelie could string together a simple sentence, she tried it out on the horse, moving in closely beside him as she'd seen the Leni do, not trying to look into the colt's eyes, just touching his mane lightly with her fingertips and speaking lowly within earshot. Serendipity's ears swivelled to focus the noise, just as they had for Leni. He was listening.

It was so strange to watch. Norman wondered if the horse really did understand, or whether it just liked the sounds of the gypsy language, liked the way it was spoken. He was the last person to question how intelligent an animal could be or how much one could understand, but in Norman's books the animals spoke English . . . and carried swords, so his experience hardly applied.

While Amelie worked relentlessly at Serendipity's side, Norman eased up to the fence beside Leni.

"What is she saying?" he asked.

Leni never took her eyes of the horse. "She's telling him her name."

"Oh," said Norman. "Is that all?"

"You could do better?" Leni fired back.

"I suppose not," he conceded. He thought for a moment before asking, "Does it matter what you say to him?"

Leni turned and regarded him curiously, wrinkling her forehead. "What do you mean?"

"Is it just the sound of the words, or does he understand? Could you be counting or just saying any word that comes into your head? Does it have to make sense?"

Leni tilted her head to the side, amused by the question. "I suppose he'd listen even if it didn't make sense, but it helps if you do."

Norman nodded, as if everything she said also made perfect sense.

Amelie was getting no further with the horse. Serendipity was listening, but little more than that. Occasionally he still stamped the ground and snorted in frustration or anger. It was beginning to wear her out. Finally she slumped back to the fence, looking defeated and tired. She gave Leni a thin, weary smile, but ignored Norman.

"It's hopeless," she said to Leni. "He's so different than he used to be. What happened to him seems to have chased the real Serendipity away. It's like he's gone into hiding." To Norman it was as if Amelie was describing herself. This distraught, defeated girl was not the Amelie admired by Dora and Leni, the Amelie who had charged off into the bush to look for her horse.

"He's still in there," Leni assured her. "You can see it in his eyes. He hasn't run away. He's still here. He wants to be here. He's listening to you."

"He's listening, but I have nothing to say to him," said Amelie. She wrapped her arms around herself as if warming herself, and cast a mournful glance back at the agitated horse. "When he was first born, I didn't need to say anything. I could just look at him and know what he was thinking. He would look at me and know what I was thinking. It will never be like that again."

"It can," Leni insisted.

Amelie looked up at the sky, so that no one could see her tears. "It's so cruel. It's so horribly unfair," she sniffed. "Dad says that we can keep him. He says that we have to keep him now because he's so traumatized. No one will want him. I can keep him, but I feel like I've lost him anyway. It's the worst feeling. I want to be thankful, but it's all so unfair."

Norman knew somehow that this was the wrong time to console her and that he was the wrong person to be doing it anyway, but he wanted to say something. He still clung to the idea that he could make things right. It was his fault, after all. Something he had done had let the wolves in here, and despite everything, this story was still broken. It wasn't enough to kill the wolves in this book; something else needed to happen to give it a happy ending. The happiness of three girls seemed to rest on Norman's shoulders—not just Amelie's and Leni's, but also Dora's. He'd told himself he wouldn't leave the book until he'd fixed it for Dora.

"Listen, Amelie . . ." Norman had started talking before he'd fully formed his thought. It came to him slowly. "Maybe he just needs to hear from you that you understand." He looked to see both girls watching him blankly, as if they weren't quite sure they were hearing him properly. "Maybe he needs to hear that you were frightened too . . . that we were all frightened." It was weird to hear himself say it. It was something his mom might say. He even said it like his mom would, measured and assured, completely unlike what he was feeling, which was guilty and unsure. But the more he thought of it, the more it sort of made sense. "Just knowing that might help, and then maybe he'll believe you when you tell him that it's going to be all right."

Amelie opened her mouth to speak, but for once she did not voice whatever comeback was on her lips. She stared open-mouthed at Norman for a few more seconds as if she too couldn't believe what had come out of his mouth.

There was more insistent whispering between the two girls. Amelie's head nodded, her brow furrowed and her bright eyes fixed on Leni as the younger girl explained something with her usual earnest focus. They seemed to take forever. Whatever Leni was teaching her to say wasn't as easy as "Hello my name is . . ." Finally the two girls broke apart. Amelie turned directly to the horse. Her lips were moving silently, rehearsing whatever phrase of traveller language Leni had taught her. The gypsy girl glanced quickly at Norman. He could not decipher the look on her face.

"Were you really scared?" she asked Norman in a whisper, as she joined him at the fence. After a moment, Norman just nodded. They were both intent on Amelie and the horse now.

Amelie approached Serendipity slowly from the side. The foal seemed to feel, rather than see, her coming, and sidled away. But Amelie kept easing toward him. Quietly, confidently now, she repeated his name in the gypsy tongue, while ever so slowly closing the gap between them. The horse watched her out of the corner of his eye, pawing the ground with one hoof and shaking his head as if he was bothered by flies or a buzzing in his ears. Amelie resisted the urge to look him in the eye. Her mouth was near his ear, which twitched and bent as Serendipity strained to hear, or perhaps to understand what the girl was saying to him.

The two were still for a long time. Amelie seemed older to Norman now. It wasn't just that she had cleaned up and put her brown hair back in braids—there was something else. She had now moved one hand to the horse's neck and was stroking it slowly. She looked more like she was consoling a friend than training a horse. The animal was responding by turning slowly, not away from Amelie, but toward her. His muzzle was now almost in her ear, as if he too had a story or a secret to tell. Amelie was still whispering, repeating her story, reassuring the horse that she understood, that she had felt the same terror when she faced the wolf. Because they shared that, she was telling him, they would be all right. They would get through it together. Norman could barely hear her speak and couldn't understand the words he did pick out, but it seemed to him that this was exactly what Amelie was telling Serendipity.

Now suddenly Amelie wasn't talking at all. He arms were wrapped around the horse's neck and her face was buried in his mane. The horse bowed its head and breathed slowly. It looked, from where Norman was standing, as if they were supporting each other. He and Leni held their breath while this moment lasted. When Serendipity pulled away, it wasn't with a jolt of fear or nervousness. He just seemed exhausted. He no longer pawed the ground or shook his head. Instead he stared directly at Amelie, held her gaze even longer than she could bear.

When Amelie turned around to face Leni and Norman, tears were streaming down her cheeks, crossing the wrinkles of a wide smile. Serendipity's eyes followed her as she stepped back to the fence, then it was more than his eyes that followed her. He took a few tentative steps toward her then halted, as if gathering courage before starting again in her footsteps. When she reached them, he stopped, just metres away, calm at least for now and no longer cowering in a far corner of the paddock. Amelie's wet eyes flicked momentarily to Norman. She never said, "You were right, Norman. Your idea worked. Everything is going to be fine now." Norman didn't really want her to.

Hours later, listening to Leni's muffled snores as they slept by the fire in the Saint-Saens living room, Norman worried momentarily about how the little girl would deal with his disappearance. His doubts didn't last long. Leni was a smart and resourceful little girl. She'd do fine.

He took a moment to write a note to Amelie on the paper scraps he had borrowed from Leni's notebook. It wasn't a long note—he didn't know how to write a long note—but he apologized. He wasn't sure exactly what he was apologizing for, but he knew he felt sorry. He just wrote, "Sorry for all the trouble," and another line about how "Serendipity will be fine." It wasn't like he knew for sure, but it was the sort of thing you put in cards and letters. After that the note still seemed too short. He thought of what else he usually put on Christmas cards and on thank-you notes to his grandparents.

In the end something else occurred to him. His last line wasn't about Amelie or the horse at all. He didn't know if it would be any use, or even if the book was supposed to work out this way, but he thought it was what Leni wanted. "Leni thinks you are amazing," he wrote. "She wants to be just like you. She wants to go to a real school. She's pretty smart. Maybe she could she stay with you sometimes? Ask her dad."

When he had finished writing this, Norman turned on his side toward the fire and took out the page from Aida's red book. The old woman had said that he'd know when to use it. He'd done his job, he thought. He'd brought the horse back. He'd brought the girls together. He'd done as much as he could. Now was as good a time as any to disappear. But he hesitated. How could he be sure that he'd done all he needed to? Maybe he should stay a few more nights to see if Serendipity improved. There were no rules for this. You broke all the rules when you entered a book, he told himself. You couldn't ever really undo what you did. It's best to just minimize the damage and get out as quickly as you can.

In the light of the fire he read the page over and over again, slowly tearing off tiny bite-sized pieces, which he placed on his tongue. Chewing them gingerly, making them into little balls in his mouth that were easily swallowed, he made it last longer than he really needed to. He did not remember falling asleep, and he did not remember dreaming of pancakes and homework.

At Home Things Are Even Less Normal

Dora's thumping at the door woke him up.

Norman rubbed his eyes and sniffed. The scent of wood smoke permeated the clothes in which he'd slept. "What?" he asked groggily.

Dora opened the door far enough to stick her head through.

"Mom says . . ." She stopped and came farther into his room. "Hey, that's my book."

"What?" Norman still wasn't awake enough to just bark "Get out of my room!"

"What are you doing with my book?"

Norman looked down at the slim paperback lying open, cover up, on the floor beside his bed.

"You asked me to read it," he replied, exasperated. "You wanted me to tell you how it ended."

"You better not!" Dora warned shrilly, grabbing the book. "Mom," she cried, "Norman's reading my book and he says he's going to tell me how it ends!"

Norman breathed deeply. Was this really better than being in the horse book? It wasn't even worth arguing that she'd already read the book and knew how it ended. It was a stupid argument, and for once he didn't let himself get drawn into it.

"He'll do nothing of the sort. Will you, Norman," his mother called up. It was a warning, but a cheerful warning.

Dora instantly found another way to be annoying. It was her gift. "Norman reads girl's books. Norman likes horsey books," she began chanting, in her own special taunting, sing-song way.

"Just get out of my room, will you?" Norman growled, too tired to work up any real anger.

It didn't take any effort to find out how *Fortune's Foal* ended. Dora couldn't keep anything to herself. She always had to tell everybody about everything that ever happened to her. That night at dinner, after telling everybody about her day at school, including both recesses, snack time and the bus ride home, she regaled them with every needless detail of the book she was reading.

"Everybody thought that Serendipity had been kidnapped by the gypsies to be sold at the fair, but the gypsies are actually wanderers who know all about wild horses," she narrated breathlessly. "So Leni, who is a gypsy girl—I mean, a *traveller* girl—she rescues the horse because she knows that the wolves are going to get him." Norman wondered if she was going to take a breath. "But Amelie finds them on an island, where they are attacked by wolves again, but it's okay, even if that Nolan kid can't help 'cos he's totally useless. The gypsies shoot the wolf and they all come back to the farm, and there—"

"Wait a minute. Who's Nolan?" Norman had forgotten to pretend not to be interested.

"Oh, he's hilarious," Dora declared, continuing with her relentless storytelling. "He's this kid from the next farm that has a total crush on Amelie. He's always trying to help, but he always messes up."

Norman couldn't hide his outrage. How could she get it so wrong? "What do you mean, he messes up?"

"Well, it's him who leaves the barn door open for the wolves to get in, and when the gypsies are about to get the wolf the first time, he tackles them. He's such an idiot. Every time they're on the horse's trail, he wants to go the opposite direction."

Norman wondered if he'd have been able to piece the book together from Dora's rambling, excited recap if he hadn't read it himself.

"Does Amelie ever cure Serendipity completely?" he asked. "Does Amelie train him for that horse therapy thing like you said?"

"It's true, you *do* like girl books," Dora said tauntingly. "Do you want to borrow some other books?" She didn't seem to remember having been so worried about the book the night before, or having asked Norman to read ahead for her.

"No, I don't want to read more of your stupid books," Norman replied exasperatedly. "Nothing even happens in them."

Dora was unmoved by Norman's dig. "What? You need some Samurai Gerbils or something to make it exciting?"

Norman bit his tongue. All in all, it was a fun sort of argument to be having after everything he'd been through. He was thinking of a reply when his mother interrupted. "Norman, darling, shall we go to the library after dinner? You sound like you need some new books."

Pleas Procedural

“Hmph,” muttered Norman’s mother, slapping her paperback closed and sliding it onto the side table beside the couch. “That’s weird.” Her thin eyebrows rose in that funny judgmental way of hers. Rummaging through her papers on the coffee table, she pulled out a different book.

Norman was no longer watching television. The moment his mother had said the word “weird,” his attention had been fixed on her. It had been more than a week since he’d returned from *Fortune’s Foal,* but he was still sensitive to anything said about books. He’d taken to asking his family what they were reading. His mother had complimented him on his interest, but cautioned him that her book wasn’t really suitable for him. Norman didn’t care. He didn’t want to read her psycho-killer murder mystery. He just needed to make sure nothing odd was happening in it. He wanted to believe that it was all over. Maybe, he’d thought, eating the page back at Amelie’s farm had fixed it—evened things out and put everything right that had gone wrong since he’d eaten the first page—but the way his heart thumped when his mother said “weird” showed just how convinced he was of that.

“What’s weird?” his father asked, saving Norman the trouble.

Norman looked from his mother to his father and back again. Between them on the wall was that painting of wolves in the wild. He found it impossible to look at now without a slight shiver. He took pains to avoid their eyes.

"Conran's really losing it now," his mother replied.

Conran was the author of her novel. Norman was used to seeing that name in big silver letters on the well-worn paperbacks that were usually to be found face down on the coffee table.

"The last few books have been weaker than usual," she said. "He seemed to have no new ideas and was just recycling old ones, but now he's really lost the plot."

Norman could hide his interest no longer. "What do you mean, Mom?"

"Well, you might like it actually now, since you're into Dora's books," she replied teasingly.

"What's that supposed to mean?" he said, in a voice more hurt than he had intended.

"Detectives Darwin and Rorschach are on the trail of this serial killer called the Magpie, who, by the way, sounds a lot like the Bower Bird killer from the first Darwin and Rorschach novel. Anyway, when they arrive at the crime scene, you're expecting the usual gory stuff that impressionable young boys like you don't need to know about yet. Instead they come face to face with . . . here, let me read it to you."

She grabbed the paperback again and opened it at the page she'd last dog-eared. She read clearly and brightly in a tone that was awkwardly familiar to Norman. This was the voice that had read to him for years, the voice that had repeated the strange magic of foxes in boxes and told him the stories of borrowers and magicians and friendly giants. It was so strange now to hear it cheerfully relating the following scene.

Rorschach winced as he hoisted his thick limbs out of the car. The tension bandage the doc had given him was useless. The slightest movement tormented his cracked rib, and this getting in and out of cars, it was like breaking the thing all over again. Darwin saw the grimace on his partner's face but knew better than to ask about it or offer sympathy.

"Suck it up, Rorscho," the smaller man said. "It's game time."

Rorschach only glowered back.

"Who called this in?" he asked as they flashed their badges and edged through the growing crowd of bystanders.

"Beat officer, just finishing his rounds. Called it in about an hour ago."

"And we're just hearing about it now?" Rorschach growled.

Darwin shrugged. They had reached the band of yellow police tape that stretched across the mouth of the alley.

"Anyone touched the body?" he asked the uniformed cop who guarded the entrance.

"No, sir," she replied. "The crime scene techs are waiting for you."

Darwin nodded. This was the way it was supposed to go, but it seldom did. Some eager Sherlock six months out of the Academy always thought he could solve the crime in the first five minutes. The smaller man did his best to lift the yellow tape high enough for his big partner to duck through painlessly, but the big man still had nearly a foot on him. Darwin read the curse on Rorschach's lips as he ducked under.

"Where's the vic?" Rorschach asked hoarsely, his voice taut with impatience and lingering pain.

"Over there behind the dumpster." The uniformed officer pointed.

The two detectives turned the corner at the same time. Neither said anything at first. Darwin reached into the inside pocket of his leather jacket and pulled out a stick of gum. Rorschach rubbed his hands over his eyes in tired disgust.

"What the heck is this supposed to be?"

The thing that was waiting for them there behind the dumpster looked back at them with big, bored brown eyes, stomped a hoof and exhaled condensation from its nostrils into the cold city air.

"Where the heck did this come from?" Rorschach demanded.

"What?" Darwin deadpanned. "You've never worked with the Police Pony Squad?"

"Did he really say 'heck'?" Norman's father asked smugly when his mother had put the *The Magpie* down again.

"I think Norman probably has heard the actual word he used before, but he doesn't need to hear it from his mother's mouth," Meg Jespers-Vilnius replied with a smirk.

"Is it really a pony?" Norman asked, a quaver in his voice betraying his anxiety.

"Apparently a very well-behaved Shetland," his mother answered.

"What happened to the body—the '*vic*'?" Norman's father pronounced the word "*vic*" with a fake gruff New York accent.

"Gone, disappeared," his mother replied, ignoring his mocking tone. "And according to the book, there's no way in or out of the alley. There's no way someone could have moved the body and put a pony in its place without crossing the crime scene tape."

"Ah, well, clearly you've got a corrupt cop there. Isn't there always a corrupt cop in these things?" his father continued cheerfully. "I'll bet it's the woman officer. She's probably got some pony thing—posters and little pink pony ceramics all over her apartment. She's the notorious Pony Killer."

Norman's mother replied with her "are you done?" look, but it didn't take the smirk off his face.

"All right, Norman," she said, as if suddenly remembering. "Bedtime."

Norman lay in his bed awake as long as he could. This wasn't getting better at all. So far all he'd done was mess up kids' books. That somehow seemed semi-okay. But now his book problem had spread to adult books. That had to be worse. People would surely start to notice now. It would get on the news. It would get back to him somehow. Norman imagined the creepy librarian pulling a concerned face while denouncing him on the TV: "Well, there was this one kid . . ."

Fretting about someone from the book fraud squad knocking on the door kept him awake, which was a good thing, because he was more afraid of falling asleep than of being caught for book-wrecking. This wasn't like the other times. He was afraid to go into an adult book. His mother wouldn't even let him read it. It couldn't be a pleasant place to visit.

He couldn't be transported into *The Magpie* anyway, Norman told himself. He hadn't actually read any of it. To go into the book, Norman reasoned to himself, you have to actually read. Another argumentative voice in his head wondered if it was enough to have heard someone else read it to you, but he worked hard to dismiss the suggestion. Even if being read to could bring on the weirdness, surely you'd have to hear more than just a page. That's where Norman wanted to leave the argument being waged in his head. He told himself that he was confident and that nothing would happen, but anyone watching might have asked why he was lying in bed fully dressed, wearing not only his shoes, but also his jacket.

Waking up standing up is as surprising and uncomfortable as it sounds. Norman's first sensation was of falling backward, and by the time the reflexes to lock his knees kicked in, it was already too late. A lesson from karate class whispered to his body. He tucked his chin in and brought his arms in close, ready to slap out and break his fall. It was a good thought, but he needn't have bothered. The pony cushioned his landing.

Norman made more noise than the pony, letting out a muffled "whaaa . . . wmph" as he fell and his breath was knocked out of his lungs from the contact with the animal's flank. The little horse merely turned and snorted. It was, if this was possible for a horse, an amused kind of snort, exactly like the involuntary snigger Norman's so-intellectual father let out when he surreptitiously watched TV blooper shows. The pony, on the other hand, didn't seem embarrassed by his amusement. There was a glint in his big brown eyes, as if he enjoyed the odd bit of human stupidity every now and then.

"Hi," Norman said, pushing himself up from the pony's side as gently as he could. "I'm Norman."

The creature smiled with his eyes. If he was half as surprised to find himself lying in a dirty city alleyway behind a stinking dumpster as Norman was, he was doing a very good job of hiding it. He lay there casually, legs folded underneath him on the pavement, head back against the graffiti-covered brick wall, his breathing steady.

"I, ah . . . I don't speak horse," Norman explained apologetically. "I mean, I can't do that gypsy thing. One of my friends can, but . . . well, she's not here. At least I don't think so."

The pony nodded its shaggy head and exhaled a cloud of condensation from its nostrils. Overhead, the morning sky was as overcast and grey as the pony's coat. This was not a foal, like Serendipity. It was a fully grown pony.

"Are you the missing pony from Serendipity's stall that everyone seemed to have forgotten?" Norman asked, not really expecting an answer. "Sorry about the wolves . . ." Norman didn't have to hear the pony's thoughts to feel the calm power as the animal rose in one smooth motion to his feet. It was as if he knew the policemen would be coming around the corner at that moment.

"What the hell?"

Norman's mother hadn't read Rorschach's words accurately. The fat man said a lot worse now, too. The gist of his angry rant was that he'd like to know who thought it was funny to pull a stunt like this, when the good people of the city were out there murdering each other. Once this was off his chest, he stormed off to find someone to hold responsible and berate. "You deal with the kid," he told the smaller guy as he left.

Darwin remained where he was, a few yards distant, both hands in his jacket pockets, studying Norman and the grey pony with an inscrutable look on his face while he chewed gum. Then he strolled nonchalantly around the alley examining it disinterestedly, removing one hand from the pocket of his leather jacket only to rattle a fire-escape ladder while his eyes followed its steps up to the rooftop.

Apparently satisfied that the fire escape could not be successfully navigated by a horse of any size, Darwin turned to Norman and asked in a cool, nasal voice, "That your horse, son?"

Norman realized that he was standing close to the pony, his finger buried in the animal's grey mane, as if trying to reassure himself. He shook his head no in reply to Detective Darwin's question, and they were silent again.

Norman's mother definitely wouldn't have repeated the curses that the uniformed policewoman swore when she and Rorschach came around the corner and saw a shaggy grey pony and an eleven-year-old boy standing where a murder victim had previously lain in a pool of blood.

An hour later, Norman was sitting in an interrogation room at the police headquarters. It was exactly like every interrogation room he had ever seen in a TV police drama, bare and dingy, with just four metal chairs separated into pairs by a peeling Formica table. Norman was seated on one side of the table. Rorschach sat diagonally across from him. The other two chairs were empty. Darwin leaned against the wall in the corner, chewing gum. So far their interrogation hadn't amounted to much. They had brought Norman an orange juice and a chocolate chip muffin and chatted back and forth between themselves about the case.

"I had a word with the boys down in the mounted squad about that horse," Rorschach told Darwin, as if he was just making idle conversation.

"They reckon it escaped from the circus or something? We get any calls about stolen ponies?" Darwin asked.

"Naw, they said it probably wasn't worth stealing. That old pony has seen better days. It was probably headed to the boneyard anyway."

It was all Norman could do to remain silent, but he saw Darwin watching him from the corner and knew they were trying to get a reaction.

"It's the darndest thing, they say," Rorschach continued. "All the horses down there are acting weird since they brought that grey one in. They're all skittish and refuse to be saddled up. Not one of them will look that grey horse in the eye. It's like the king of horses has arrived at the stables."

It really was difficult not to interrupt them and tell them why. Norman only stopped because he knew they wouldn't believe him. He just sat there and looked at the wood-grained Formica while he sipped his sugary juice and nibbled the dry, machine-dispensed muffin. It was depressing food, but it suited the situation.

They'd asked him a dozen times already for the names of his parents and his home address. Norman didn't even know what world he was in, never mind what city. His street, his house and his parents probably didn't exist in this book. As an excuse, Norman just repeated what he'd seen on TV cop shows.

"I need to see my lawyer first."

Rorschach was getting more and more frustrated with this answer.

"For the hundredth time, kid, you don't need a lawyer. You're not being charged with anything. We just need to call your parents. They're probably worried about you."

Norman avoided the big man's eyes and concentrated on picking the last few muffin crumbs from the crinkled wax-paper baking cup on the table. His parents probably weren't worried about him, but they should be.

"Listen, we've already called Child Services. If we get your phone number now, we can have your parents here before they send a social worker over. Otherwise you're looking at a group home for the night."

Norman just shrugged. There was a knock at the door. Darwin, standing against the wall by the doorway, turned the knob and pulled the door open a few inches without taking his eyes off Norman at the table. The door was pushed open the rest of the way from outside, and a tall, awkward figure shuffled in. He was dressed in black with a crumpled suit jacket and with a pair of running shoes at the end of his long legs. As he tried to close the door behind him, he juggled and nearly dropped a stack of books and file folders. Darwin reacted quickly to catch a yellow file folder sliding off the top of the stack. The clumsy new man scowled, as if it was Darwin's fault. He managed to get his pile of papers to the desk without further incident and sat himself noisily in the chair next to Norman.

"Fuchs, Child Services," he said, by way of introduction, nodding first to Norman, then to the two police officers opposite.

"Okay, then, Fuchs, maybe you could explain to your client here that he's not in any trouble," Rorschach continued. "He's not under arrest. We just need to get in touch with his parents so that we can get him home."

Fuchs opened the yellow file folder in front of him, answering without looking up from it. "Mr. Norman's parents are out of the country at the moment," he said officiously. "I've spoken to the administrator at his boarding school and arranged for someone to pick him up. They're very worried about him. Seems they lost track of him on a school trip to the Met."

Rorschach and Darwin looked almost as surprised as Norman by this news. Norman stared at Fuchs as the man from Child Services slid the yellow folder toward him. There was something familiar about this Fuchs character. How exactly did this person know half of his name, and why had he made up this story about his parents, a boarding school and some place named after a baseball team? Norman couldn't help following the stranger's long, pale finger to the top page in the folder open in front of him, a sheet of neatly typed text. Norman read it to himself.

There was something familiar about this Fuchs character. How exactly did this person know half of his name, and why had he made up this story about his parents, a boarding school and some place named after a baseball team?

Exactly what Norman had just thought! Shocked, Norman scrutinized the stranger's face again. Where had he seen him before? This was about as weird as it got.

"Okay, now we're getting somewhere. Norman. Is that a first or a last name?"

Norman and the Fuchs character spoke up at the same time.

"First," Norman blurted out, glad to be able to answer a question.

"Last," said the Child Services man.

Rorschach turned incredulously to the still silent Darwin, who shrugged just slightly.

"Okay, then, Norman Norman, maybe we could ask you a few questions before this person from your school gets here."

Norman gave a hesitant nod.

"So you wandered off from your school group and ended up in that alley," the detective began.

Norman kept his mouth shut. It wasn't that he didn't want to talk. It was just that he had no idea what to say.

Rorschach pushed on impatiently. "When you got there, was the alley empty?"

Norman looked to Fuchs for some guidance, but the man merely crossed his arms and regarded him with a curious raised eyebrow, as if he was mildly interested in the answer.

Rorschach repeated the question. "Was the horse there behind the dumpster when you entered the alley?"

Finding no answer in Fuchs's face, Norman peered down at the file folder, but Fuchs's narrow white fingers were spread out flat to cover the entire page.

"Was there police tape across the front of the alley when you went in?" There was an edge of frustration now to Rorschach's voice. "Yellow tape that says 'POLICE LINE DO NOT CROSS.' Was it there when you entered the alley?" Norman gulped. To his surprise, he found himself on the verge of bursting into tears.

The big detective didn't seem to notice. He kept pressing his questions. "Did you see anyone else enter or leave the alley while you were there?"

Frightened a little bit now by Rorschach's tone, Norman looked desperately to Fuchs for some clue as to what to say or do. The Child Services representative wore an amused expression on his face, like someone who's watching a movie he's seen before and knows that the good part is just coming up. A motion of his hand brought Norman's eye back to the page in front of him. Fuchs had exposed the top half of the page. Norman read the sentence just above Fuchs's finger.

And then Norman knew exactly what to do. He had stumbled into the bookweird by accident, but he was starting to understand it, and he saw it gave him a slim chance to escape.

But Norman did not know exactly what to do. He did not understand what "bookweird" was supposed to be and he had no idea how to escape. He gaped back at Fuchs, trying to show his incomprehension and frustration by raising both eyebrows in a shrug. In response, the man in black twitched his ear in a way that no human could. With that motion, Norman recognized him. It was the strange librarian who knew about the missing page and who could put a pencil through the hole in his ear. But it was also the fox abbot of Tintern Abbey in Undergrowth. They were the same person, or the same fox.

"You," he gasped. It was so obvious now.

Fuchs smirked ever so slightly and repeated the trick with his ear. Calmly and quietly, his big fingers began tearing the page out of his book.

"You who?" Rorschach asked, confused. "Who are you talking to?"

With a grand, sweeping gesture Fuchs removed the typed page from the folder. He closed the yellow folder with a slap and slid the page across the Formica table top to Norman, who stared at it desperately for a clue as to what to do next. It had no instructions for him, just a description of the very scene he was in the middle of. He scanned down the page.

This was no book for a kid like Norman. Even Fuchs, who thought kids should be tougher, could see that. Even he couldn't leave the skinny Norman kid by himself in the middle of a bloody New York murder investigation. Fuchs would have loved to stay himself and play the game with the two detectives, but the little part of his good judgment that remained overruled this idea. He would help the kid out sooner, rather than later.

As strange as it was to see his own thoughts on the page, it was stranger still to see Fuchs's. And it was frightening to think that his fate depended on the help of this unreliable character, who wasn't a librarian and who wasn't a fox abbot and who seemed to be able to move at will between the real world and books. Knowing that Fuchs thought that this was a dangerous book and no place for a kid made him more anxious. The page was shaking in his hands as he desperately searched for an escape route among its paragraphs.

Rorschach was only going to get angrier and ask more questions about the alley, about why he was there, where the horse had come from and whether he'd seen the body—nothing to tell him how to get out of this. According to this, Norman was supposed to have known how to escape half a page ago. In his nervousness, he ripped off a corner of the page and brought the paper to his mouth. The moment it touched his tongue, he understood.

"Can I have a glass of water please?" Norman asked in his most polite voice. He tore another corner off the page.

Darwin slid out the door as Norman continued to chew nervously on the balled-up paper.

Fuchs covered for him while he ate. "I don't think you need to be asking questions in that tone. This is a scared boy lost in the city. Look how anxious you are making him."

In the next fifteen minutes, Norman made his way methodically through his paper meal. It went more quickly after Darwin brought his water. As he chewed, Norman realized that the paper actually tasted better than the muffin he'd been served as an appetizer. When he was done, he had a moment of doubt. Didn't he have to fall asleep for this to work? He looked over at the strange fox man, wishing he could ask him a few questions. When he got back home, he was going to visit every library in the city until he tracked him down again. He was beginning to hate the fox man a little bit.

Fuchs seemed to read his mind. He *could* read his mind, of course. If the book in front of him really was the book that they were in now, then Fuchs could read everything Norman was thinking right there on the page. The moment Norman found himself thinking up insults and accusations, Fuchs turned to him, his smirking foxlike eyes flashing a silent rebuke.

Rising to his feet, Fuchs suggested they take a break. "There should be someone here for Mr. Norman by now. I'll just check at the front desk."

Norman gaped at him incredulously. His face pleaded, don't leave me, but leave he did. As the Child Services man passed Norman's chair, he kicked a leg hard. His clumsiness wouldn't have been a problem if Norman hadn't been leaning back on two legs. The chair slid out from underneath him, and Norman began to fall backward. He had no time to react. In karate, they didn't teach you how to break your fall when you were sitting on a chair. Norman's legs flailed in front of him. This was going to knock him out cold, he thought, but his head never hit the floor. He merely fell into blackness.

Losing It

"Put a coat on!" his mother cried, as Norman hastily gathered his shoes at the door.

"Okay," he called back from the doorway.

"That's some coat," she said, her voice closer now.

Norman, caught in the open doorway, could only grin back guiltily.

"Where's your coat?" she asked.

"I can't find it."

"Your new one? The yellow one with the black trim we just bought you?" Nothing exasperated his mother more than Norman's absentmindedness. "Where did you see it last?"

Norman shrugged. He could hardly tell her that he'd left it on the back of a metal chair in the interrogation room in one of her murder mystery books. Norman had checked and it was still there. There were no stray ponies anymore, no fox-men from Child Services and definitely no kids called Norman Norman, but in the scene when they bring their first suspect in for interrogation, Rorschach picks up a kid's yellow and black windbreaker from the back of the chair and asks Darwin, making a joke about his height, if it is his. That was all. The rest was all pretty normal for these kind of books, Norman guessed—it was kind of creepy and gross. He understood why his mom wouldn't let him read them, but he couldn't understand why *she* read them. She was pretty nice as moms go. What was with the serial murder stuff?

"I guess I'll have to buy you a really cheap geeky one to replace it," Meg Jespers-Vilnius warned. She probably should, but Norman knew she wouldn't. His dad definitely would have. Dad was all about teaching him lessons, but his mom understood. While a geeky jacket might embarrass him, it wouldn't help him remember things. Her letting him off the hook like this might make him more careful next time.

"Are you going to the library? Put a sweater on then instead." She disappeared up the stairs for a moment and returned with a grey sweatshirt. Rolling it into a ball, she tossed it to him from the top of the stairs, nailing him in the head.

"Nice arm," he said, rubbing his head where the Undergrowth scratches were just beginning to heal.

"Nice eye," she replied smugly as he closed the door behind him.

There was little point in going. He'd been to the local branch every day for a week. Yesterday he'd done a long tour on his bike to the other nearby branches. He'd asked every librarian he'd met if they knew the name of the tall replacement librarian who wore black and had a hole in his ear. Nobody seemed to remember him, and he didn't seem to be the sort of person you easily forgot. Maybe hole-in-the-ear man wasn't a real librarian, Norman thought as he slipped on his running shoes. "That's right," he said aloud as he kicked and tugged at his shoes to avoid unlacing them, "he's an impostor!"

What did he want then, this impostor librarian, and how did he move so easily between books and real life? Was he just like Norman, a kid who had fallen into one book and then just got the hang of it? Another thought struck Norman as he rummaged through the mudroom closet for his bike helmet. What if Fuchs actually came out of a book? After all the crazy stuff that had happened to Norman, the idea shouldn't have been so frightening. But it was. It was enough that he himself had already messed up three books, but so far he'd always come back home to his own life, unchanged. He didn't at all like the idea of somebody coming out of a book and disturbing real life.

"Who is the impostor?" a soft voice asked behind him. Norman jumped, surprised to see his mother holding the door.

"No one," he answered sheepishly. "Someone from a book."

His mom smiled and regarded him affectionately. "I know how that is. Sometimes you get so wrapped up in a book it stays with you all day. You feel like you're in it."

Norman nodded. She said she understood, which was nice of her, but she couldn't really understand.

"Just try to keep the conversations in your head," she warned. "People might think you're crazy." She widened her eyes to show the whites and raised her eyebrows manically.

Norman half smiled. No, he wouldn't want that.

"Your dad would like to talk to you before you go out," his mom added.

"What about?" There must have been an edge of worry in his voice. He was nervous these days, always prepared for something else to go wrong as his book problems snowballed.

His mother's answer was meant to be reassuring, but it was nothing of the sort.

"Don't worry. It's nothing to do with you. Your father's lost something. He just wants your help to reconstruct his steps."

"What . . . what has he lost?" Norman stuttered. Deep in his heart he knew what had gone missing. A twinge of foreboding went through his chest as he slowly slid his shoes off again.

"Just go on up. Your dad just needs to talk it out."

It was not possible to climb the stairs any more slowly or to push the door to the study open any more quietly. Edward Vilnius stood facing his desk by the window where Norman could see him in profile. His hand was on his chin and he was staring, not exactly at his desk, but at some spot of nothing in between himself and the desk. Norman stood there, not wanting to interrupt, but his father didn't acknowledge his presence immediately. He just stood there stroking his chin. There was an empty espresso cup on the desk. Somebody obviously thought he needed the strong stuff.

"Hey, Norman," he said finally, speaking in a slow, tired-sounding voice. He called him Norman, not Spiny, which was a bad sign.

"Wh—what's up, Dad?"

"Norman, I've lost something, and I'm at my wit's end now, hoping somebody else can think of something." His voice sounded tight, as if he was straining to keep control of it.

"Oh, okay . . ."

"You remember the poem I brought home, right?"

It was as if a stone had dropped down Norman's throat and bruised the bottom of his stomach. He couldn't have said a word at that moment, so it was for the best that his dad kept talking.

"It's called *The Battle of Maldon*," his father continued. "It's very old. You remember I had a copy that had been transcribed by Tolkien, with his notes pencilled in the margins. I was writing a paper."

Norman didn't need to be told about it. He remembered too well what his father was talking about. His attention turned to the desk. The plastic-covered pages were laid out on the desk like patio stones. One, two, three . . . six, Norman counted. How many of them were there supposed to be?

"I'm missing a page. I can't for the life of me think of what I've done with it." Edward Vilnius ran a hand through his hair.

Norman gulped, desperately trying to bring moisture to his dry throat.

"You haven't seen me walking around with these, have you?" His father peered at him earnestly.

Norman shook his head. No words would come, but his father pressed. "I wasn't working on them downstairs in the dining room or anywhere?"

"Not . . ." Norman stammered. "Not since that day you showed them to me."

"No." His father didn't seem surprised by the answer.

"What the devil have I done with it?" He turned to Norman

again. "I don't suppose you've been in here, looking at them . . . or at other stuff? I know you sometimes borrow pencils and paper."

Norman croaked a hoarse "no." He hadn't been in his dad's office. He hadn't touched the plastic sheaths with the old poem pages inside. But that didn't make him feel any less guilty.

His father heard it in his voice and saw it in the way he was narrowing his shoulders, trying to make himself smaller, as if he'd be harder to see. Edward Vilnius's own voice changed with his next question. "Is there something you need to tell me, Norman?"

All Norman could do was shake his head stiffly. He couldn't even look his father in the eye. Instead he stared blankly at the plastic-covered pages on the desk. Everything he did now made him look more guilty. It was like being back on the farm with Amelie. He wanted to explain, but how could he?

"Norman," his father said through gritted teeth, "I'm not a fool, you know. I can tell when you are not telling the truth."

Norman tried to look him in the eyes but couldn't.

His father removed his glasses and ran his palm over his head. "Have you any idea how important this is, Norman? This is not just my job at stake. This is a piece of history."

Norman gulped. His throat felt clogged, as if he had just swallowed a page whole. He couldn't get any words out.

"You are only going to make this worse." Anger continued to mount in Edward Vilnius's voice. It was there, but he was trying to hold it back. "If you tell me now, maybe we can sort this out, but I will not tolerate lying."

"I . . . I am not lying," Norman croaked.

"You aren't telling me the truth, either," his father barked back. He crossed his arms and stared, harsh and judgmental, his jaw set. Edward Vilnius was not an especially big man, but there was a look in his eyes when he was pushed to real anger—an animal look, maybe, the way his jaw twitched as he ground his teeth and squinted. Perhaps only a son could feel the full intimidation of this fierce scowl. Norman's head wilted under it, unable to hold his father's glare.

"Is that it? Is that all you have to say for yourself?" His father held that stare for a long time before shaking his head and turning away in disgust. "Go to your room and think about it."

Norman stood rooted in the doorway.

"Go!" he shouted, so loud it made Norman jump. He backed out of the study as quickly as he could, but not fast enough to avoid hearing the door slam and bounce open again, or to hear his father shout a word that Norman had only ever heard him say once, when he'd hit his thumb with a hammer. It was a word that seemed to come more frequently to Darwin and Rorschach.

Norman stood in the hallway staring at his father. Edward Vilnius counted the plastic sheets on his desk oncemore, put his fists on the desk and muttered the word again before turning to rummage through some cardboard file boxes. As he did so, he caught Norman standing there in the hall staring. He didn't say a word, just glared as he stepped forward to slam the study door fully closed.

The wind raged against Norman as he cycled to the library. He stood up in the pedals, pumping as hard as he could, his hair streaming out behind him. In his haste to get out of the house without anyone noticing, he'd forgotten his helmet. He ignored it now like he ignored the inevitable punishment that would come his way when his dad discovered he'd snuck out. He just needed to get to the library as quickly as possible. The wind thought differently, howling down the bike path between the rows of cedars, turning them into a wind tunnel. So there was a very good excuse for the stinging in his eyes, for the protective film of moisture now forming over them and streaking out of the corner of his eyes across his cheeks. And a perfectly good reason for his nose to be running.

It could not be that Norman was scared. Hadn't he been through much worse? Hadn't he dodged raven's arrows in the mountain passes of Undergrowth? Hadn't he heard the blood-curdling howls of wolves honing in on him through the dark? Hadn't he also been interrogated by two hardboiled big-city cops? Losing the pages of some old poem—that was nothing. Right? So why did Norman's hands tremble, no matter how hard he gripped the handlebars?

This was too close to home. Somehow being inside those books had made all the danger he'd faced recently less threatening. Sure he'd been scared, but scared for himself only. And always in the back of his head, he'd known that there was somewhere more real, somewhere where everything was safe and normal. As long as the weirdness happened only inside books, Norman could just about handle it. But now it was spreading to the real world. This chain reaction of page disappearances got worse every time. First it had been kids' books. Then it had been his mom's cheesy thriller, as his dad called it. Now it was a book people cared about it. There were courses at university about it. His dad had a job because of it. Maybe he'd lose his job now . . . and it would all be Norman's fault.

Norman was breathless when he swung through the door or the library. Mrs. Balani shushed him silently from behind the counter with a slight pursing of the lips and rise of her finger. He hadn't really expected the ear-hole librarian to be there. He hadn't had any distinct plan when he'd bolted from the house and grabbed his bike. He'd only known that the library was his best place to start. As he stood there though, blinking the moisture out of his eyes and sniffling as quietly as he could, an idea came to him.

"You know that librarian I was asking about?"

Mrs. Balani gave him a look that was supposed to express impatience but was really the opposite. You could always tell when a grown-up was only pretending to reprimand you and was actually amused.

"Well, he lent me a book of his own, and I feel bad that I haven't returned it to him." How better to get a librarian on your side than to make it about returning a book? "He told me his name, but I can't remember it. I'm sure I'd recognize it if I saw it, though. Do you have a list of all the librarians . . . you know, if you have to call them when someone's sick?"

Mrs. Balani studied him for a moment, as if considering whether to indulge him further. Probably she decided it would do no harm, because next she shuffled through a set of files behind her. It didn't take her long. She handed over four sheets of paper stapled in the corner.

"Don't even think of taking it away from this counter," she warned.

As Norman took the sheets, he realized that his fingers were shaking. The contact list had four columns: a name, a phone number, an email address and a home branch. Norman scanned them all quickly. He had no idea what he was looking for, and nothing leapt off the page. After flipping through them once, he started again and looked through them more methodically, focusing on the ones that had "itinerant" in the home branch column, guessing this meant they had no home library and were called in when someone was sick, like the day Mrs. Balani had been out. It was generally hopeless—who knew if "Martin Wyeth" or "Paul Bryznicki" was a tall teenager who always wore black? It was possible that "R. Russet" or "Prem Pahlajra" had holes in his ears that you could pass pencils through, but how could you know? Norman ran his finger across the line for each of them, checking their phone numbers and email addresses in case they meant something. It was desperation time now. Wyethm at whatever dot com didn't really help, but Norman's finger hovered over one address: reynard_russet@libro.li. Something about that made him stop.

"Mrs. Balani? Reynard means 'fox,' right?"

"Yes," she said, without looking away from her computer terminal. "It's from the French word *renard*."

"Can I borrow the phone, please?"

Norman's hands still hadn't stopped shaking. If anything, they trembled more than ever as he dialled. The phone rang three times before an answering machine kicked in.

"Hello, you've reached Reynard. I'm either reading a book or out getting a new piercing right now, so leave a message. And if I were you, I'd read up on my Anglo-Saxon. See ya."

Norman hadn't really known what he was going to say, and the beep of an answering machine prompt always gave him a kind of stage fright.

"Erm, this is Norman, you know the kid with . . . the kid with the ah . . ." He lowered his voice to a whisper. "The, ah—" He tried to remember what Fuchs had called it. "—the bookweird problem. I'd like to talk to you. You can reach me at . . ." For some reason he hesitated to give Reynard his phone number. The weird librarian had intruded too much already into Norman's life. He didn't want to invite him further. "I'll be at the library all afternoon." The second beep told him that his time was up.

Norman didn't doubt that Reynard's message had been left for him—he had better read up on his Anglo-Saxon. It wasn't hard to figure out what that meant. It meant that Reynard knew about *The Battle of Maldon.* Did it mean he was going there next? Maybe he should learn a little more.

If he was going to have to wait here for Reynard, he might as well follow his advice. Scanning the article in the encyclopedia, Norman found that a lot of the stuff about the Anglo-Saxons was familiar. Was it possible that despite trying to ignore his dad, some of his rambling stories had actually got through? It was true, his father had told him all this—that the Anglo-Saxons were Germanic tribes, that they had given their name to the country England and the English language. So they spoke English; that was reassuring.

Norman hunkered down in the history aisle to wait and to start filling in the details. The Angles and the Saxons had come from the continent and taken over from the Britons, who had ruled the British Isles before them. Norman filed this as an "interesting fact" because he'd always thought that "British" and "English" meant the same thing.

King Alfred was the first king of England and was called the Great, even though he seemed to be most famous for hiding in swamps. They were defeated by William the Conqueror in 1066, a date that Norman thought he remembered. It didn't seem like a good thing for him that the conquerors were called Normans, from a place in France, but the lucky thing was that the Battle of Maldon had been in 991, when the Anglo-Saxons were more bothered with Vikings than Frenchmen and the King was someone called Aethelred the Unready.

"That's where Dad got the name for the cat," Norman muttered to himself. "It's still a stupid name for a cat."

This Battle of Maldon thing was more confusing than he thought. Norman tried to read the poem in what he guessed was the original but was confronted with bizarre letters that weren't even in the English alphabet—curvy *d*'s with slashes through them, elongated *p*'s and lots of vowels stuck together.

I thought this was supposed to be English! he thought.

Finding a real English version didn't help much either. It seemed to start halfway in, and mostly it seemed to be a list of all the people who were there and all the insults and boasts they had made. His father had told him that the poem celebrated "the great English character in the face of adversity," but even after reading it, Norman couldn't tell how they had actually won. That part seemed to be missing.

Would he be expected to understand these people if he arrived in the poem? Would he be expected to talk in rhyme? Norman had never been in a poem before and wasn't sure how he would have to behave. And he had no doubt that that was where he was going the next time he fell asleep. He just hoped that he could last until Reynard arrived and he could go home. The stifling air of the library was making him drowsy, and the sea of *ð*'s, *þ*'s and *æ*'s wasn't helping. To be safe, he'd stuffed a copy of a bicycle-safety pamphlet into his pocket. It was best to be prepared with an escape route. He held out for the better part of two hours. His last thought as he dozed off was to wish that he hadn't left his coat in *The Magpie*. Anglo-Saxon England sounded cold.

The Battle of Maldon

A jacket would have been nice. So would some rubber boots. Anglo-Saxon England wasn't just cold; it was wet and muddy. Today's wake-up spot was a ditch beside a hayfield. Norman woke up dry enough, but he got up and stepped forward into an ankle-deep soaker. "Jeez," he muttered, pulling his sneaker out with a squelching sound. The extra weight on his other foot drove it too into the mud. "Make that two soakers," he said aloud. He stepped back to the hayfield side of the ditch and prepared to long-jump it. Nearby, a group of grazing rabbits rose on their hind legs, startled by the sounds of his fight with the mud. It was hard, after Undergrowth, not to see them as somehow human. Norman squinted and wondered if that was a staff the large brown rabbit was holding or whether it was just a stick in the mud. The flash of blue and silver in the grass could have been a flag, perhaps, maybe the blue banner of Logorno. Was he back in Undergrowth? Was he far from Malcolm?

A cry from the road that ran beside the ditch turned his attention.

"What are you doing down there, boy?" Norman understood the sense of the question after a while, but not immediately. It was the strange almost-English of his dad's old poem. His vision of Undergrowth faded away.

"I said, what are you doing? Are you a fool, lad?" the man on the road repeated slowly. He wore a sort of leather and chain-mail armour and carried a steel helmet behind him on the saddle of the small, shaggy horse he rode.

His daydream about the rabbits forgotten, Norman shook his head slowly and replied even more slowly, "I was sleeping."

The armoured man's face registered his confusion. Norman's speech must have sounded just as strange to him. He dismounted his horse and peered over the edge of the ditch to frown at Norman. "Get out of that ditch, lad, and come up here," he ordered.

Norman did his best. He could hear the man chuckling as he scrambled across. There wasn't enough room to get a good run at the ditch. He cleared the deepest parts, but the far embankment was still muddy enough to cause him to slip and muddy his jeans from his shin to his knees.

"Here, lad, have a hand." A hand reached down into the ditch, grasped his firmly and yanked him up. He'd been hauled up with such force that it was a surprise to find himself looking almost directly into the eyes of the man on the road. The man seemed just as surprised. His bright blue eyes narrowed and blinked.

"You're quite the beanpole, aren't you," he growled, tugging his beard. "Are you a boy or a man?"

"I'm eleven," Norman eventually replied.

"Well, you speak too oddly for my ear. Where do you hail from when you aren't sleeping in other men's ditches?"

Norman was stuck for a safe reply. Where was it safe to say he came from? He hesitated and stammered for a while before the man gave up.

"You are well addled, boy. Have you taken a blow to that high head of yours?"

Norman nodded. If it gave him time to get his bearings, he could blame his disorientation on head injuries.

"Well, do you know your name?" the man asked more softly.

Reassured, he replied without thinking, "Norman."

The man started at the sound of this. His hand reached instinctively to the hilt of his sword. "That's an ill-omened name. Was your father struck on the head too when you were born?" He shook his head in disbelief that any good Saxon would call his son Norman. "Now I look at you, you've the look of a young North Man, you do. It would explain the ungodly height of you. What was your father called?"

Norman stuttered his reply. "Edward—my father is Edward."

"That's an English-enough name. Good enough for a king. Where is this Edward the Ill-Namer?"

"I don't know," Norman muttered. This too had the benefit of being true.

The armoured man frowned. "Well, Son of Edward. I am Aetheric. Many men would leave you here in your ditch, but I don't send my two cattle a year to the Bishop unwillingly. We're Christian men here. It's what separates us from the Vikings. You had best be coming with me."

There didn't seem much point arguing with this. Aetheric handed Norman a rough canvas sack. "See how you do with that," he commanded. "If you handle it as far as the abbey, I might let you carry my sword the rest of the way to Maldon." Norman blinked, not understanding how this was supposed to be a reward.

Aetheric was not silent on the road to Maldon. He talked endlessly about his journey, walking beside his horse and leading it by its reins in order to make conversation easier. For the first while he could not help giving Norman the occasional disbelieving look, but he seemed to get more comfortable with the strange sight of the boy in his jeans and sneakers. It was good for Norman to listen to the older man talk. It attuned his ear to the strange version of English that Aetheric spoke.

"I am a kinsman and thane to Brythnoth, that earl that as we speak amasses his troops at Maldon. There we shall drive away the sea thieves that have harassed our shores this summer long. My brothers go ahead of me, but think not that it is through cowardice that I dawdle. My wife gave me a son, not more than two days ago, and I had to be on hand to make sure that he did not have a fool's name." Aetheric punched Norman in the arm and grinned. Norman guessed that it was supposed to be a friendly shot, but it hurt either way. Aetheric laughed as Norman rubbed his biceps. "I can see you've not spent much time in the field, lad. Perhaps your father means to send you to the monastery, as I send my cows." The short, swarthy man laughed again at his joke. Norman just smiled in a way that he supposed reinforced the burly little man's impression that Norman was not quite right in the head.

At least Aetheric didn't follow through on his promise to let Norman carry his sword. The canvas sack was heavy enough. When they passed the church at the hill, Aetheric merely crossed himself and carried on. By the time they crested the hill at Maldon, Norman was too tired to be excited by the sight of the sea or of the small band of men who were assembling at the shore. He had seen too many movies with hundreds of extras and thousands more soldiers drawn in by computer to be impressed by a few hundred men in metal hats and breastplates. Aetheric smiled proudly as he looked down, though.

"There are my kinsmen. They have all come. Our boasts in the mead hall were not hollow. It will be a fell day for sea thieves today."

The stocky warrior actually spat as he insulted the raiders. Norman followed his eyes out to sea. In the mouth of the river, not far from the shore where the Saxon troops were forming up, was a small island. The bows of two long boats moored on the island could be seen from here. Perhaps there were more.

"Vikings," Norman whispered. His pulse was racing now. Something about the shape of that hull and that square sail meant danger to him.

"Aye," affirmed Aetheric. "This lot are Danish, but don't you worry. They will not blight these West Saxon shores much longer. Brythnoth is a great earl and a fearsome fighter. This black-water river will be red with Danish blood before sunset." Somehow this image did not reassure Norman at all.

Aetheric immediately sought out his own family and retainers. Norman stood by idly watching as they slapped each other on the back and congratulated Aetheric on the birth of his son. Only when everyone else had been greeted and saluted did anyone pay attention to Norman. Nobody said anything, but the glances from the men were curious and suspicious. The younger they were and the shorter, the more suspiciously they regarded him.

"Aye, you'll have noticed the beanpole. Would that he had width to match his height. He'd have made a fine fighter. There's time yet, perhaps. He says he's only eleven, but he's been struck on the head at least once, so you can't rely on his counting." The men all guffawed, the boys even more, and Norman felt himself reddening in anger. Aetheric noticed immediately.

"I see there's some fight in you, after all. Perhaps your father spoke too soon when he promised you to the monks."

The warrior nodded to one of the older boys. "Wulfmaer, why don't you see if you can teach the sapling to draw a bow."

The boy called Wulfmaer scowled. He looked as vicious as his name. A head shorter than Norman but obviously a few years older, with scruffy long hair and a snarling lip, he had the same angry look as the kids Norman avoided in the schoolyard. He grunted and motioned for Norman to follow him to a far end of the field.

Wulfmaer's instructional technique involved firing a dozen arrows at a hay bale while Norman looked on, then sending him to fetch the arrows. Next it was Norman's turn. He did his best to remember how Wulfmaer had held the arrow and the bow but had to endure the older boy's snickers as he fought with each arrow. He stung his fingers on the bowstring and scraped his forearm with every second release. None of his arrows hit the hay bale. When he was out of arrows, Wulfmaer sent him to fetch them all again. This sequence continued. They would take turns shooting the arrows, but only Norman ever fetched them. He paid closer attention to the way that the Saxon boy notched the arrow each time. Wulfmaer wasn't nearly as fast or as accurate as Malcolm or the other stoat archers of Undergrowth, but there's only so much you can learn from a weasel's bow technique that can be applied to human hands and fingers.

Despite Wulfmaer's dismal teaching methods, after six or seven rounds Norman was putting half of his arrows into the hay bale. This seemed to bother Wulfmaer. For once several of his own arrows had gone wide of their mark. Norman was gathering them from the mud beside the target when he heard the whistle of another arrow. He turned just in time to see it pierce the hay. Shocked, he turned to see Wulfmaer standing smugly with the bow at his side.

Norman reacted instinctively. "Hey, what do you think you are doing? You could have killed me!" he shouted. He strode angrily back to the shooting area. "Idiot," he shouted as he grasped the bow. He couldn't help himself. The Saxon boy might not have understood a word he said, but he knew he was being insulted and he wasn't about to hand over his bow.

Norman's anger at being shot at got the better of him. "It's my turn, jerk. Give me the bow."

Wulfmaer let go of the bow, but only to fling it behind him. Norman could see what was going to happen next. The other boy clenched his face as well as his fist before he swung. Norman was already in guard stance. He parried Wulfmaer's wild swing with a side block and followed with a backfist. The Saxon boy might be stronger, but Norman the advantage of height, arm length and two years of karate lessons. It was a yellow-belt move, and he did it as instinctively now as he would in the dojo—only in the dojo they all wore pads and mouthguards and were careful to avoid the face. Norman was shocked that he'd actually done it. He watched dumbfounded as Wulfmaer wiped his nose with his hand and found it streaming with blood. The Saxon boy's eyes widened in surprise. His lip curled in animal ferocity, and Norman could see him coiling himself to bull-rush and tackle him. If the older boy got in close and got him to the ground, his superior strength and weight would settle this fight easily.

They were interrupted by the sounding of a horn. The sound snapped both boys' heads toward the beach, where the troops were forming up in rows. Wulfmaer appeared to consider finishing this fight but thought better of it. He flared one nostril and pointed a threatening finger at Norman's chest that promised he'd sort this out later.

Norman reached the beach first. The tide had gone out and revealed a narrow causeway between them and the island where the Vikings had moored their boats and encamped. A single Viking had crossed the causeway and stood now just feet from the shore. One figure emerged from the crowd of Saxon warriors at the end of the causeway. He was neither taller nor more handsome than any of the warriors around him, but something made him stand out. Others around him had finer armour and flashier swords, yet none had the same bearing of authority. He raised a spear in the air and the host around him first roared then fell absolutely silent.

"You hear what answer we've given you. If you want a tribute, we'll give you one. How about we pay you in spears and swords? Tell your heathen lords that this is Aethelred's country and I am Aethelred's Earl and I will fight to defend this homeland of ours. You'll not leave here without a fight."

So this was Brythnoth, the leader Aetheric boasted of. The Viking messenger was nearly a head taller. The white scars that criss-crossed the Viking's face showed that he was no stranger to battle, but this Brythnoth was fearless. He scoffed at the Viking's demands. There was not a trace of fear or indecision in his demeanour or voice. It was no wonder they'd written a poem about this day. Norman's father had called him a tenth-century Churchill, whatever that meant. When the roar went up from the Saxons, Norman joined in.

A wall of Saxon shields rushed to the shoreline, blocking off access from the causeway. Three of the largest Saxon warriors stood at the point where the causeway touched the mainland. Their helmets were pulled down tight now, their shields held close to their bodies, leaving room only for their spears to poke through. Then the Vikings came streaming across the causeway. Their war cry made Norman's throat go dry and he felt his knees weaken beneath him. This knee-weakening seemed to be happening all along the shield wall, because it wavered just slightly. All it took was a rallying cry from Brythnoth to strengthen those knees.

The Vikings could not attack en masse. The narrow causeway allowed them to cross only two abreast and gave them little room to swing their swords. The first two raced to the end of the causeway and threw themselves at the shield wall. Norman was close enough to the battle now to see their faces. Their ferocity was shocking. He had seen that look in the eyes of the wolves of Undergrowth, but never in the face of a human. Had Norman been there holding a shield, he knew that he would have turned and run, but the three warriors who guarded the end of the causeway were obviously a little more brave than him. They held their ground as the Vikings charged. The Saxon spears drew back just enough to allow the invaders to get in close, and then, much more quickly than they'd been drawn back, the spears were thrust out again.

The two Viking attackers halted. They looked surprised, as if something completely unexpected had happened. One fell immediately into the marsh beside the causeway. The other composed himself for another attack. But his sword was met with another that came from higher ground. The Viking, already wounded, struggled with his footing and swung weakly. The Saxon's blow was swift and decisive in retaliation, and this second Viking too slumped to his knees and keeled over into the marsh.

Another two Vikings followed, but they were dispatched just as quickly. Wave after wave came after them, but it was no use: the Saxons stood on firmer footing and held higher ground. The Vikings were handicapped by their poor position and the muddy ground beneath their feet, and the causeway wouldn't allow them to broaden their front. Brythnoth had his three best men at the end of the causeway, and the Vikings could not bring more than two against them.

Carried away by the excitement of the fight, Norman and Wulfmaer forgot their own quarrel and crept close to Aetheric in rank of Saxon thanes just behind Brythnoth.

"It's hopeless," Norman said gleefully. "We could hold out all day like this!" He didn't realize how loudly he'd spoken. Brythnoth himself turned and peered at him inquisitively.

"What's your boy saying there, Aetheric?"

Aetheric laughed nervously. "Praise for your battle plan, Earl. He says the sea scum don't have a chance."

Brythnoth looked from Aetheric to Norman, his eyes narrowing. "Hmph," he grumbled.

Out on the causeway, the Vikings finally stopped their senseless attack, pulling back away from the shield wall. The Saxons on shore let out a roar of derision. "Go home, sea scum," someone shouted. But the Vikings did not go home. The messenger stepped out onto the causeway again.

"Mighty Brythnoth!" he shouted. "You call this a battle? You promised us a clash of swords, a test of men and metal. This is a duel for but a few. My men are eager to fight. Are not yours?"

Brythnoth drew his sword and strode to the edge of the cliff. Aetheric and the other Saxon thanes followed immediately, anxious to show that they too were ready return this insult.

"How can you look at the fallen bodies of your brethren and ask that?" Brythnoth growled through his teeth. "Ask *them* if you like. Ask them if they found us eager to fight."

"Oh, we can see that two or three of you are ready for it," came the answer. "Those few stout spearmen at the end of this causeway here have shown their mettle. But what of the rest of you? Are there only three real warriors in England?"

Brythnoth was so angry now that he couldn't speak. You could hear the sly smile in the Viking messenger's voice as he went on. He seemed to know exactly what he was doing. Norman could do this to Dora sometimes. His mother called it "pushing someone's buttons."

"Let's see the how you fare in an equal fight then, Englander!"

the Viking continued to heckle. "In that position, any three men could hold out all day. Why, three Viking girls could do as well."

Brythnoth turned back quickly to aim a dark look at Norman. Norman had said almost the same thing a few minutes ago.

"A real warrior wouldn't stand for this," the Viking went on. "Let us onto the shore. Let us all share in this battle. Let us have a real fight, a fair fight."

Norman stood speechless as Brythnoth glanced back at him. Two grey-blue eyes glinted on either side of the iron nosepiece of his helmet and settled momentarily on Norman. It reminded Norman of the judgmental, accusative look his father had given him in the study. The Earl turned away before Norman regained enough of his wits to shake his head. His throat was dry and the words came out in a hoarse whisper. Only Aetheric beside him seemed to hear.

"No, don't do it. Don't let them."

But it was too late. The Earl was giving the order to move back from the embankment. There was only a moment's hesitation. Then each rank of spearmen stepped back slowly. The lines were orderly and unhurried. They retreated at most six metres, but it was enough. The three men at the causeway lingered. They raised their spears and shook them defiantly at the invaders on the causeway. There was a murmur of anger in the Viking ranks, but Norman could hear the whispers telling them to be quiet, to wait for their time. He found enough courage and voice to speak up one more time.

"Brythnoth, no! Don't do it. Don't let them onto the shore. You don't have to prove anything."

The Earl turned back suddenly and glared, his blue eyes full of icy fury. "Get this insolent whelp out of here," he growled.

Norman felt the heavy hand of Wulfmaer on his shoulder hauling him back. A bow and a quiver of arrows were thrust into his hands, and he stumbled clumsily through the mud as the older boy dragged him away. The Saxon boy let go of him only when they reached the area where the archers were assembling.

A shout from behind him made him look back where they had come from. The Vikings were charging. The defenders of the causeway had stepped back and the way was clear for the invaders. The sea warriors streamed from the narrow land bridge to the wide shore but did not halt for a moment. From where Norman stood, they looked like a single mass, like liquid pouring out from a bottle into a widening pool. This illusion was shattered when the spill hit the Saxon shield wall. The force was too obviously solid—the sound was abrupt and sickening. Steel rang against steel or thudded against thick wooden shields.

The shield wall didn't hold. It buckled in two, then three spots and then was breached. At each of these points, the Viking horde applied more pressure, pushing into the second and third ranks of the defenders. Within minutes the shield wall was no more. There was no separation between the two armies. English thanes on horseback rushed in to support their foot soldiers but were quickly pulled from their mounts into the hand-to-hand combat. Norman felt a sharp thud on his shoulder. Gasping, he whirled, quickly expecting blood and angry Viking faces, but it was no Viking mace but the fist of Wulfmaer that struck him.

"Stop gawking and start shooting those arrows!" he snarled.

Norman had been too engrossed in the enfolding battle to notice that the rest of the archers were busy firing arrows down at the Vikings who continued to stream across along the causeway from the island. Norman's fingers trembled as he notched his arrow. A sharp twinge of pain shot down his arm when he pulled the arrow back. Wulfmaer had hit him hard. His arrow went straight, but fell short. He bit his lip and grasped another arrow. Down below in the hill, the English were falling back. Some of the banners had fallen. Norman knew what that meant: a thane had fallen with it. If too many of their leaders fell, the English would lose heart.

Below, there was a mighty push into the heart of the English defence. It was as if the Vikings had read Norman's mind and meant to crush the Saxons' morale. Norman wished he could do something. He hauled his bow string back with all his might, grunting as he let his arrow fly. His eye followed its flight. It was long enough this time, and high, but he saw it fall harmlessly on the causeway.

When Norman looked again at the melee down below, the English numbers seemed severely depleted and the fighting was much closer. They were in full retreat now. Some of the thanes had grabbed their horses and were fleeing to the woods.

"What's going on? Why are they running?" Norman asked, appalled.

Beside him, Wulfmaer had stopped firing too. His voice was no longer confident and gruff. "There . . ." He pointed to the centre of the battle, where a man slumped on one knee, his sword arm limp at his side. His helmet had been knocked askew, so that his grey hair stuck out. It was Brythnoth. Norman had not realized that he was so old.

Though the Earl could no longer fight himself, he exhorted his followers still, rallying them to him, urging them on. Some few brave fighters stayed at his side, but more fled. Norman and Wulfmaer watched in shock as riders mounted and fled to the safety of the woods.

The archers looked on passively now. The enemy was among the defenders. None of them trusted their aim enough to fire into the crowd that was now pushing toward them up the hill. One after another the English champions fell. With increasing desperation, Wulfmaer spoke their names as they fell. "That is Offa, there, the big man. He is down. Those are Oswold and Thurstan." The battle was close enough now that Norman could see the faces of the dying men. Moments ago he had stood at their shoulder shouting insults at the Vikings; now they were falling to their knees in the mud. His stomach churned as he saw Aetheric fall. From the ground where he kneeled, unable to get to his feet, Aetheric looked back, fixing his eyes on Wulfmaer.

"Be gone now. Get the boys to the woods. This day is over," he cried hoarsely.

Wulfmaer lunged forward, drawing a small dagger from his belt. Norman grasped his shoulder. The boy wheeled and glared at him, a wild look of grief on his face.

The young Saxon's face was a mask of indecision and pain. He longed to help his thane, but there was nothing he could do. When he finally turned away from his stricken master, the grief in his eyes had hardened to hatred. He knew whose fault this all was. He placed the point of his dagger at Norman's throat.

Norman gulped and looked around desperately for help, but all around him Saxon archers were dropping their weapons and fleeing. Then a Viking war cry turned both boys' heads. A mass of Viking warriors surged up the hill.

"Another day," the Saxon boy threatened hoarsely, and they both fled.

The protection of the forest seemed miles away. Norman regretted not having run sooner. He should have known the battle was lost as soon as he saw Brythnoth fall, but he had remained for some reason. A sense of responsibility tied him to this fight. It was his stupid comment that had made Brythnoth give up his position at the causeway.

Wulfmaer had sprinted ahead of Norman. He had ditched his bow and arrows and would make it to the forest in time. Norman had slung his bow and quiver across his back, like he'd seen the stoat archers do, and he was regretting it now. The bow made it hard to run at full stride. He wondered if it was worth stopping and getting rid of it now. One glance over his shoulder told him it was too late for that. The pursuing Vikings were close enough to see the grins on their faces.

Norman didn't think he could run any faster. In desperation he reached for the pamphlet he'd stuffed in his pocket back in the library. He tore off one page and stuffed the rest back in his jeans. There was no time to slice and dice on the battlefield. He'd have to eat this one whole. He crumpled it into a ball and threw it into his mouth. It made breathing difficult and slowed him down even further. It was like trying to eat the world's nastiest-tasting gobstopper in less than a minute. His jaw worked away at it in rhythm with his running stride. Norman thought bitterly about that old joke about walking and chewing gum—it was supposed to be simple.

Norman reached the shallow gorge that marked the edge of the field. It was amazing that he'd made it this far. His lungs were bursting, and he still hadn't managed to work the ball of paper in his mouth to a size he could swallow without choking himself. Three steps down the incline of the gorge, he slipped. The ground was greasy with mud here, and it was deeper than it looked. Norman felt his sneaker sink into the soft muck and heard a familiar squelch as he tried to yank it out. The mud held his shoe fast and only his socked foot emerged. He was reaching back for it when he saw the Viking over the edge of the gully. The barbarian wielded a huge battle axe that Norman probably wouldn't even have been able to lift. There was a greedy, wide-eyed look on his face that said, "I've got you now!"

Norman actually gulped with shock. With that motion, the compressed ball of paper squeezed past his tonsils and into his throat. It might have caught there, or else this is where the expression "having your heart in your mouth" came from. It certainly felt like that as his throat burned and throbbed. It was amazing the things that went through your head when you were running for your life, for he had abandoned his shoe now and was churning across the muddy gorge. If he survived this, his mother would be furious. She hadn't been happy about the jacket, and these were new sneakers.

Norman could hear the Viking close behind him now, laughing and taunting him. Suddenly everything seemed hopeless. What was he thinking, eating the page from the bike pamphlet? It wasn't like he could fall asleep here. He was going to be murdered by a bloodthirsty Viking in a muddy English poem, bludgeoned or skewered with only one sneaker on. His legs were weak underneath him now and he was trudging, rather than running, up the other side of the gully. He barely noticed that his eyes were watering and his nose running. He had lost this battle for the English. If his dad ever found out, he would be furious. His poem was wrecked. This wasn't a day that English poets would be celebrating at all. And suddenly Norman knew that he wouldn't be seeing his father or mother. It really was over this time. He lost his footing again and lurched forward. There was a sharp pain like fire in his temple, and then everything went black.

The Castle by the Lake

It might not have been the cold that woke him, but it was certainly the first thing he noticed. Norman was lying in a ditch again. If he ever tracked down that Reynard dude, he was going to ask him why the bookweird always left you in ditches. Why couldn't it be nice warm beds or sleeping bags every now and then?

Norman remembered then that he was supposed to be dead. How had he survived the Viking attack? Had he been taken prisoner? Had they just knocked him unconscious in an English ditch and carted him off to be held in some Viking ditch for ransom? This certainly wasn't the same ditch he'd fallen in. The ground wasn't muddy, and he couldn't hear the sea. The air was also much colder. He sat up to get a better look, and a bright pain flashed above his right eye, making his stomach nauseous. Somebody had hit him with something again.

Now that he was sitting up, it was obvious that he was no longer at Maldon. The sea was nowhere in sight, and he was much higher up. The trees were all pines here, and above them he could see the tips of snow-covered mountains. Maybe he *had* been knocked unconscious and being knocked out was as good as falling asleep for the bookweird. But if this had done the trick, shouldn't he be home now, hearing his mother scold him for losing a shoe and listening to his father complain in Danish? Shouldn't he at the very least have woken up in a bicycle safety pamphlet? Some day he'd really like to learn how this actually worked.

Norman rose to his feet shakily, gathering up his longbow and the quiver of arrows from the ground beside him. He should have dropped them when he was running, he thought belatedly. Slinging them over his shoulder, he felt reassured that he had a weapon of some sort and that he'd had at least a morning's training in how to use it. He'd yet to wake up in any book where he didn't have to defend himself.

It wasn't long, though, before Norman was wishing he could trade his bow and arrow for the sneaker he'd abandoned in the mud at Maldon. The ground was rocky here, and cold. He hobbled along the ridge of a hill for an hour before he found a clear path. He saw no one and heard nothing. It was strangely quiet.

The path presented him with a dilemma. Should he go up or down? He hadn't thought of it while he was trudging along the ridge, but the path clearly travelled up and down the mountain. Though an hour's walk had warmed him up a little, he was still reluctant to climb higher, into even colder, less protected regions. Norman actually did turn around at one point, but something stopped him after the first step. Later he would think that it was because he had been running uphill away from the sea at Maldon and that in a way he was still running away from the pursuing Vikings.

Another half hour's walk made him regret his decision. The pathway narrowed considerably as it ascended and veered into the forest. The headroom continually grew lower and lower, and soon Norman found himself crouching and ducking beneath the boughs of pine trees. He scrambled though the narrowest and lowest passage yet and muttered to himself aloud, "Jeez, it's as bad as Under—"

He unbent himself and looked up as he spoke. What he saw on the mountainside in front of him had interrupted his thoughts: a tall, grey castle well placed behind thick battlements. Surrounded by snow-capped fir trees, its three towers loomed over the silver surface of the lake it commanded. The view was exactly like the cover . . .

"Lochwarren," he whispered, amazed.

He broke into a run. The prospect of seeing his friend Malcolm again chased every chill from his body. Even his sore head felt better. If he wasn't home, then this was the next best place. Reaching open ground, he began to jog across the uneven heath toward the castle.

He was well within shouting distance of the castle walls when he pulled himself up short. That was not the red flag of the Stoat Kingdom flying from each of Lochwarren's three towers. Instead Norman spied the ragged yellow pennant of the forest wolves. Lochwarren was still a wolf stronghold.

Norman realized that there was no way of knowing where in the story he had arrived. Had he arrived during the Princes' exile? Were Duncan and Cuilean still growing up somewhere, or had the war begun? Either way, wolves would be everywhere now. The forest would be full of them. Feeling suddenly exposed, Norman crouched and surveyed the battlements for a sign of its defenders. No movement could be seen in the notches of the parapets. Nothing obvious stuck out from the arrow loops, but the drawbridge was up and the portcullis down. The wolves were on the defensive. They had withdrawn to the castle and were prepared for an attack. Had Lochwarren only just fallen to the wolves, or had Duncan and Cuilean's rebellion reached this far?

Try as he might, Norman could see no evidence of a stoat army anywhere around him. This was no proof of anything, of course. If the stoats didn't want to be seen, it would take sharper eyes than Norman's to pick them out. But perhaps this was just wishful thinking.

As Norman crouched in the shrubs, a wolf appeared at the top of the lowest tower. He was a haggard creature who must have seen many battles. Norman shuddered and remembered his flight from Scalded Rock.

"Come out of your holes, vermin!" the wolf howled. "Come take your puny castle back if you dare!" There was a hint of desperation to his voice. This was a last stand of some sort.

There was no reaction to the wolf's taunt. Norman scanned the forest line around the castle for any movement, any glint of steel in the shadows of the pines. Nothing—only the trees swaying in the breeze, the forest creaking with their motion. No other sound was to be heard. That clinched it: the stoats had to be out there. The whole forest was hushed in anticipation. No birdcalls, no chattering from field mice or voles—all the woodland animals of Lochwarren knew that a battle loomed.

Up on the battlement more wolves appeared. They whistled and jeered and rattled their spears against the stone encastlations.

"You coward weasels, come out and fight. Come out and take your worthless little hovel. It's not fit for wolf kings," the shaggy predator on the tower called.

It was easy for them to be brave. Up there on the battlements, they knew that they were out of archer range. They could heckle all they wanted. Norman wanted to shout back. He wanted to tell the wolf to come down and fight if he was so brave, but he wasn't about to reveal his position.

The grey wolf snarled in frustration and disappeared again into the tower.

What was the stoat battle plan? Norman wondered. How did they intend to take back their castle? Surely they would need siege engines. Archers and swordsmen alone would be useless against the thick fortifications of Lochwarren castle. He scanned the forest again for any sign. Still nothing.

A shout from the castle caught his attention. Norman caught his breath as he saw the scruffy wolf emerge once again. He stood high on the wall now so that he could be seen. His sword was drawn in his right paw. He turned it menacingly so it glinted in the sunlight. In his left paw he held something else up high. Norman squinted to try to identify it. It was brown, too small to be a shield. Suddenly it moved, and Norman knew exactly what it was.

"Such cowards you are," taunted the wolf. "Cower in the woods, you vermin. Don't bother trying to save your little friend."

The young stoat struggled vainly in his captor's vicious paw.

The squirming captive was too far away to recognize, but a sickening feeling gripped Norman's stomach. It could be Malcolm up there twisting in the wolf's grip. The more he thought about it, the more he felt it must be true. They had taken Malcolm hostage. It was his own friend up there with the sword at his throat.

A deep rage welled up in Norman. So much had gone wrong since he'd first fallen into this book. He had screwed up so much. But one thing had gone right. One thing was worth it all: the friendship of the little stoat prince, Malcolm. If he was up on that parapet right now, Norman wouldn't hesitate to confront that wolf. It wouldn't matter that the beast had been raised to kill, and that he could do it equally well with his claws and teeth as with the sword. Norman would stand up for his friend.

Only then did Norman recall the bow at his side. The castle was farther and higher than any shot he'd made back at Maldon, but he didn't care. He had to do *something.* He could give that filthy wolf something to think about. Gripping the bow just as Wulfmaer had shown him, he notched the straightest of his remaining arrows. He could feel a snarl growing on his own face as he drew the string back. The anger surging through his body lent strength to his arm, but his hand didn't shake. It was steadier than ever as he pulled back and raised his aim. The fingers released just right. The flight didn't snag on his fingers. The string didn't snap on his arm. The arrow flew high and straight. Even as he heard it whistling in the air, Norman was shouting.

"For Tista Kirk!" he yelled, bellowing it from the bottom of his stomach, packing all his anger and his love for the little stoat into his breath. The volume of his voice startling him. The echo resounded through the valley. Shocked wolves on the parapets of Lochwarren castle turned toward him, their long snouts agape in amazement. Then a gurgling cry from the parapet snapped their heads the other way. The grey wolf was on his knees, clutching his chest. His captive had scampered away and was nowhere to be seen.

The echo of Norman's shout was just dying out when he realized what he'd done. He'd actually hit the wolf. He almost couldn't believe it. You could give him this shot a hundred more times and he'd never make it again.

There was a moment of shock before he could speak again. There was still anger in his voice, but also a strange bewildered awe at what he'd done. He cupped his hands around his mouth and bellowed, "For Duncan and Cuilean! For the sons of Malcolm!"

Bewildered wolves on the castle wall looked around for the source of the battle cry. Most cowered behind battlements. A few fired back, their arrows falling harmlessly in the field in front of him. Norman sent another arrow back. It whistled past harmlessly this time, rattling off an inner wall, but the wolves had been warned and ducked hurriedly behind the parapet.

Norman was reaching for his third arrow when he heard a swelling roar of voices from the woods. Those stoats were small, but they could make an oversized racket when they wanted to. Norman unleashed another arrow toward the castle. The wolves, shocked by his range, ducked behind merlons on the castle battlements and did not reappear.

The stoat army poured from the forest now. Norman could see the red cloaks and gold banners of the old stoat kings along with the buccaneer flags of Duncan's Rivernesters. At the centre there was even a small body of hares marching under the banner of the Five Cities. So Duncan's and Cuilean's forces had united. The brothers were marching together to free their ancestral home. A desperate hope filled Norman's chest—maybe that hadn't been Malcolm there in the clutches of the grey wolf in the tower after all.

From within the castle a horn blast sounded. Norman had heard that call before. It was no wolf clarion. That was a river raider horn. A new banner thrust now from one of the drawbridge towers, Duncan's black battle ensign. There were stoats inside the castle already! The mechanical clank of the drawbridge cogs could be heard now too, and sure enough the portcullis was creaking upward and the moat bridge was descending.

"Of course," Norman whispered to himself, "the tunnels." Years ago, the stoat princes had fled Lochwarren through hidden passages that led out to the lake. They would return the same way. A small party of Rivernesters had slipped in through the tunnels, silently securing the gate towers while the garrison focused on the drama up on the high parapets. The bridge fell into place with a thud, its timing perfect. Stoat troops streamed into Lochwarren castle. Norman could hear the panicked howls of the wolves within. They were trying to defend again now from the castle towers, aiming crossbow bolts directly down at the drawbridge, but Norman harried them with his longbow. It no longer mattered if he hit them or not. Just the sound of arrows rattling off the stones sent them scurrying. With each arrow, fewer and fewer wolves dared to show their snouts.

It could not be going well for the defenders inside either, because another door had opened at the side of the castle, from which wolves were now fleeing in twos and threes. Norman hurried them along in their flight by sending a few arrows their way. There were no returning shots now from the castle. The defence was crumbling. Undone by the shocking fall of its commander and the surprise attack from below, the wolves were in disarray. One by one the wolf banners had been replaced by the red and gold flag of the stoat kings.

As the clamour of fighting died down, Norman edged closer to the castle. His quiver was empty now and there was nothing more he could do from the forest edge. Perhaps it would have been wiser to wait there until the battle was over and the castle fully secure, but he could not wait. He needed to know if that was Malcolm up there. He needed to know that his friend was okay. Soon he made no more pretence at caution. As he jogged across the heath, he glanced up occasionally to appreciate how much bigger the castle was when you got close to it. It no longer looked like a plaything or a model. And the carcass of a slain wolf that lay across the castle gate was no toy either—it was as long as he was high. A chill of fear went through him finally. He had forgotten how big these predators were. Norman just stood there staring at the fallen wolf. If any defenders had remained on the high tower, his bare head would have been an easy target.

A shout from above snapped him out of his reverie.

"Where'd you learn to shoot like that?"

Norman grinned up at the little animal standing atop the gate tower. The young stoat looked bigger, stronger and if possible cockier than when Norman had last seen him.

"In England!" Norman shouted back, the grin wide on his face.

Malcolm laughed his gleeful stoat laugh. "England? Tell me another one. Every stoat-body knows that England is the stuff of fairy tales."

Norman heard the full story of the stoat campaign that night. A fire roared in the great hall of Lochwarren and a grand feast was served. It was only the second room in Undergrowth that actually accommodated Norman, and it was certainly warmer than the ruined shell of Tintern Abbey. Norman sprawled down the length of the hall, warming his socked feet by the fire. Someone, most likely Malcolm, had lashed Norman's one sneaker to an iron peg high up on the wall beside the ancient armour and trophies of the stoat kings. Malcolm sat beside him at the banquet table, chatting away vigorously. Norman did his best to follow the story.

"I'm sorry we didn't stay and look for you when you disappeared like that, but Uncle Cuilean said we had to move on. There were too many wolf spies in Edgeweir to hang about looking for a great oaf like you. That old fox abbot at Tintern told us you were probably gone for good.

"We spent the spring gathering men to fight in the uprising. At first there were just a few of us. We hijacked the wolf mail convoys and set fire to their weapons stockpiles, little things that showed the people that we could fight back. Every time we struck out at them, we drew more stoats to the struggle. By midsummer we were an army of hundreds."

Cuilean's old companion James turned to face them from his place on the feast bench. There was a look of grandfatherly pride on his face as he smiled and nodded at the young stoat. "This young scoundrel would have fought the war on his own, but the new recruits kept coming. The hares came to deliver swords and crossbows, a gift from the Duke of Logorno, but stayed when they got their first taste of real fighting after so many quiet years in the Five Cities." He amicably nudged the russet brown hare who shared his bench.

Malcolm bounded onto Norman's shoulder and made himself comfortable there—like old times—and continued breathlessly. "With reinforcements and the proper weapons, the wolves could nae handle us. They locked themselves up in their strongholds. They were afraid to stick their noses out without armed knights, but we ferreted them out of their towers one by one. It was almost too easy."

"The boy's right," the hare added. "The towers and fortified towns fell with minimal resistance. The cretins waited for reinforcements that never came, then tried to escape in the night."

"Uncle Cuilean couldn't understand why the tower garrisons weren't reinforced, but I always knew. I knew that Dad was on the march, too. I knew he had drawn the wolf armies out. Soon we heard the news from the other side of the mountains. Another stoat army had massed in the west hills. I wanted to be the one who took the message to Dad, but Uncle Cuilean sent James instead."

James placed a friendly hand on the young prince's shoulder. "The boy was already too valuable. He led two regiments of archers at that point. The lads shoot farther and with more accuracy when a Mustelid prince gives the orders," the old stoat boasted. James had only just met Malcolm when Norman last left Undergrowth. In the interim he had clearly developed a soft spot for the boy.

Malcolm suppressed a proud smile. "James snuck through enemy territory to Dad's war camp at Castle Craigweel. Dad knew I was alive all along. He knew you and Simon would get me out of Scalded Rock."

Norman thought back to that harrowing escape and that moment of confrontation in the forest. The last time Norman had seen Simon Whiteclaw, he was facing down a wolf assassin.

"I don't suppose Simon . . . ," he began.

James shook his silver head. "No sign of him. I never had much time for the man, but the scoundrel did right by the boy, and he went down fighting, like a true soldier."

Norman felt a shiver go through the young stoat on his shoulder. "Like my dad," Malcolm whispered.

It took a second for Malcolm's words to sink in. When they did, Norman didn't know what to say.

"Aye, lad," James said, eyeing his young charge sympathetically. "He lived like a hero and died like one. They'll be telling his tale in this hall for generations to come."

"But what happened?" Norman couldn't help worrying that it was something he'd done, some change he'd made in the book that had precipitated Duncan's death and orphaned his young friend.

"'Twas at the second battle of Tista Kirk, a masterful bit of warcraft by this lad's dad and uncle. Some might say that a stoat is no match for a wolf. Your wolf in fighting trim is often four times the weight of even the largest stoat. But a stoat's got speed, speed of hand and of brain. A well-trained sword-stoat is more than a match for a lumbering wolf in hand-to-hand combat. What you don't want to do with wolves is engage them in pitched battles. On open ground, a well-formed wolf army would smash through the strongest shield wall. That's what happened at the first Tista Kirk. Duncan dared the wolves to do it again. His army had fought its way up the mountains in a series of bloody battles. His war was tougher than ours. We stayed in the forests, harassing the supply lines, hiding our real strength. When Duncan formed up his battle lines on the fields of Tista Kirk, those wolves must have been licking their chops—a good old pitched battle, just their kettle of tea. Those Rivernesters are brave lads, I'll give you that. They stood firm behind their shields and taunted those wolves until they charged. There's not many a stoat who can stand firm in the face of an armed wolf charge, but those lads did. They knew we were hiding in the woods there, waiting for the wolves to break cover, but they wouldn't have kidded themselves. They must have known that many would die that day."

"I shoulda been there with 'em," Malcolm muttered through gritted teeth. "I ought to 'ave been at my father's side."

"Ah, lad, but then who would have won the battle for us?" James asked the young prince gently. He turned back to Norman. "It was Malcolm's archers that made the difference. They'd been lying low in the woods just behind the wolves all day. Once the wolves moved out into the open, we brought our archers up at the tree line. Just before the wolves reached the shield wall, Malcolm's lads unleashed their fury, used those slobbering bags of fur like pincushions. They didn't know what hit them. They ran about like madbeasts scrambling to get out of range. When they finally formed up again, we rained more arrows down on them and made ready for another charge. By the time they reached Duncan's lines, their force was half what it had been. It was enough to do some damage, though. Duncan's men fought them every step of the way. Thankfully, the archers had done enough, chopped the wolf regiments up into little bite-sized chunks that Duncan's men could digest.

"By noon only the fiercest wolf lairds remained, those that knew the battle was lost but fought on anyway, hoping just to take a few stoats with them to the grave. It was one of them that did it, Nighthowler, a fierce old warrior, strong and sly. He was there at the first Tista Kirk. He boasted of knocking the banner out of old Malcolm's hand and of dealing the last blow.

"Duncan called him out there on the battlefield, challenged him to single combat. It didn't matter that Duncan was wounded already and had fought all morning while the old wolf prowled and hid behind his bodyguards. Within minutes Duncan had him at swordpoint. It was a done deal, but the treacherous beast wasn't having it. Nighthowler knew he'd lost the duel, but he couldn't allow it, couldn't end it with dignity. Before any stoat could do anything, three wolf bodyguards jumped Prince Duncan from behind. He took two of them with him to the grave as well as old Nighthowler, but between them, they did him in."

The whole table was quiet now. Hares and stoats alike had put down their tankards and lowered their eyes. Perhaps, like Norman, they could not bear to look at Malcolm. James lowered his voice as he continued.

"Cuilean is as able a healer as you'll find in these hills, but nothing he'd learned back in Logorno could have saved his brother. They said their farewells at Tista Kirk."

James motioned with his head to where Cuilean was lifting a cup in toast. The campaign had changed him, too. He looked older, more solemn than when Norman had met him in the Borders. While his soldiers celebrated, he moved from table to table shaking hands and patting backs. When he smiled it was a slow, sad smile that showed he remembered too much of the battle's carnage to celebrate wholeheartedly. He noticed Norman watching him and made his way across the hall.

"You lived up to your name today, Norman Strong Arm. My brother's faith was not misplaced. I owe you a debt of gratitude, both for today's intervention and for your earlier help." He seemed to paused, and looked meaningfully at the stoat upon Norman's shoulder. "For bringing the boy out of Scalded Rock."

When Norman had first started reading this book, he had longed to join the brothers to help them figure out the riddle of the gifts and determine the rightful king. Now that Cuilean stood in front of him, they were both equally speechless. When the silence could not be borne any longer, the stoat prince nodded, smiled that same wise smile and saluted him before turning away.

The Writing of Wrongs

Norman slept that night in the granary of Lochwarren castle. It was the most comfortable night he ever spent in Undergrowth. But if he'd slept less soundly and been less groggy, he might have been alarmed to see the fox abbot's silhouette hanging above his head. The Abbot had already drawn back his cowl and was well into his lecture by the time Norman was fully awake. Norman rubbed the sleep from his eyes and squinted. He was certain he recognized him now.

Norman greeted him grumpily. "You're a little late, aren't you? I was waiting for you in the library."

Bemused, the fox licked his chops and scratched his ear distractedly. A sharp fox claw poked momentarily through the round hole at the top of his ear.

"Surely not, son. Castle Lochwarren has a fine library, but it could not accommodate a creature of your size."

"Come on," Norman protested. "I left a message for you on your answering machine."

The abbot fox squinted at him as if he might possibly be mad. "A machine for answering, you say? A mechanical oracle? I've never . . . You must tell me about it sometime. Tonight, though, we have work to do."

Norman rolled his eyes. "Whatever," he said. Rolling over to face the stone wall of his chamber, he pretended to go back to sleep.

The Abbot coughed a sharp barklike cough. "You do want to get home, I suppose?"

Norman replied without moving, "I don't need your help. I know how it works now."

"Oh, you do, do you?" The fox snickered. "You have it all figured out? You are able to arrive exactly where you like? I'd never have thought it. You will have to teach me, O great lumbering adept of the bookweird."

Norman wasn't nearly as confident as he pretended. Eating a page from a book certainly seemed to be the trick, but it wasn't an exact science. He had never eaten a page from Dora's horse book or his mom's novel or his dad's poem, but he'd been transported into them. And when he ate the cycling brochure to get out of Maldon, he'd expected to arrive home. Why did he arrive in Undergrowth again? Why not in the land of cycling safety?

He threw the covers off and sat up. "Okay, then, you explain it to me. I only ate the page from the one Undergrowth book. What happened to get me into the horse place and the murder mystery? What made a page from Dad's poem disappear? That's really bad, you know. I need to get that back."

The Abbot raised a foxy eyebrow. "Ah, the gangly warrior would be a scholar now?"

Norman made an impatient face. A "ha ha, very funny" sort of squint.

"Bookweird is a powerful force, and a complicated one. It can't be explained in a few minutes, nor understood, likely, in a single lifetime," the fox continued. "Suffice it to say that you have found one of the ways in—a previously unknown way in, I should add, or perhaps just long forgotten. Few things are unknown in the lore of bookweird, but many things are forgotten.

"As a destructive *ingresso,* your consumption method was bound to disturb the structure of the weird, but you are lucky. Imagine if you had burned or erased those pages. Those are calamitous methods, and I'll warn you now, don't even consider them. Your consumption *ingresso* seems to have a more local effect, spreading to the books of your household. I'm considering calling it the Norman Domino Effect."

He regarded Norman expectantly, as if he was supposed to be flattered by this name.

"So can I fix it?" Norman demanded impatiently.

"Fix it? Why, no, of course not. Nothing in bookweird is ever *fixed*," the abbot replied, as if astounded by Norman's ignorance. "Repaired, perhaps, if I'm right—patched." He paused a moment to think over his plan. "You can write as well as read, can't you?"

The Abbot must have had the book under his tunic the whole time, but he removed it only once they'd reached the little chapel in the woods behind Lochwarren castle. It was a tiny structure, about the size of Norman's garden shed back home. The only doorway was both low and narrow. Norman might have been able to crawl through it, but that would only manage to put him in position to crush the miniature wooden pews within. The fox abbot unbolted the door and went ahead. Norman stuck his head and arms through the arched doorway.

"Why can't you just give me the page?" Norman complained. "I can eat it outside."

"*This,*" admonished the abbot, clutching the book to his chest, "is not for eating."

"Well, let me read it out here, if that's what we're doing. Reading out loud worked last time. Is it your goofy bestiary again, the one that says that humans are hatched from eggs?"

"It is not a *goofy* bestiary," the Abbot responded haughtily. "It is a well-respected reference book, long maintained by my abbey. You'd do well to study it." In the moonlit interior of the chapel, it was impossible to tell if his outrage was genuine. "Tonight, though, we have other matters. This is not the bestiary. It is the Great Chronicle of the Mustelid Kings. Tonight, you must restore the page of history that you so greedily consumed. This cannot be done outside or in the castle. It must be done here in the Chapel of St. Sleekyn, as this is the place where the Mustelid Kings are crowned."

Norman furrowed his brows, not quite getting it. "And you want me to . . ."

"Rewrite the legacy of King Malcolm, declaring which of the two gifts is the gift of the successor."

"But I don't know what either of the gifts is, never mind which was meant for the future king," Norman protested. "I didn't read that far before I ate the page."

"Well, that wasn't the smartest thing you've done." Norman was growing to really dislike this fox. "It's not like you burned the page or cast it to the wind. It is . . ." The Abbot paused. "It is inside you, after all. You must imitate the style." He handed Norman the book solemnly and busied himself with the preparation of the ink and pen.

"I don't know," Norman whispered as he glanced through the Chronicle. "It's pretty fancy writing."

"Normally the king dictates to a trained scribe. How's your penmanship?" He handed Norman a tiny pen. "This should fit those monster hands of yours. I had it fashioned from a rake handle."

Norman found the blank page in the book and stared at it for a very long time. What exactly was he supposed to write here? How could he decide who would be King?

"I can't do this," he protested. "It's not my decision. I can't guess what King Malcolm wanted. I don't know what gifts he put in those boxes. How am I supposed to know what to write?"

The Abbot just shrugged and held out what to him was a giant pot of ink. "Whatever you write, you had better do it quickly. The sun will be rising within the hour."

Norman bit the end of his pen nervously for a while and considered his options. This was his chance to change history, or at least to change the outcome of the book. When he'd begun reading *The Brothers of Lochwarren,* hadn't he thought that Cuilean would make a better king? Didn't Duncan's death make the choice easy?

"Come on, get on with it. This ink pot isn't exactly light, you know," the Abbot growled.

The Unveiling of the Gifts

The next morning Norman dragged himself to the chapel once again. It seemed like he'd only just left. Even snugly back in his bed in the granary, he had been unable to sleep. His mind kept wandering back to the decisions he'd made and the words he'd written in the Chronicle. Had he made the right choice for the future of the Mustelid dynasty?

If Malcolm noticed his giant friend's sluggishness that morning, he didn't say anything. The young stoat was unusually solemn. There was none of his usual flitting and chattering. He must be thinking about his father, Norman thought. It must be terrible to lose your father. He remembered suddenly that Malcolm's mother was dead too. He was an orphan now. Norman couldn't think of anything more terrible.

He thought suddenly about his own family. Were his father and mother still looking for a page of the missing poem, or had he changed history twice today? When the page from *The Battle of Maldon* was found, it would not be the same page. The English had lost at the Battle of Maldon because of Norman. There would be no such thing as England, and no Department of English for his father to teach in. His ancestors would have been speaking Danish for centuries. Would he even understand his family when he returned?

The chapel was built atop a rise behind Castle Lochwarren. Half hidden in the pine forest, it was reached by a narrow path strewn with gravel and moss. It was a strange place for a coronation—for that was what this was, though they were a modest group for a royal procession. Four ferret clerics led them up the winding path. Behind the clerics strode two squires carrying the fateful gifts of King Malcolm. The boxes were identical save for their condition, simple wooden boxes with unpolished iron hinges and locks. Duncan's—scratched, dinted and oddly out of square—bore the effects of its fall from the cliff and hasty reconstruction in the early chapters. Cuilean's was clean and tidy but no less austere. You wouldn't guess that one contained a gift fit for a king.

Cuilean and James followed the squires who carried the boxes. They were as silent as Norman and Malcolm. A small party of stoat nobles completed the party. They alone broke the silence. Though they walked some distance behind the clerics and the royal party, Norman could hear them whispering all the way up the hill. More than a few of them marvelled at the outlandish appearance of the giant Norman. The less polite whispered indiscreetly about the half-civilized beast that might at any time turn on them. Mostly, though, they traded speculations as to what the boxes contained and what the old king had decreed all those years ago before marching off to his death at Tista Kirk.

Norman had had a long time to think about the gifts. From what he had read from the book, Duncan had not been impressed with his. The warrior prince would have hoped for a sword or dagger, some weapon to symbolize his strength and leadership. Perhaps that was why he had been so surly and so eager to forget he had a brother. Did Cuilean's box contain the symbol of a soldier's power that Duncan hoped for? It wasn't long enough to hold a sword—but a dagger, perhaps, or a buckler. Norman was nervous now, not knowing for sure what he'd been able to do the night before. Reality could contradict what he had written and expose his fraud. He had tried to be vague, but there was only so much you could *not* say.

The procession had reached the chapel. The royal party entered solemnly, making the sign of the cross as they stepped over the threshold. Only Malcolm hesitated, turning back at the door where Norman himself had inevitably stopped.

"Wish you could come in here." The little stoat's voice caught as he spoke, instantly making Norman's eyes sting. The young prince looked so alone.

"I'll be watching from the back," Norman whispered hoarsely. Unable to say anything else, he just nodded toward the front of the chapel, where the rest were waiting. Even then Malcolm hesitated. Norman gave him the thumbs-up sign. A perplexed look crossed the stoat's face, but he smiled quickly and gave the sign back with his own furry paw. The sight brought a silent chuckle to Norman's belly. Malcolm turned and strode confidently to the front of the chapel. Norman watched for just a moment more before standing aside for the rest of the attendees.

The stoat nobles passed through the arched doorway hastily, casting wary glances at Norman as they slipped past him. He resisted the urge to startle them with a lunge or a shout of "boo."

When they were all settled, the senior cleric stepped to the lectern and cleared his throat. After a pause, he declaimed in a loud but high voice, "Before he fastened his sword to his belt and donned his battle helm to lead the defence of our people at Tista Kirk, King Malcolm dictated his last entry in the Chronicle of his lineage. The King set aside two gifts for his sons by which they would know his intention." The priest cleared his throat again and gazed down from the pulpit dramatically before continuing. "May I have the boxes please?" he asked officiously.

The two gift bearers stepped forward. The locks on their boxes were unfastened now, and all that remained was to open them. At a nod from the priest, they opened the hinged lids. The cleric gazed down at their contents for a moment, taking in their significance. Norman was holding his breath as he watched. Finally the priest stepped forward and reached into one of the boxes—Norman could not tell whose—and slowly, he withdrew the gift. Stepping back to his pulpit, he raised the gift in one hand and held it there for all to see.

It was a book. Norman recognized it as the Chronicle of Mustelid Kings that he'd written in the night before. So it had worked. He smiled to himself. Somehow it had worked. He had written that one of the gifts was a book, *this* book, and now it was happening.

The priest had opened the book to the last page and was reading from it. He was reading King Malcolm's last testament—ghostwritten by Norman Jespers-Vilnius.

"In this year of peril for our people it is my responsibility to ensure the security of my people, not only with the sword, but with words. Let them both move true and sure."

Strange, thought Norman—it was sort of what he had written, but not exactly. He hadn't been that, what was the word, poetic. This bookweird was hard to fathom.

"Should I not return to this fine castle and this ancient seat of our kings, the future of our people does not rest with one man, but one man must be their support, their shield and their defender. One man too must be their memory, their guide and their wisdom. I am fortunate enough to have two sons, two sons of talent and valour, each worthy of this throne and this responsibility. Each could rule and each could lead, and each shall lead in his way. Alas, only one stoat can wear the crown.

"I have left each of my sons a gift. In choosing, I have been mindful that a father must consider what his child requires as well as what he desires. To one I have left this Chronicle, for a king must consider the past if he thinks to determine the future. To the other I have left a gift similarly suited to his responsibilities, for one should lead and the other protect."

Peering in from the open door, Norman wondered if anyone thought it unusual that he had not named the second gift. There wasn't much he could do now. He thought overall it had come out miraculously well. It not only sounded regal: it had become true.

The priest stepped back down from the pulpit and replaced

the Chronicle in its box. The retainers closed the lids and turned to face the assembly.

The royal party had not thought the reading would be so short. When they realized that there was nothing else, Cuilean and Malcolm advanced to the spot where two retainers held the boxes. Cuilean leaned over to his young nephew, placed a hand on his shoulder and whispered something in his ear. The young stoat nodded nervously and stepped forward. Reaching out tentatively, he put his hand on the lid of the battered crate and held it there a moment. He appeared not to want to open it. No one spoke. The moment stretched on. Finally Malcolm reached out with his other hand and, with both paws, slowly lifted the lid. Again there was stillness and silence.

Malcolm must see it now. He must know what his gift was and what it meant. Without removing it, he looked to his uncle, an apologetic frown upon his face. Cuilean must see the book too. Surely he would be disappointed. Hadn't he trained all his life to be King? Maybe he held out hope. A thought struck Norman: what if the second gift was a book too? Maybe this is what Cuilean hoped now. How would they solve it then?

Old King Malcolm's only surviving son now reached forward. More assured and graceful than his nephew, he opened the box before him with one swift movement. Why not? He had been waiting all his life to do this. It was like knowing where your Christmas presents were hidden. He could have forced it open at any time, but he had resisted. He peered in for just a moment. No one behind could see the look on his face. Norman held his breath and hoped. Let it not be another book. Let him be okay with not being King. Whatever was in the second box, Cuilean did not waste time pondering it. He reached in with two hands and lifted it out. Still he shielded it from the audience with his back. Upon a nod from Cuilean, Malcolm removed his own gift from its case. They turned to reveal the gifts in unison.

There were gasps of surprise from the attendees. Norman looked first not at the gifts but at the face of Cuilean, the man he just might have robbed of the throne. He was smiling—not the tired, sad smile that Norman had seen on his face the night before in the great hall, either, but the one that reminded Norman of young Malcolm's cheerful grin. Cuilean held up the ornately engraved silver helm for all to see, and with a gentle tap on the shoulder, urged his nephew to lift his own gift. Malcolm looked stunned, unprepared for his gift or the result. His eyes were lowered as if unwilling to recognize the book in his hands. Cuilean leaned over and whispered something in his nephew's ear. A gleam returned to Malcolm's eyes as he listened. He nodded, looked up and stood taller.

"King Malcolm divided the two traditional gifts of the Mustelid Kings between his sons," the haughty cleric declared. "To Cuilean he gave the Helm of Govan, symbol of the protector. To Duncan he gave the Chronicle of the Mustelid Kings, the one true record of our history." He held up the book.

"From Malcolm to his son Duncan and to his son Malcolm the throne passes," he proclaimed.

"Long live King Malcolm!" Cuilean's voice rang out, calmly and warmly.

"Long live King Malcolm!" the audience in the chapel shouted enthusiastically. It was echoed not only in the church but behind Norman, where a large crowd had assembled to witness the emergence of their new king.

"Long live Cuilean the Protector!" the audience now cried. The bells above the church had begun a joyful peel. Norman's legs felt weak beneath him.

One glance toward the two princes convinced him that he'd done the right thing. Cuilean stood proudly and protectively at Malcolm's shoulder. The young boy looked up for reassurance. The older man nodded encouragingly, and the new king again brightened and stood tall.

It would all work out. The bookweird would make it okay. Whatever he had written last night was now the truth. Norman might have changed the story, but he had done it right. Malcolm would be a good king. His people clearly loved him, and his uncle would protect and guide him.

Malcolm's gleaming eye caught his own as he stared down the aisle of the chapel.

"Long live King Malcolm," Norman yelled, giving his friend the thumbs-up sign again. At least he thought he yelled. It came out quietly, as if the volume had been turned down. He still felt faint and his vision was blurring. By the time he realized what was really happening, it was too late to say or do anything more in Undergrowth.

Grounded

There was no scent of pancakes this time, or of bacon, or of banana milkshakes, for that matter. Norman just woke up. That didn't make it any less confusing. Wherever he was, it was dark and very, very quiet. He rubbed his face and sat up. He'd been sleeping on something hard, and it had left an impression on his cheek that he did his best to rub off. Where was he, anyway?

It looked liked he was back in his own time, or at least close. Carpet had been invented at least, he noticed, as he stood up and felt it with his sock feet. He peered down at his feet for a while, trying to remember why he wasn't wearing shoes. It came to him eventually. One shoe was stuck in the mud of an ancient English battlefield. The other was now displayed on the trophy wall of the great hall of Castle Lochwarren.

Norman hardly dared to hope that he was home again. It certainly wasn't his own house he was in. He knew the sounds of his house—the hum of the furnace, the rattle of the old fridge—but there were none of these here. And yet this had to be modern times. There was carpet on the floor and the sound of the occasional car going past outside. He was in a large room, with no windows. The only light was the faint red glow of an illuminated exit sign. God, Norman hoped, let this not be Mom's gross murder book again. He reassured himself that it didn't smell like a police station.

As his eyes adjusted to the dim light, the room became clearer. The tall shapes that filtered the light on either side of him were not cell walls. Those were books, not iron bars. It was beginning to dawn on him where he was.

"Hello," he whispered cautiously. He'd listened to the silence about as long as he could. There was no answer. He tried again, louder this time. Now he was sure that the library was empty, that it was long past closing time. Only a few cars had driven past since he'd woken up. During the day, the street outside the library was much busier than that.

Keeping his hand on the shelf beside him as a guide, Norman slowly made his way out of the history section, where he'd fallen asleep. There was a phone by the desk. It should be that easy to get out of here.

It could have been just the lack of light, but the library seemed more of a maze than he remembered. He hit a few dead ends at the end of the rows of shelves as he groped his way through the dark. When he finally emerged from the stacks at the library's front desk, the first thing that confronted him was the illuminated face of the clock. It couldn't possibly be that late, could it? The clock insisted it was 1:30 A.M., but he was reluctant to believe it. That would mean he was in some serious trouble.

Norman stared at the telephone keypad and listened to the drone of the dial tone for several moments. He wondered if it might not be better to be back in a book being chased by a wolf or a crazed Viking. Darwin and Rorschach's interrogation room didn't even sound all that bad at the moment.

When Norman finally worked up the courage to dial, it did not take long for someone to pick up. It hardly rang once. His dad must have been sitting by the phone.

"Norman, is that you? Where are you? Are you all right?" he demanded.

Norman must have said he was all right about fifty times before his mother picked up the other extension and asked some sensible questions.

Norman's parents arrived at the library about the same time as the police. Edward Vilnius had called Norman back on his cellphone and talked to him while he drove to the library. The police, he insisted, said it was okay to go out through the emergency door, but he was to wait until they were in the parking lot.

The alarm going off made it pretty dramatic. The police didn't have any way of turning it off. They'd already phoned the fire department and explained the situation. They weren't sending a truck. The chief would drive over in his own car. That, at least, was a little less embarrassing than it might have been. Still, it was surprisingly difficult to explain.

Nobody seemed to want to believe that he'd just fallen asleep in the library. Not his parents, not the police. The fire chief, at least, didn't care. He just wanted to get the alarm off and get back to bed, which sounded like a pretty good idea to Norman himself. Instead, though, he had to answer a dozen questions from his parents and the police—or rather, the same question over and over. Everyone wanted to know if he had really fallen asleep in the library or if he had tried to run away. The police officer wasn't at all like Rorschach or Darwin. She reminded him more of his grade 2 teacher, Ms. Morin. She always made a big deal out of little things, too. When he finally convinced them all that he really had just fallen asleep in the library, it was after 2 A.M.

If his parents were angry, they did a good job of hiding it. His mom sat in the back with him while his dad drove. She kept stroking his hair back from his forehead while she told him how worried they had been.

"I haven't seen your father look that worried since the day you were born."

Norman's dad looked back at them in the rear-view mirror. There was a deep frown on his face.

"Honestly, Edward," his mom said, talking to his dad's face reflected in the rear-view mirror, "your forehead was creased exactly like that."

His parents didn't mention the missing page from the poem, even when they arrived home. Norman wasn't complaining. If he could avoid talking about it, he would. Maybe he would never have to talk about it. Maybe they didn't know that the old poem had been changed at all, never mind that it was his fault. It would be a terrible secret to keep. Worrying about it tainted his relief at being home even as he fell back asleep, exhausted.

He was still thinking about the damage to *The Battle of Maldon* when he awoke. He was more than a little surprised that he was in his own bed in his own room in his own life. Once you've woken up inside a book a few times, it's hard to go on through your life with the same expectation of normalness.

The clock told him it was 9:30, but he was sure it was a school day. Hadn't he left on a school day? His mother was working at the kitchen table when he finally dragged himself down there. There was no reprimand. She just looked up, smiled and said, "Good morning, sweetheart," as he lurched into the room. Norman poured himself a bowl of cereal and waited. Perhaps he ate with an elbow on the table and slurped to hasten the scolding, but really Norman was too exhausted to be this calculating.

"Isn't today a school day?" he asked finally, cautiously.

His mother smiled the same indulgent smile she'd given him when he'd first come down. "We thought you could use a little extra rest."

Boy, if she only knew, Norman thought. He gulped another spoonful of cereal before another thought came to him.

"Is Dad at the university today?" Norman's mom tended to be more lenient than his father. When his mom went easy on him, there was always the chance that this would only make his dad come down harder on him.

"Your dad's here too. He's working in the den." She got up

from the table to steam the milk for coffee. "Why don't you take this up to him? He'll appreciate that."

Norman studied her face. She didn't *look* like she was sending him off for his punishment, but his mother could hide her intentions better than most. She was hard to read sometimes.

On the stairs, on his way to his father's office, Norman decided that honesty was the best policy, or at least as much honesty as would be believable, which, now he thought about it, wasn't really much. This might be a case where he'd have to lie in order to be honest. This conundrum made him hesitate as he knocked on the door of his father's den.

"Is that coffee I smell?" his father asked cheerfully. "I certainly hope so. I feel the last one wearing off." It was the old familiar joke, but Norman would not let himself be lulled into a false sense of security. He kept his guard up and placed the coffee carefully on the desk.

"Ah, cappuccino, just what the doctor ordered. Your mother is a lifesaver." This was really weird. Maybe it would be better to just leave his father alone with his coffee. Norman backed away toward the door.

"Listen, Spiny . . ." That stopped Norman in his tracks. Dad never called him Spiny when he was angry. Norman was a bundle of nerves. He could feel his lip quivering and bit it to make it stop. His dad had every right to be furious. It *was* all his fault after all. When he'd eaten that first page out of his book, he'd broken some ancient law of books. He'd caused a chain reaction of destruction that had culminated in his father's work being destroyed. Now history was all messed up and his dad would get fired, and he'd have to learn to speak Viking. He was probably already speaking Viking and just didn't know it.

"Spiny—"

"I'm sorry, Dad. I'm sorry about your poem. I didn't mean to. I don't know how it happened . . . I just, accidentally one night. I ate . . . I didn't even know I was doing it."

His father got up from his chair and approached him with his arms open. "Spiny?"

"There's a librarian, though. He's also a fox. He knows how to fix it. He won't tell me, but maybe if you . . ."

His father had wrapped one arm around him and pulled him close. With his free hand he wiped Norman's cheek. "Hey, relax. There's nothing to be sorry about. Fox librarians, eh? That's what happens when you have a sleepover in a library. Listen, I owe you an apology."

Norman was sniffling now. When had he come down with a cold? It was probably from running around outside in hills of Lochwarren without shoes.

"Yesterday when I was looking for the page I'd lost, I was frantic. I let my anger at myself get out of control and I blamed other people for something that was entirely my fault."

"But, Dad, it *is* kind of my fault. Even though it doesn't seem like it. It's something called bookweird."

His father chuckled. "Bookweird? That's a good word for it. It's funny how you can lose your head over a book. I found my missing page, Spiny. It was here all along." He pointed to a large leather-bound book. "It was here, in between the pages of this dictionary. I was up late—not as late as you, perhaps—but like you, I lost track of things."

Norman nodded. "But the battle at Maldon. The English lost, and it's all my fault."

"Your fault, eh?" His father laughed. "Now you're getting delusions of grandeur, Spiny. That must have been some crazy dream you had in the library last night. Stress can make you dream strange things. I'm really sorry, Norman. I shouldn't have blamed you for the missing page."

"But the English lost," Norman repeated. His father clearly didn't understand.

"Of course, they lost. Brythnoth let the Vikings across the causeway, and as soon as things got rough his allies ran off."

"But was it always that way?" Norman asked.

Another chuckle from of his father. "Yes, it was always that way. It's the whole point of the poem. It's what makes it interesting. Is

Brythnoth a sucker, or is he another example of this crazy English idea of fair play?"

"But don't the Vikings go on and conquer England? Didn't you tell me that this was an important point in the war against the Vikings?"

"It was, but not because they won—because they kept fighting. English history is full of stories like this, fighting on in the face of sure defeat."

Norman didn't really know what to say to this. He wasn't sure he believed it.

Norman's father smiled again and tried to cajole one out of Norman. "Your mother figured you could use a day off school. I think she's right. You couldn't have slept all that well in the library."

Still deep in thought, Norman shook his head slowly.

"Listen," his father said. "I have a book on this you might like. It's about the first great English king, Alfred the Great. Do you want to read it?" Norman's father ran a finger across the spines of the books on his bookshelf until they came to rest on a slim green clothbound volume. Norman jumped back involuntarily when his father held it out toward him.

His dad chuckled. "You haven't developed bibliophobia, have you? Fear of books? It's very serious. The treatment is quite painful."

Norman couldn't stop a small grin from wrinkling out from his mouth. "I just think that I should give my brain a rest for a day or so."

"You're probably right. That's another possible diagnosis: you could have bibliotoxosis, book poisoning. I'd suggest a day of bike rides. I could pull my bike out after lunch, if you like."

"Maybe until then I'll just play on my computer."

His father took a sip of his coffee and nodded in mock solemnity. "Yes. For now, that's probably the safest course of action."

Norman did finally return to book reading later that week. He borrowed his dad's book on Alfred the Great and got through it without incident. And *The Scythian Scimitar* finally came in at the library on the weekend. Mrs. Balani handed it over and took his library card with a sly smile.

"You know this is a day pass? It's not good for overnight stays. Right?"

Norman had no answer to that. Mrs. Balani would hardly be the last person to tease him about his night in the library.

He read *The Scythian Scimitar* carefully at first, worried that this was just the sort of book to draw him in—all ancient intrigues, customs and magic. But he couldn't hold off very long. On his second night with it, he found himself reading by his desk lamp, which was bent and pointed in a tight cone of light toward his pillow. It had just been revealed that the sword, long protected in a crystal case in the Scythian vaults, was a fake, just when they needed its powers the most. The city was sure to fall to the evil monk Savanorola now. Norman knew it all along. The monk had tricked a young groom in the Scythian stables into hiding the true scimitar. If only he were there, Norman could explain it all to the groom and save the city. He was just about to rip off the corner of the page when he stopped himself. That was close, he thought to himself. He put the book down for the night.

He finished *The Scythian Scimitar* the next day, in the daylight. The next few books were a little easier. He was slowly curing himself of his habit of eating paper. After a while, not eating parts of books became as natural and unconscious as eating them had once been. For a very long time after that, the strangest thing that happened to Norman was a dream in which he was failing a cycling safety test given by a bunch of pencil drawings. That seemed to be the end of bookweird for him.

By the time summer holidays rolled around, Norman was pretty sure he had dreamed it all—the Vikings, the gypsies, even his friend Malcolm. He might not have forgotten so easily if he hadn't lost the map that Duncan had given him. When it went missing, he just assumed that it was one more thing that he had imagined. It wasn't as if he could, as he usually did when he lost something, ask his mother if she'd seen his authentic stoat heirloom map of Undergrowth. Had he asked, though, he might have received an unexpected answer. It would have been interesting to hear her explain why, when she found the map on Norman's floor that day, she peered at it curiously for some time before folding it up and putting it in her pocket.

Acknowledgements

I'm grateful for Lara Hinchberger's sympathetic editing, which made *Bookweird* a much better book. I must thank Denise Bukowski for introducing the book to the world and Amy Black for making sure it emerged in the best possible shape. *Bookweird* would not exist without the early encouragement of the Stickman and his sister, the book's earliest readers, editors, and critics. One of them also knows a secret or two about *Fortune's Foal.*

About the Author

Paul Glennon is the author of an adult book, which was a finalist for the 2006 Governor General's Literary Award for fiction and was selected as one of *The Globe and Mail*'s 100 Best Books of the Year. *Bookweird* is his first book for young readers. He lives in Ottawa.